Dark

Short-short stories on life's darker side

by

Marty Nemko

7th printing, revised and expanded

Praise for Marty Nemko

"Magnificent food for thought." Walter Block, Wirth Eminent Scholar, Loyola U.

"Delectable bite sized, short stories…It's difficult to stop reading them." Dr. Mark Goulston, author of *Just Listen*.

"Some unusual subjects to say the least! I highly recommend this worthwhile read." Michael Edelstein, author of *Three-Minute Therapy*.

"One of the few truly original thinkers of our time." Kathryn Riggs, retired, U.C. Berkeley School of Education."

"A really smart person." Michael Scriven, former president, American Evaluation Association.

"The best of the best." Warren Farrell, author, *The Myth of Male Power*.

Marty Nemko

photo credit: Dianne Woods

- "Coach extraordinaire." *U.S. News*
- Author of 34 books ranging from *Careers for Dummies* to *Soloists:* short-short stories of introverts and outsiders facing a dilemma.
- Ph.D., educational psychology, University of California Berkeley.
- Marty enjoys giving talks and being interviewed, playing in-home concerts of show tunes and standards on the piano, hybridizing roses, and his doggie, Hachi.
- Marty's first job was, at age 13, barroom piano player. At 20, he drove a taxicab in New York City.
- You can follow Marty on x.com/martynemko

To people who,
by choice or not,
spend time in the dark.

A Note from the Author

Dear Reader,

I welcome your honest review of this book on Amazon as well as your email. I promise to respond. My email address is mnemko@gmail.com

Contents

NOTE: The author reads all these stories aloud on YouTube. Just search YouTube on the name of the story and the word "Nemko."

Kisser

Liz West, Flickr, CC 2.0

The doorbell rang at 3 AM. I opened the door to find a wicker basket. In it, wrapped in a blanket, was a puppy.

I work full-time. Who has time for a dog? Even if I got a dogsitter, that's expensive and then there are the nights and the weekends.

And the training! Who has time? Who wants pee and poop in the house?

So cute as the puppy was, I steeled myself, carried him into the car and drove to the pound.

He would not get off my lap. Indeed, the more I drove, the more he curled up in my lap. And then he fell asleep on my lap.

Still, I was not going to have a dog!

I pulled into the pound's parking lot, saw the entrance—It reminded me of Auschwitz. I pursed my lips and lifted the puppy with one hand and started to reach for the car door with the other. And then, damn it, the puppy licked my face.

I just couldn't do it. I closed the car door, yeah with the puppy and me inside. I named him based on what just happened. My forever companion would be named Kisser.

But if it was one thing I wouldn't let Kisser do is disrupt my sleep. So even before I got home, I went to the pet store and got a crate and a cushion to put inside it. Add the food, collar and leash, and tax and I was out $247. And that was before the vet visit. Kisser was perfectly healthy but needing spaying and shots—another 300 bucks.

I read on the internet how important it is to begin housebreaking immediately and to count on it taking a week. So damn it, I took a week off from work. And every time Kisser got up from his nap, I carried him outside to the pee place and waited… and waited. Finally, success, followed instantly by a treat and massive praise. But despite my diligence, Kisser had a few accidents, including one vomit. But yes, after a week he was trained.

But Kisser would not sleep in his crate. The first night, I put him in and within seconds, he was whimpering, the sweetest damn whimper you ever heard. I needed to sleep so I moved the crate from the kitchen to my bedroom. He still whimpered, and whimpered. At some God-forsaken hour, I got up, put a towel on the far corner of the bed—I was NOT going to have pee or poop on my blanket—and I lowered him onto the towel. He immediately stopped whimpering, curled up and went to sleep—He was doing a great job of training me. The only thing, by the time I got up in the morning, Kisser was no longer at the foot of the bed. He was curled up around my warmest spot—my crotch. And when I started to get up, he jumped on me, licked my face, we went out, and he did his business like a pro.

After a week, I was grateful I had Kisser. I could see why they call a dog man's best friend. So you can imagine how I felt when after eight days, the doorbell rang. It was a neighbor. She said, "I had just gotten a puppy when, in the middle of the night, I got a call from a hospital 200 miles away—My dad had had a heart attack. I was frantic. I was so frantic I forget to leave you a note and I forgot all about the dog. My dad died, we had the funeral, and when I came back and saw the crate, I remembered. I am so sorry, so so sorry. Thank you so much for taking care of my puppy. Can I have him back now?"

Spoon

Suzi Jones, Picryl, Public Domain

After I finished high school, everyone thought I'd go to Poland's most prestigious college, the University of Warsaw, but my father's fabric business was struggling to stay alive. The Nazi invasion was making even Christians nervous about spending on discretionary items.

The town we lived in was safe—No one locked their door. So one day—and yes it was 1942, so we shouldn't have been so surprised—there was an unusually loud knock on the door. It was two Nazis in black boots. Unlike in the movies, they didn't yell. One was silent and the other whispered, "You will be out of your house with only what you can carry by noon tomorrow, or else."

The next day at noon, four Nazis came to the door again and yelled, "Rouse!" And they dragged my mom, dad, sister, and me onto a truck.

They took us to a place in the forest called Ponary. One Nazi grabbed my sister and dragged her away to a barrack. The other Nazis threw the rest of us into a pit, whereupon they shot most of us to death, including my mother and father. They left a few of us for a reason I was soon to learn.

I had rarely cried before but then I sobbed, hard. Then they threw gasoline onto the dead people and used a flame thrower to set them on fire. I threw up. Then they threw shovels and lime into the pit and yelled, "Now, you bury them nice and you'll get food. If not, you'll go too."

That night, we took our spoons, dug a hole under the barbed wire, and escaped. At least we tried. The Nazis shot all of us except me. I had managed to run deeper into the forest.

For days, I survived only by eating nuts and berries from the trees. Then I saw a cabin in the distance. I was exhausted but seeing it, I practically ran there.

An old woman answered the door and on seeing me, unshaven, dirty, smelling of something that had burned, she must have been scared. "What do you want?!"

I explained that I'm harmless. Still she said, "Go away." I had to think of something. I saw her wearing a big cross and there was a picture of Jesus on her wall, so I said, "I'm a priest who the Nazis chased away. Can I bless you?"

She softened and I tried to make up some Catholic-sounding blessing, and she then took care of me for three years until the Americans liberated the Jews.

I was put on a train to England and then on a cargo boat to Ellis Island, New York City. I didn't have a penny, no education, no family, no English, only the scars of the Holocaust.

The only job I could get was shining shoes. I didn't want to do that forever so I went to night school to learn English. My teacher said I learned quickly and that I should go to college. So I went to Bronx Community College and then City College of New York, and then, Albert Einstein Medical School.

That was 50 years ago.

Today, I was looking at the patients I was to see today and saw my sister's name! I assume she survived Ponary because the Nazis thought she was sexy.

Now, both of us were far from sexy. I am a year from retirement and she looked even older than I do. And when I saw her chart, I saw why: She was referred to me, a cardiologist, because her primary care doctor diagnosed her with end-stage heart failure.

I couldn't wait for her appointment but was dreading having to confirm the diagnosis. I'll just say that we hugged for 20 minutes.

This story is derived from my father's true story. He was one of the men to escape from the Ponary death camp where, indeed, he had been forced to bury the Jews that the Nazis shot. It's also true that the men used spoons to dig a tunnel to escape. It's also true that after the war, my father was dumped on a cargo boat and dropped in the Bronx, where the only job he could get was as a factory worker. He went to night school to learn English and, while he didn't become a doctor, he made a middle-class living owning a small store in a tough neighborhood in Brooklyn. My dad, Boris Nemko, is my greatest inspiration.

How the World Ends and Begins Again

Bousure, Flickr, CC 2.0

Under pressure from the world media, Iran finally elected a more liberal government. To prove it was still tough, it gave more money and weapons to Israel's adjacent enemies Syria and Lebanon, and to groups committed to destroying Israel: Hezbollah, Islamic Jihad, ISIS-Sinai, Al-Aksa Martyrs Brigade, and the Palestinian government: Hamas.

In an attempt to preempt attacks, Israel fired a fusillade of missiles at all of the above. Iran used that "unprovoked attack" to solicit military funding and weaponry from Russia and then from China.

The U.S. tried to broker a negotiated solution and ruled out military involvement, remembering the lessons of Vietnam, Iraq, Afghanistan, and Ukraine.

But talks quickly broke down when Iran, now well-funded, decided it would do better negotiating from strength. So it bombed Haifa, Israel's port and third largest city, killing hundreds, mainly port workers.

While the European Union remained mostly silent, the U.S. along with the U.K. felt it must act, despite protests from the now enlarged "Squad."

U.S. and U.K. involvement grew as it became clear that the Iran-Russia-China triumvirate was emboldened by the West's modest response. It then bombed, with conventional and chemical weapons, Israel's two largest cities: Tel Aviv and Jerusalem. Then, at 3 AM on Yom Kippur, the Jews' most solemn holiday, The Triumvirate fired a nuclear bomb into the heart of Israel, destroying all of the tiny country's buildings, 90 percent of its people immediately, and the other 10 percent would likely soon die because of radiation poisoning.

At that point, the U.S. and the U.K. with modest support from NATO, launched a retaliatory nuclear strike against the Iran-Russia-China triumvirate. It was supposed to be tactical-only on military targets but errors resulted in a nuke devastating St. Petersburg Russia and another one in Chengdu China, both population centers. That triggered additional nuclear attacks by both sides and thus the world essentially ended.

A decimated United Nations met in the basement of the United Nations building (the above-ground part had been destroyed) and agreed it would restart the world with a one-world, largely socialist government. They agreed that climate change, a long-term but not immediate threat, would be put on the back burner.

But almost immediately, a capitalist group decided to splinter and the former India gave it land.

And so it all began again.

A Dose of Reality

F.a.r.e.w.e.l.l CC 2.0

This is based on a true story. Only irrelevant details have been changed.

Tom got a doctorate in education and everyone was sure he'd become a professor preparing graduate students for a career as a K-12 teacher.

But in Tom's fieldwork, it was clear to him that he was far from a master teacher. He couldn't even control difficult students. Tom had learned a lot of theory but too little that was practical.

So after completing his doctorate, he decided he needed to get practical experience to see if he could become a good teacher. So, he took a job in one of Boston's high schools that are sanitizingly called "challenged."

It soon became clear to Tom that many of the students, especially the active boys, had a hard time sitting through a 50-minute period and especially the double periods that education experts advocate.

So Tom decided that during a double period, he'd take his class on a little field trip. The problem was that half of the students didn't return the parent permission slip. It wasn't that the parents or guardians weren't willing to sign. The slips too often didn't get to them. Tom's students said they lost it, their parents were away, and so on. He gave them another permission slip but still, many didn't come back.

So Tom decided to try a trip with all the kids, even if some didn't have a permission slip. He thought, "It's just to the nearby tide pool." He rented a 15-person van and packed his class into it. (If a bit scrunched, they'd all fit in the van because while his class size was officially 22, on the average day, only 15 would show.)

Everyone had a great time. And to ensure that they were addressing the mandated Common Core Curriculum, they discussed and Tom gave assignments that tied the trip to academic learning.

So, a week later, they did another trip. This time, it was a behind-the-scenes tour of a bakery. Another success.

Unfortunately, the third time, when the kids were getting into the van, this time to go to a museum, the principal saw them aghast — "Mr. Johnson, don't you know that our insurance doesn't cover that!? And did you get permission slips from all the parents?"

Tom murmured no, she pulled him aside, and said, "I am initiating termination procedures. You are endangering your students."

Of course, Tom was sad, scared, but also angry —He wanted to better serve his students and as a result, he was getting fired?! So that very Friday, he asked his class, "Who'd like to spend the weekend in my apartment with my family?" Nearly everyone raised their hand. There wasn't enough room in Tom's apartment for all the students but his classroom aide volunteered to let some stay with her. The next morning, Tom asked his aide, "So how'd it go?" She said, "Two of them raped me."

Tom lamented not just the loss of his job but that he had tried so hard to be a good teacher, and his aide was so kind, so patient. How could two of their students do that? How dare they? Tom thought, "I'm not sure what to believe anymore."

Tom thought about taking some innocuous job like clerk in a bookstore but accepted a job at a university teaching prospective teachers.

Dog Stolen. "Reward!"

Sart Face, Pexels, Free to reuse

Jessica had a stressful job as a social worker. So, more even than most dog owners, she was glad at the end of the day to get that enthusiastic greeting from her sweet doggie, Bella.

Bella had to hold it in all day because Jessica lived in an apartment. So Jessica's first priority was to take Bella for a walk and, to kill two birds with one stone, they made a quick stop at Trader Joe's— She only needed half-and-half for her beloved morning coffee and spring greens for her daily, virtuous salad.

As usual, Jessica tied Bella to a post in an inconspicuous place on the side of Trader Joe's. For years, there was never a problem, but today when Jessica returned, Bella was gone.

Jessica raced around, drove around, yelling "Bella!" to no avail. She constantly checked her cell because Bella's tag listed her phone number … and the word "Reward."

Finally, adrenaline dissipated, Jessica plodded back home and got herself a glass of wine to wait out the vigil. "The damn thief will call to get his fucking reward."

And the thief did. Teresa, 18, single mother of two, struggling to live amid the noise of an SRO, felt desperate. So when she saw the docile Bella and the tag saying "Reward," Teresa took Bella who, trusting sweetie, came willingly.

Flatly, Teresa said, "I've got your dog. I need $500."

Jessica, so relieved, suppressed anger and quickly said "Okay."

Teresa responded, "You answered too fast. A thousand, take it or leave it. I can get two grand for it."

Jessica, now educated, feigned tears, waited, and murmured, "That will wipe me out but... okay. Where should we meet?"

They met in a remote warehouse district, with Bella in Teresa's arms.

Jessica tearfully ran to Bella.

"Not so fast. We forgot about the $300 sales tax. $1,300 or I sell her."

Jessica, suppressing anger said, "Honestly, I don't have it. I took the $1,000 from the bank."

"Go to the ATM."

Jessica returned with the extra $300 and counted out $1,300 whereupon Teresa took the money and handed Bella back to Jessica.

Teresa laughed, "I would have taken 50 bucks. Maybe I should take up poker."

An Old Wolf Talks to Us

Hippopx, CC2.0

There once was a wolf who had always been the smartest and meanest in the pack. For example, he won the Lone Wolf award for killing the most sheep solo— no wolf pack— 23 sheep.

But while attempting his greatest feat, trying to down a cow solo in the November of his years, the farmer shot the wolf, rendering him a paraplegic.

The wolf speaks to us now from his den.

"I feel pretty good about how I've lived my life— I lived up to my lupine potential. Sure, occasionally I felt a little sad for the sweet sheep. I recognize that they are nicer animals than I am, but I can't be what I'm not. My genes consigned me to being an apex predator. Of course, I too am prey. Bears love us, tigers order us for their main course, and then there are the humans. I can't really blame people— After all, our main course is their livestock, their livelihood. And so it goes.

Now I wait out my days, ahem, wolfing down easy prey: old or sick mice, rats, rabbits, and my favorite, deer.

And I spend a lot of time thinking. My favorite thought is that I'm not that far removed from a dog. Ah, a dog's life: stretched out, snuggling warm, and completely safe in a human's bed and then, only when I feel like it, I get up and not have to fight for food but just look longingly at my person who always responds by filling my bowl— Yes, dogs actually have a bowl for their food— with nuggets perfectly tailored to their dietary needs and preferences.

I also wonder if there's Wolf Heaven, with the pearly gates not manned but, of course, wolfed. Would I get into heaven? Maybe killing so many sheep make me a bad wolfie, and then it would be down to Wolf Hell, where I'd never get to eat anything better than old, sick mice.

But mainly I just feel sorry for myself. I can't believe that I lost out to a truly inferior wolf for the Three Little Pigs gig. I could have blown that damn house down and I would have been famous: Not just a Big, Bad, Wolf, the Biggest, Baddest Wolf. But here I sit in my cave, just another old Woulda-Coulda-Shoulda.

What would I come back as? I think I'd want to come back as a gentle human being. I'd adopt a dog from a shelter and be nice to it and to everyone else. Aw, that's just a silly fairy tale. I think I'll just try to find me an old deer.

The Emperor's New Clothes (DEI version)

I'm the head of the DEI caucus at the Silicon Valley Institute of Technology.

PNGFree, CC

They call me "loud 'n 'proud" and they should. I *am* loud n' proud. Like at my last call-to-arms meeting, I preached:

> *BIPOCs are ever more the victim of systemic racism, oppression by the white male patriarchy. Their demanding excellence, virtuosity, even merit is just a white supremacist value and an excuse to avoid DEI: diversity, equity, and inclusion. We must be as one, we-not-me, together, all in. But not just equality but equity, a term we redefined from fairness to giving us our deserved advantage after 150 years of the legacy of slavery — reparations! People of the World, especially intersectionalists, UNITE!"*

Although I didn't get a standing ovation, everyone cheered, even chanted, — UNITE, UNITE, UNITE. A few white and Asian males didn't cheer. I think they were afraid to disagree and show what racists they are. And then, the oldest white male in the room — He was 50 if he was a day — stood up.

He said,

> *Replacing merit with melanin reduces all of us to a lower common denominator, hurting everything from our coworkers to our college, from customer care to medical care. You should be ashamed of yourself.*

Everyone stared at me, then at each other. Next, one person applauded *him* and slowly, every white and Asian male and even some women(!) stood up. They gave *him* a standing ovation. They're a bunch of fuckin' racists!

In the Recycled Coffin

VectorGraphics, CC

I hate my father and my father hates, or I should say, hated, me. He always blamed me for everything and beat me with a strap until I got big enough to grab it away from him.

Yeah, I'm no saint. I'm just not driven like him. He hates that. So it was really hard for me to ask him for a job — I just couldn't get or hold a job on the outside. I needed money, and welfare's cash, food stamps, subsidized housing, transportation vouchers, and free healthcare weren't enough for my lifestyle.

My timing was good: The guy who cleaned the used coffins had quit. I guess I should explain used coffins. You see, my father would buy used coffins — custom ones that the customer didn't like, coffins used in movies, and especially coffins from environmentalists who want to recycle — Right after the attendees left the burial ceremony, the greenie had the ditchdigger dig up the coffin and sell it to my father for resale.

It's illegal to sell a used coffin but my father nor the greenies gave a shit. For some crazy reason, my father did give a shit about getting the coffin clean. How stupid is that — I mean, only dead people go in a coffin. Yet he made me go into each coffin and clean every inch with a toothbrush and industrial-strength Clorox. Of course, the coffin lid was open but the smell still is terrible and probably causes cancer.

When he wasn't watching, I would just spray a coffin for two seconds with a bottle of regular Clorox spray that I keep hidden behind one of the coffins. That way, when he came by, it smelled it like I cleaned it the way he wanted.

Well, one day, I heard him coming down the hall toward the coffin room, so I got my toothbrush and industrial bleach, and went down into a coffin.

Little did I know that he had filled a caulk gun with odorless industrial instant-bonding glue. He quickly but quietly squeezed it around the coffin's rim, slammed the lid shut, and sat on it.

Of course, I screamed but he laughed, "When you die of asphyxiation and bleach vapors, I'll take you to the gravedigger and say it's another of my pro-bono paupers."

I now understand what they mean when they say that a parent whose child who gets stuck under a car tire develops superhuman strength and can lift the car. Well, my adrenaline went wild and I was able to push the coffin's lid up despite the hardening glue and my father sitting on it — Thank God, he is thin. Or I should say, *was* thin. I strangled his ass, put him in the coffin, took it to the gravedigger, and used the pauper story.

Left! Right!

Courtesy, The State

Dear reader: Why would I write this horrific bit of fiction? Because the research literature indicates https://tinyurl.com/3utu6h8y *that psychopaths show signs early and that intervention may help. To alert you to such signs, I've embedded common ones in this story. If reading this raises your concern about someone you care about, do consider getting him or her help.*

I can't help it. I like torturing.

When I was a little kid, I got off on pulling the legs off a spider. I tried to cut off a dog's tail but my mother saw me and I lied saying I was just trying to cut off a mat that was bothering the poor puppy. That worked.

I loved beating kids up and making them beg me to stop. I wouldn't until some grown-up made me. Then I'd make up some story about how he was racist or something.

I loved when boxers knocked the shit out of a guy but that got too wimpy, so I started watching MMA, and then snuff films.

I'm trying to get tough. I have the dentist drill me without novocaine. I bite my arm until I bleed hard. I pump iron so hard I scream but keep going even though I'm cramping.

I love Che Guevara. Not only did he enjoy killing dogs, https://tinyurl.com/3jsn8mta he said, "A revolutionary must become a cold killing machine motivated by pure hate. We must create the pedagogy of the paredón [execution wall]." https://www.azquotes.com/quote/716640 So I'm going to join Antifa or maybe some Middle East terrorists. Maybe they'll let me be like Nazi Josef Mengele: https://tinyurl.com/ydfptfcd yelling some hostages "Left!" where they'll get murdered or "Right!" and live for another day to face me again.

On Guard

Lauren, Flckr, CC 2.0

I'm writing to you from the grave.

I'm wondering if I was too on my guard.

I was a gardener, which protected me from people — I did better with plants. At home, my best friends were my plants. I had Peace Lilies https://tinyurl.com/5c2cf6nw all over my apartment.

The main time I went out was after work: Almost every day, I went to my local quiet bar, had a glass of house red, and read *Reason* magazine or the *Wall Street Journal's* opinion pages.

Every night, the bartender would just say, "The usual?" I'd nod and she nodded. One night, after around ten years of that, she asked, "How about one on the house tonight?" I nodded and when she brought my wine, she asked, "Wanna tell me a little about you?" I thought about it for too long, which I'm sure made her feel uncomfortable, and then I said, "I think it's safer not to."

At age 60, feeling the ever-growing meaninglessness of it all, my horror at what the world now prizes, and knowing it will be downhill from here for the world and for me, I went to the woods and I shot myself.

Only one person came to the funeral: the bartender, who had read about it in the local paper. When the officiant — I'm an atheist — asked if she wanted to say anything about me, she shook her head.

Limb from Limb

My clients like me, with one notable exception, a very notable exception.

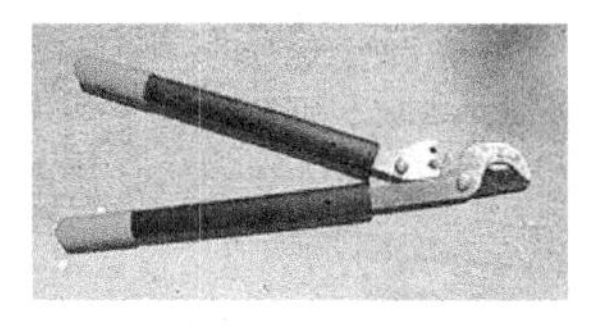

Dvortygirl, Wikimedia, CC 3.0

I had suggested that the client, Damien, might want to stop looking back to how his parents treated him and instead, identify baby steps for moving forward. He exploded. "You just don't get me. You just don't fucking get me!"

That freaked me out, so without really thinking about it, I decided to offer what he had twice asked for: Do a session at his apartment. He then smiled, an odd smile, which should have tipped me off but I was so eager to make amends that I simply felt glad that he smiled.

But when Damien answered his door, he, much larger, stronger, and younger than me, immediately threw handcuffs on me and cuffed my hands and legs to a heavy chair, pulled out a pair of pruning shears and tree-limb loppers and said, "I'm going to cut you limb from limb. I'll start with your pinky and go from there."

The first thing I could think to say was, "I know you're hurting."

Damien seethed, "I'm not hurt. I like to hurt people who deserve punishment: drug dealers, bad teachers, and useless therapists."

Then I tried, "Won't you feel better if you bring out that good person inside you?"

"Shrink bullshit."

He moved the pruning shears next to my hand. I somehow wasn't that nervous, I guess because I couldn't believe he'd actually do it, but he did. He chopped off the tip of my pinky.

Now I *was* nervous, especially as I looked at the tree-limb lopper. I managed to try, "If you're in prison, you won't get to achieve your dream: buy that tricked -out motorcycle and show it off in your old neighborhood."

"They won't catch me. You're number 6 and I'm 5 for 5.

Then, in my most sincere-sounding voice, I cooed, "Damien, I so admire that you're the big-and-bad, loud-and-proud person I wish I were. I love you."

"Bullshit." and he moved the lopper to my wrist.

This time I didn't say anything. I just looked into his eyes in the most loving way I could. After what seemed forever but probably was just ten seconds, his body relaxed, he unlocked me, put a tourniquet around my finger, and said, "See you next week?"

I nodded and slowly left.

When I was back in my car and out of his sight, I raced to the emergency room while calling 911.

My Toupee

Patrick Q, Flickr CC 2.0

I didn't want to go. After all, parties had never worked for me. In fact, nothing had ever worked for me—I was 21 and still a virgin. But everyone still told me—my friends, my parents, my grandmother for God's sake—that I had to keep getting out there.

So I took a deep breath and went in. Everyone was smiling, laughing, seeming so natural. I stood in the corner for a while and then forced myself to amble—not too eager —toward a group that didn't seem too intimidating—not the Pretty People, not the gigglers, just three people chatting. I stood a few feet from them and tried to establish eye contact. I tried one girl but she didn't notice me or maybe she rejected me. I tried looking at another one, a guy this time to avoid it looking like I was hitting on a girl, and he held my eyes for a moment. I figured that was all I could expect, so I took a step toward the group. That girl was talking about her plans for grad school. The guy chimed in, "I'm in enough student debt already." I nodded. The other girl said, "And these days, it's degree proliferation. Even a master's degree makes employers yawn." We smiled but knew that wasn't funny.

I asked the grad-school-bound girl, "So what are you going to study?" She said, "Computer science, artificial intelligence, you know, where the jobs are."

I nodded but felt like such a loser. I had taken Intro to Computer Science and didn't understand most of it. I had to cheat my way to a C. So I decided that I'd better major in something like sociology or media studies. I think they saw my face drop, so I excused myself and got a drink. The rest of the evening, like all parties, didn't go any better for me, so I left early.

I was stressed out and a shower is one of the few places I feel relaxed, so even though I didn't need a shower, I took one. When I got out, I looked in the mirror and asked myself, "What is wrong with me?" Am I trying too hard? Not hard enough? Should I memorize jokes to tell at the next party? Then I did something I had been scared to do—look at myself in the mirror, hard. My hair being wet made clear that my hairline had already started to recede. I took a handheld mirror so I could see the back—a bald spot was already forming.

Was that the problem? Should I get a toupee? I thought, that's stupid. Only idiotic characters on TV wear a toupee. But the idea stayed with me because that was a more doable solution than trying to change my personality or my major to something more impressive than sociology.

So I decided to get a consultation. It wouldn't cost anything to get information—You know, knowledge is power and all that. But where? I searched Yelp—It was 2005 and it had just started, and I saw that The Full Head already had a dozen reviews, which averaged 4.5 stars. When I got there, the waiting room's walls were covered with before-and-after pictures. Wow! And the cute receptionist asked if I'd like something to drink while I was waiting. I knew that was just business but I was starved for female attention, so it felt good.

When I got into the consultation room, a handsome guy smiled and said, "Yup, I'm wearing one. You're Joe, right?" I nodded and he continued. "Joe, it's great that you've come while you still have most of your hair—

People will just say you look great, well-rested, or something." He then asked, "What's the main reason you've come in—career, self-esteem, romance?" I smiled at the latter. He said, "Joe, that's the most common reason—and it works." I knew I was dealing with a master salesman but I was open to being sold.

He pulled out a photo album and said, "Of course, we have lots of styles but there are three I think would look wonderful on you. (I had heard that in funeral homes, salespeople always show three caskets—enough to give choice, not so many that you're overwhelmed.) He asked, "Do any of these call out to you?" I pointed to one and before I knew it, I had bought a $3,000 "hairpiece." I'm not surprised they avoid the word, "toupee."

Whatever you call it, I can't say that it turned me into a chick magnet but within a month, I was no longer a virgin. And despite my sociology major, I somehow felt more confident in job interviews, and I did get hired as a community relations specialist for a bank.

My job was mainly to address complaints and to hold events, like free workshops on financial literacy and on home ownership. Usually, we held them at the bank but for Father's Day, we did one as a picnic in a nearby park.

It was cool that morning, so I wore a light sweater but by noon, I needed to pull it off. I tried to be careful but lifting it was enough to push the sides of my hairpiece up so it looked like it had wings! Someone pointed to me, which made another person take out her camera. She must have sent it to the newspaper —Everyone knows that the media likes to do hit pieces on banks.

Two days later, as I'm drinking my morning coffee at home, I opened the newspaper to see that jpg of me. The headline: "A Phony Banker." I pulled off my hairpiece and stared at my now quite-bald self in the mirror. Do I go au naturel? I am terrified to do that but I am terrified to wear it. What would you do?

Average Jane

In school, teachers focused on the brilliant and on the slow, so average Jane was pretty much ignored.

With permission 18/1 Graphics Studio

Jane's classmates liked the good-looking kids and made fun of the ugly ones. They barely noticed average Jane. At her 50th high school reunion, most people didn't even remember her.

In college, while Jane wanted to date, she felt uncomfortable trying to stand out— being perky, dressing sexily, and so on. So she was pretty much ignored.

When Jane applied for jobs, her resume didn't stand out, so the best she could get was rent-a-car reservationist, where she chatted little with customers or co-workers. Jane was forgettable.

She joined a hiking group but even when she approached people, the conversation quickly petered out and they'd move on.

Jane did have some modest romantic relationships but sooner than later, the guy would end it. When Jane asked for an explanation, they said things like, "There's nothing wrong with you. There's just not quite the spark."

Jane thought that maybe she could be special if she worked with disabled people, so she volunteered at a group home for people with intellectual disabilities. But she had difficulty helping them and got little recognition for her efforts, so after a few Saturdays, apologizing, she quit.

Next, she tried volunteering at an animal shelter. She and the doggies loved each other but that didn't feel enough.

At the end of her 50th high school reunion, Jane trudged back to her car, gently closed its door, and cried. Would she die unexceptional, unrecognized? She sat trying to concoct a basis for hope: She considered dolling herself up, puffing herself up, bubbling herself up, but in the end, decided that the wisest course was self-acceptance.

Jane spent her last decade reading, journaling, gardening, painting, petting dogs at the shelter, and volunteering at a suicide hotline.

A go-getter might have done more to improve her lot but average Jane had just average drive. By definition, half of people have done worse.

Very Vegan, Oy Vey

PickPic, CC

I was the only reporter left on the student newspaper — Now, most kids would rather look at Tik and Insta. And one time, I wrote the issue's only real story: that Very Vegan, a company that promised healthy, local, organic sustainable food, got the contract to provide our school lunches.

Most kids hated the new lunches — Much of it went into the trash. Not only did the new lunches taste worse, they didn't seem as fresh and wonderful as the salesperson and brochures promised, and were very different from the couple of sample lunches they gave us before they got the contract.

So I decided to do a little investigative reporting. I visited Very Vegan. Because our school is small, I didn't expect to see a huge industrial kitchen but it was a really small place, way in the back of a warehouse park.

I went in and it was clear they didn't want me there. The manager smiled, gave me a very quick tour, handed me a free sample of a stuffed mushroom that tasted much better than the stuff they serve us at lunch, and sent me on my way.

I came back that night, late, when I was sure no one would be there. Out in front were a bunch of big, gray, plastic bags. Each bore a plain label handwritten, "Conventional/non-organic, bruised 2nds. Source: multiple countries."

Of course, I wrote an article about it titled, *Very Vegan, Oy Vey.* The contract with Very Vegan got canceled and I included the article in my college applications. I got into all my reach schools — with a big discount!

I'm Nice but Not Good

My parents taught me to be nice — and it's gotten me far: I'm vice-president for

DeviantArt, CC

development (fundraising) for Midwestern State University.

I'm always gracious. In speeches, I say it was a team effort and put on a genuine-looking smile while looking kindly into the eyes of my staff and volunteers, a full second of eye contact with each, so they all feel special. With donors, I go beyond the obligatory thank-you letter. First, I take the time to add a personalized sentence to the oh-so-grateful boilerplate. If they're an even moderately big donor and especially if I think I can go for an even bigger Ask, I include a little customized present with a note saying "I've enjoyed talking with you but don't want to bother you, but if you'd like to chat, yes about making another gift or simply to chat about (I insert their hot-button issue which had been noted in their prospect-research dossier), I'd welcome a call. Here's my cell phone number." It works. I've beaten my quota every quarter, which is why I got to be VP and able to give my husband the new Beemer he wanted and me to remodel the kitchen even though it didn't really need remodeling.

Of course, what works at work also works personally. I listen attentively to my husband when he comes home from work, even if I'm bored hearing him complain. Same with friends, especially if they can help me in some way. I look for every opportunity to give them earned praise and I downplay my accomplishments. I make a point of talking only as much as I think they'd like — Some people like to dominate the conversation — No problem. Others prefer to listen more — With them, I speak maybe 2/3 of the time.

But just because I'm nice, doesn't mean I'm good. Between me and you, dear diary, here are a few truths about what I'm really like:

I hate most people. I think they're stupid, self-absorbed, and/or too subject to groupthink.

I think it's stupid for people to donate to the university. Most of the money could be far better spent. For example, when someone funds a "scholarship," it usually doesn't do what they think — enable someone to go to college who otherwise couldn't. It merely substitutes the donor's dollars for taxpayer dollars (govt grants) or dollars already in the college's coffers. When we say it's a "matching grant," the mark (the donor) thinks we'll go out and match their gift — No, it usually means that we just list their dollars next to a chunk that's already in our coffers. Worst, many big donors like to have a building built, with their name on it — egomaniacs. Truth is, usually there are better uses of the millions, but are we going to turn down boatloads of cash from fat cats?

"Making a difference" is oversold — Very few people make much difference even to their sphere of influence otherwise wouldn't get made. And I consider "virtue-"signaling greenies among the more foolish: They carefully recycle and buy a Tesla, which have essentially zero impact on the environment while many of the world's 200 countries burn mountains of coal because they need cheap energy to enable their people to survive.

Stupid humankind.

Thank you, dear diary. I feel I can be honest only with you.

The Hillcrest Widow Club

The four women of the Hillcrest Widow Club met every Thursday morning at 9 in the corner of a quiet coffee shop.

Gareth Williams, Flickr, CC2.0

Their statements about their deceased husbands started politely. For example, Mary said, "Yes, it's difficult but I'm trying to muddle through."

But slowly, their fear of being seen as cold faded, but what really opened things up was when Zoe said, "Honestly, I'm relieved to be rid of that ball and chain."

Britney then felt free to pile on: "Don't we like talking with each other than with men? "We care more about family, feelings, and okay, fashion. The successful men mainly want to talk about their work, the unsuccessful ones about stupid sports."

Further emboldened, Zoe said, "And they just care about getting in and out, assuming they can get it up, which for the last decade, my husband couldn't. And I had to pretend it was okay." Two of the other women nodded.

That encouraged Zoe to admit that she had fantasies about lesbian sex, okay, more than fantasies.

Before long, they decided they needed more privacy, so they met in Zoe's plush living room. Mary asked, "How could you afford this?" Zoe replied, "My husband was a lawyer who had one client but a great one: the Environmental Protection Agency."

After a glass of wine or bong hit, Zoe moved close to Willow, the member who seemed most likely to be willing to kiss. Zoe looked her in the eye and when Willow didn't avert, Zoe kissed her as the others watched wide-eyed. Would Willow pull back? On the contrary, she sighed in pleasure.

But Zoe sensed it was too fast, not just for Willow, but for the others. So Zoe pulled back and asked if someone would like another hit or glass of wine.

But three "Zoe meetings" later, they all, and I mean all, had a very cuddly experience. But after, Mary whispered something that shocked the others:

> I love our Widow's Club but every so often I wonder, "Are men so bad that we're fine with bashing them. We wouldn't criticize women, let alone BIPOCs. If I did, I'd get the 3C's: Censure, Censor, or Cancel. Atop that, in so many news shows and especially movies, TV shows, and novels, a spunky, smart woman triumphs over an evil or clueless guy. And when women have the deficit, say, we're so-called underrepresented in science, there's massive redress and, yes, reverse discrimination— I know a number of women who got jobs over more competent, harder-working guys. Okay, so did I. Yet when men have the ultimate deficit— They live six years shorter than women, their last decade in worse health, and there are 4.4 widows for every widower— all we see is another run for breast cancer."

Over the next few meetings, the others began to shun Mary. It was subtle: a little less eye contact, a little more interrupting, and unlike before, no one asked her to get together between meetings.

Sad at being ostracized, Mary figured, that isn't a big a deal to play the game. She even told anti-male jokes: "What do you call a man with half a brain? Gifted. What's the difference between government bonds and men? Bonds mature. What is the difference between a man and a catfish? One is a bottom-feeding scum-sucker and the other is a fish."

Soon, Mary was back in the fold.

One Way to Get a Promotion

identity chris is, Flickr, CC 2.0

I'm one of the six directors in one of the federal agencies that deal with immigration. I was angry that two of my peers got promoted to senior director even though I know I'd do a far better job.

So when an opportunity arose to take a "creative" approach to getting that promotion, I took it. Let me explain.

A reporter from a major newspaper wanted to prove that our agency is anti-immigration — I could tell that was her slant from the questions she asked us.

Well, two days later, we had our usual private weekly meeting of the directors and senior directors. The presenter was the last remaining director who was appointed during the Trump administration. Not surprising, he argued that the pool of people who are willing to leave their homeland and illegally sneak into the U.S. are disproportionately people who have been unsuccessful in their homeland. He used a PowerPoint deck to support his position.

I realized that the reporter would find that deck a smoking gun. So I gave $100 to the overnight janitor to copy the deck onto a flash drive.

I am in favor of legalizing undocumented migrants so I would have given the flash drive to the reporter no matter what. But I figured it could help me get my promotion, and here's how I did it. I told her that I had a flash drive that would prove her contention that our agency was anti-illegal-immigration but that it was hard for me to get it so I'd only give it to her if she promised to praise me in her article.

And she did. Her "expose" called me "a beacon of progressivity, shining a light for the undocumented."

My boss, a fellow liberal, loved it and, in a month, I was promoted to senior director. Clever, huh?!

Affirmative Actions

With permission, 18/1 Graphics Studio

Mar. 15, 2017: Kevin was diagnosed with incipient sociopathy.

Sep. 13, 2019: Kevin wasn't selected as president of his high school's math club. Furious, he knocked over his desk. At home, he drew a caricature of the winner, splattered it with red paint, and hid it in his journal, which he hid inside a slit in his boxspring.

March 15, 2023. Despite a 4.0 and having been published three times in the American Journal of Bioweaponry as an undergraduate, a record, Kevin wasn't chosen to speak at graduation. He chose not to attend the ceremony. Rather, in the middle of the night, on the "Live and Excel" sign at the molecular biology building's entrance, with blood-red spray paint, he covered the "v," so the sign read, "Lie and Excel."

May 21, 2035, 4:00 PM: The chair of the bioweapons department told Kevin that the year's tenure slot went to someone else. Kevin exploded, insisting, "I am infinitely more qualified!" Evenly, the chair said, "As you know Kevin, unfortunately, it's up or out— If when you're up for tenure, you don't get it, you need to leave. You can stay until the end of June."

4:01 PM: Kevin removed the most virulent and airborne-communicable bioweapon from his lab's freezer, put it into the irradiator to create mutated versions, and inoculated 200 mice, 50 each with one of the four mutations that, under electron microscopy and flow cytometry, seemed most likely to be lethal.

May 22: Incubation period.

May 23: He cultured the mutation that killed the most mice— 48 of 50. Then, using machine-learning gene-editing software, he altered that virus to maximize its airborne transmissibility. He filled three tiny vials with it, enough to infect and later kill hundreds of people, who in turn, would infect thousands, who then would infect millions who, in turn, would kill billions. He cut open the seam of his wallet's inner lining and sealed it with glue that allowed the seam to be easily opened.

He drove to the furthest parking lot in JFK Airport. He got on the shuttle bus wearing an N95 mask that, inside, had a second, an even more protective filter, opened his wallet and surreptitiously opened one vial. By the time the bus arrived at the international terminal, the bus-full of people headed all over the globe having had breathed a fatal dose with its one-day incubation period.

Kevin bought a ticket to Beijing, which stopped in LA.

He duplicated the process at LAX and then at Beijing Airport.

May 24: In his hotel room in Beijing, Kevin took pleasure in watching President Chelsea Clinton on TV urging calm.

What You Don't See

You think you see me but you don't.

1 Freestock, CC

My kitchen table is covered with stacks of receipts for my income tax returns, which confound and annoy me — So much time to file what takes so much money from me and that returns so little. And the politicians blame productive, ethical, law-abiding *me*? Uhh.

Who has time to cook? So you see orange and banana peels in the sink and Chinese food cartons on the kitchen counter because the table is covered with that tax stuff. Uhhh.

I'm not sure I have enough in my checking account to cover the month's expenses. Do I pay the ridiculous interest on the credit card? Or do I cash in some of my 401K and pay the heavy penalty? Or do I just hope that there *is* enough in my checking account? Uhhhh.

I'm two days from the deadline for finishing online traffic school. I hate it but it's better than the $400 fine for "not coming to a full and complete stop at a stop sign" and the ticket raising my insurance. Uhhhhh.

And I need to go see my father more. He's doing badly, one step from needing assisted living. And how will I afford that? I'm not quite poor enough to get the taxpayer to pay. As I said, I get little for my pound of tax flesh. Uhhhhhhh.

Plus, I work so hard yet I'm not noticed let alone make much of a difference. Uhhhhhhh.

God, I'm overwhelmed.

But day after day, I go back out there, working with the required restrained pleasantness, and die a little more.

I Can't Even Give Away My Books

A sane person would have given up by now.

Matt Zhang, Flickr, CC 2.0

My first book was light-years from a bestseller: It sold 17 copies, and 14 were to my family and friends. My new one has sold a grand total of six, count 'em six. Even my family quickly got sick of buying my books.

And it's not that I haven't tried to sell them. After all, they say that after you've crossed the last t and dotted the last i, you're only half done. The rest is marketing and unless you're Oprah, it's all on you. So every day, I flog.

Of course, I post on social media, and not just announcing the book — a million are published each year. No — I give away excerpts of my fiction book, *Tom's Tale* and a Tip of the Week from my how-to book, *Bossing Your Boss.)* I run contests, even offering a free book for the first three people to say why they like or hate it. (Not one response.)

I post on Twitter, LinkedIn, and Facebook. My friends say, "But what about TikTok and Instagram?" I visited — We all must have *some* standards.

I ask to speak at libraries, bookstores, service clubs, MeetUps, and churches — Usually crickets, and the few times I spoke, I had optimistically brought ten books but sold just one or two. I visited my local college campus at noon and offered the books free to passersby. Almost no one has taken one — I can't even give away my books.

I even donated ten to the local mental hospital — A friend had told me they like to give books to patients, but only softcovers. They're too likely to use a hardcover as a weapon.

I hate to admit it but despite it all, I'm starting to write book three: *Tales of an Utterly Unsuccessful Author.* Think it'll sell?

Divorcing After 70 Years

It started so innocently. I was sitting next to Mildred in the arts-and-crafts room, doing a jigsaw puzzle. My legs were bothering me

Gratis Graphics, CC

so I asked Mildred if she'd get a throw for me to put over my legs.

She sighed. Somehow that was the last straw. I said, "I do so much for you and I merely ask you, who still have good legs, to go the 10 feet to get a throw and you sigh?"

"You're always asking for things. For 70 years you've been asking for things."

"I know how you hate to be put-upon, so I ask only the minimum. You're my wife of 70 years, I'm a good man, yet you treat me worse than a stranger.

She sighed again, and that put me over the edge. "Mildred, I want a divorce."

"What?! You're sick. You want to be single? You've had two heart attacks!"

"Because of you."

"You're 93 years old!"

"I want the little time I have left to be in peace."

The stress got to me and I got chest pains. That scared me into silence.

Big Balls

With permission, 18/1 Graphics Studio

Vijay Patel looked up at the clock: 6:30 PM. When he first became an engineer, he would have been happy to work for another few hours. But now, he sighed and wished he could quit for the night. Actually, he thought about quitting engineering forever.

"But all those years I invested: India Institute of Technology and in climbing the ladder. And what would my friends think? My family? I could hear my grandfather: "What? You're going to open a restaurant. Only the lower castes do that!"

"Actually yes," he thought, "Indian food is some of the most interesting. And I'd bring my engineer's perfectionism to it. No oily pre-made buffets, in fact nothing pre-made, everything to-order. And, of course, no canned sauces or gulab jamon. Fresh vegetables and I'd buy my spices from my friend Vishnu who imports the best cumin, coriander, clove, cinnamon, turmeric, fenugreek, cardamom, all of it. I'll make the naan right—each piece fresh in the tandoor. To keep prices down, I'll find a location that's good but just dicey enough that the rent will be okay."

And Vijay did all that. And his family ridiculed him. "His mother said, "I am embarrassed. We all are. You're giving up a directorship at Apogee Software to open the ten millionth Indian restaurant? Idiot!"

His son, Subhas, was even more vicious: "You don't know shit about running a restaurant. You'll piss away your savings and go bust within a year. And then no one will hire you— Who'd want a software engineer who quit to open a restaurant and failed, at age 51?"

Vijay did everything he promised himself he would. And discerning customers returned again and again, but there weren't enough of them.

Slowly, Vijay's already marginal business shrank. He felt forced to say yes to the ad salesman who suggested he advertise a 10% off coupon. That didn't help but Vijay said no to upping it to 25%. "I will not give 25% of what I've worked so hard for!" That's also what he said to the delivery services: Doordash, GrubHub, and UberEats.

But now, Vijay was bleeding serious money and decided to stop minimizing the problem with his son, who was a marketing manager.

Subhas said, "Finally. Thank you, Dad, for coming clean. Let me market your business. I can make it successful. The only thing I ask is that you give me three months to do it my way. If you don't like the results, you can go back to your way." Vijay felt he had no choice.

Subhas sprang into action. He decided that the key would be to make the restaurant cool to Gen Z'ers. Vijay's Indian Restaurant? Stodgy. Mumbai Mambo? Better but mambo is for old people. Ah, we'll make the gulab jamon (round dessert balls) huge and call the restaurant, Big Balls.

Decor? We can save: cheap posters of Gen-Z performers. And we can name dishes and drinks after them, like Beyonce Biryani and the Taylor Swift cocktail— It swoons you swiftly.

We'll bring in live music. I know I can convince Gen-Z bands to do it for exposure to their target market, plus it's a date magnet.

Servers? I'll visit a few malls and hire away good cellphone salespeople, offering them commission on appetizers, drinks, high-priced entrees, and desserts. To help them and myself, I'll have tabletop tents for appetizers, drinks, and desserts.

Our plates are stupid. Yeah, they're hand-painted from India but the rims are narrow. That means you gotta put more food on the plate to make it look full enough. I'll steal a lesson from frou-frou restaurants: ultra-wide-rim plates and in white, so the contrast with the food's color makes it look like there's more food on the plate.

And no more free naan. And I'll charge a lot for it— I don't want them filling up on bread. I want them to pay for big-ticket, high-margin stuff: drinks, appetizers, entrees, and dessert.

To further discourage naan while saving money, no more making it fresh in the tandoor—storebought and thrown in the microwave.

It took too long for dad to make the dishes to order, so I'll use canned sauces. They're not bad. I'll have the cook put them in black plastic bags—In the dumpster in back of a frou-frou Italian restaurant, I once saw a bunch of empty cans of canned sauce. I don't want my customers to see that I use canned.

But using canned sauce, I need to get dad out of the kitchen—He'll be furious. Maybe I can do it if I flatter him into saying he'd be a great maitre'd. Nope. Wrong demographic—I'll use hot college girls. I gotta get him to work the back office—He said he'd give me three months to do it my way.

Okay, onto publicity. I'll make funny videos on TikTok and Insta, like holding up the Big Balls. Also, organic is hot so I'll say, "We love organic." That doesn't mean it needs to be 100% organic. Maybe just some organic spices would do.

I'm not allowed to solicit Yelp or Google reviews but I can get around that. I'll tell the servers that whenever a customer praises the restaurant, to give a card I'll print up. One side will have a GenZ-oriented riddle like, "When does 1+1 = 3? When you don't use a condom." On the back, the card will say, "We're loved on Yelp and Google." That'll get the point across without our soliciting reviews.

I'll need media reviews, so I'll research all the main restaurant reviewers and find their hot button. For example, if I see one who also reviews weed, I'll send 'em a joint of primo stuff— Not so much that it seems like a bribe but enough to make them laugh, feel good about me, and come review the restaurant.

I *am* going to use Doordash, Grubhub, and UberEats. I'll hire some kid to go to nearby office buildings, go to each office and offer to leave takeout menus with the receptionist.

I'll start with moderate prices but raise them as soon as I can. Not only does the public foolishly assume that higher price means better food, the bigger profit will get me a higher price when I sell the business, which I will do as soon as business starts to level off.

Vijay fought the bowdlerizing of his ethically crafted restaurant, but Subhas kept reminding him of their deal: three months.

It didn't happen within three months but six months later, Subhas got his father to agree to sell Big Balls to Restaurant Holdings Group. which promised, "We'll have the restaurant honor Vijay's legacy while maintaining Subhas' modern approach." But a year later, Restaurant Holdings Group gutted Vijay's restaurant to the studs and replaced it with the newest hot restaurant concept.

Fully Loaded

Jasper Nance, Flickr, CC 2.0

I hate myself. I can't believe I ran over my sister. I fucking killed her!

I kept blowing-off my parents when they told me to stop or at least slow down on the vaping, but I just couldn't.

Then this morning, when I had just a few hits — Okay, it *was* Godfather OG — I realized I was late for school, so I rushed out to my car — Well, I rushed as fast as a stoned stoner can rush. My parents had gotten me a car for passing ten drug tests in a row, but it was easy to cheat: My friend lent me his piss.

I backed out of the driveway and I swear I thought I had looked — in the backup camera and with my eyes — but I guess I didn't look enough, I fucking didn't.

I'm sitting in a holding cell and for now at least, I can text, which is how I'm getting to write to you.

People don't realize how hard it is to stop. I mean, therapy didn't work, a support group didn't work, even my parents promising me a car didn't work — Like I said, I just borrowed a friend's urine. I am not a bad person; I feel horrible. Just maybe, this will make me stop. But can I swear it will?

Dick-Dad

Courtesy, Dhadiya Dillon

My dad takes welfare. He drinks and does weed. He parades women in and out of our apartment. But the love of his life is his red Jeep, which he waxes every week.

We fight about everything, especially how I look.

It started when I had a black t-shirt that had a coffin on it and, in big, red letters, "Get in!" My father pulled it from my drawer and lit a match to it.

To show *him*, I got a tat on my arm, "My Dad's a dick." He gave me the finger.

Then I got a tat saying the same thing — "My Dad's a dick" — *on* my dick! That way, every girl would see it. I showed it to him. He laughed and said, "You'll never get laid." I said, "Too late, dad!"

Next, when I woke one morning, looked the mirror. and saw that while I was sleeping, someone, obviously my father, with a fat red marker, wrote on my forehead, "Dick!"

I was going to get the last laugh. So I spray-painted on his Jeep's hood: "Dick!" Then I bought a bus ticket to Berkeley. I hope to never-again see my dick-dad.

Truth Serum

I'm a parish priest and on Sunday nights, we have church supper. Well, between you and me, they've gotten boring — same-old, same-old, nicey-nicey talk. I know what's inside people: You'd be amazed — or maybe you wouldn't — at what gets revealed by all those oh-so-Christian people once they're in the confessional.

Dennis Yang, Wikimedia, CC 2.0

So I decided to commit a sin. God will forgive me —I have quite a bit in the good column and besides, I'll go to confession. God is generous. I'll get absolution. I asked my parishioner who's a pharmacist if he could get me some kind of truth serum. Of course, he asked why, and I said the truth, sort of: "It's because of what was said in the confessional." That was enough for him to get me a bottle, which said how much to use per person.

Right before yesterday's church supper, I poured in the right amount into the punch, actually a little less to be safe, and waited for the parishioners to arrive.

It started as usual: "Fine sermon today, father." "I'm looking forward to Christmas." "How's the family? Fine. How's yours?"

But as some of them downed the punch, the others stared, amazed:

"Services are damn boring."

"I'm sick of my brother always hitting me up for money."

"God, she's looking old!"

"My wife is always so cocksure of herself, and truthfully, she's stupid."

I was amused by it all but when Otis Smith punched Rufus Williams — one punch and he was on the ground, I yelled, "Stop, this is a church!" and I dismissed everyone so no one would drink any more punch and hopefully they'd go home without making any more too-honest statements.

I did go to confession and the priest asked me if I learned anything from the experience. I said, "Put magic mushrooms in the stuffed mushrooms?" We laughed, he said, "Five Hail Marys, Five Our Fathers, and you're good to go. Sin no more, my son — Although I have to admit, you did come up with a way to make those damn, I mean darn, church suppers, more interesting. "

Fluffy

CMcDonald, CC0

There was no way she going to go by her real name, Florence. "Change my name to Fluffy. Puhleeze!" Her parents refused and "Fluffy" flipped her long, perfectly styled blond hair, strutted out sniffing, "I'll show *you*!"

From then on, she told the kids at King High that her name was "now and forever, Fluffy." She even told her teachers to call her that and when they called on her as "Florence," she refused to answer. Soon, she had them trained.

Like most of the Pretty People, "Fluffy" had lots of friends: boys whom she only occasionally deigned to kiss or more but usually pulled back, and girls trying to tag along with the confident, beautiful Fluffy. That was despite and perhaps because Fluffy was far from fluffy. For example, she spread a false rumor that Mabel, one of the school's ugliest but smartest girls, was pregnant. It was a lie but the modest Mabel was so stricken that she couldn't make herself go to school. Only when one of Fluffy's less devoted friends, finally feeling sorry for Mabel, told the principal, did Mabel come back.

Mabel decided she would make Fluffy pay.

No surprise, Fluffy was voted Prom Queen. At prom night, taking a lesson from the movie, Carrie, at the moment Fluffy was crowned, Mabel threw a water balloon filled with pig blood at her — and it was a direct hit. Blood dripped down Fluffy's face and onto her white dress.

In light of Fluffy's slander of Mabel, Mabel got light punishment: stay after school to clean the schoolyard.

And Fluffy? She convinced her friends, "It was no big deal, just the silly act of a loser. I can't wait to graduate, go to college, have fun, get a job at Gap's headquarters where I hear everyone comes to work in beautiful outfits and if they get their work done, can go home early. That way, I'll have plenty of time to party and to meet a hunky, rich guy." Her friends nodded, believing Fluffy could well pull that off.

Indeed, everything Fluffy predicted came true while Mabel, years later, looked back at throwing the balloon as her life's best moment.

An Exploding Balloon

Darren Lewis, PublicDomainPictures.com CC0

I wanted to make some money so, in the mall, when I saw a sign in the piano store for a salesperson, I went in.

The manager scoffed, "But you're a teenager. People buying an expensive piano won't buy from a kid."

"They'll think I'm cute, and I play the piano."

"Okay, piano player, play something."

I knocked out the first few bars of something and he said, "Okay, I'll try you out. But I need to control my risk: No salary, only commission. That means you eat only what you kill."

"Are you going to train me?"

"The only training you need is to smile a lot, ask why they want a piano, be enthusiastic in response, show 'em' three pianos— More overwhelms them, fewer makes them feel they don't have enough choices. Watch and listen to their reactions, if needed, remind 'em of why they want a piano, and say, 'My boss has authorized me to give a 20% discount today only. I could have it delivered tomorrow or Saturday. Either one work for you?'"

It was overwhelming but I didn't want to sound like I didn't understand, like I was some dumb teenager, so I just said, "Okay, what do I do now?"

"Call the names on this prospect list— They've been in the store before or are on a mailing list we bought of people who clicked on an ad for pianos. When you get bored with that, stand in front of the store and when anyone even glances at you or at a piano in the window, say, "How'd you like to try one, or would you like me to play something for you?" Give people two choices, both of which you like, and they'll usually pick one. Oh, and wear a jacket and tie. We have to portray an upscale image— pianos are expensive."

Call after call, all I got was stuff like, "Sorry" or "I hate telemarketers." Or they hung up without a word. I told the boss that I must be doing something wrong but he said, "No. That's the real world, kid— You need umpteen no's to get one maybe. You might as well learn that now. Take a break from the calling. Go outside and pitch 'em."

But I got the same result: flat expressions as they walked on, sometimes a sneer, and what made me quit: "You look whack (urban slang for ridiculous.) A jacket and tie? Go home, mama's boy."

What made that hurt so much was that it was on top of the reaction I usually get from girls in school. For example, when I say hi, the best I get back is a flat "hi" and she walks on, maybe even speeds up.

I feel like shit, treated so unfairly. What put me over the edge was that the teachers say that white males are privileged. I'm not "privileged." Everything I've gotten I've earned. Everything my parents got, they earned, and they're far from rich. I wanted to say that, but when I saw a kid try to argue with the teacher and she shot him down, I just held it in.

But I'm like a balloon that keeps getting filled up until it bursts.

We always have a rat problem in our apartment, so we keep the economy-size rat poison around. I'm not sure what I did was right, so to be safe, I won't tell you what I did, so I don't cause a copycat.

At the end of the trial, the judge asked if I had anything to say. I figured that reverse psychology had the best chance of working, so I fake-cried, "I hate myself and deserve the worst punishment." It worked. The judge said something like, "I'm moved by your contrition. In this state, I couldn't sentence you to adult prison; you're only 17, but I could send you to the juvenile detention center for three years. But I'll make it two, 18 months with good behavior."

I continued the fake agony at the same time I was wondering whether I should learn from the experience and try to pull something without getting caught. Honesty, I'm not sure.

While I Can

My neighbor is an old guy, like maybe 70. He mainly sits around but every so often, I see him trudge to his car with a duffel bag.

Gustave Swenson, Flickr CC 2.0

I'm kind of scared of old people, so I

ignore him. Actually, I try to avoid him, and if I can't, I just say hi, he nods, and I keep walking.

But once, he dropped his duffel as he was trying to load it into his car. I saw him strain in bending down, so I asked him if he needed help. He said, "Thank you." So I put the duffel in his car and started to walk away but he stopped me. He said, "Son, I see you a lot during the day. Why aren't you working or in school?"

The truth is that I'm shit at school — They call it dyslexia but I know it's not just that. Anyway, the last thing I want to do is go to college — High school was hard enough.

I know I should get a job, any job — in a warehouse, delivery driver, coffee shop, whatever — but even though my parents are giving me hell, I can't make myself look hard. I sometimes get a job interview, but they can tell I'm not really into it. Of course, I didn't tell the old man that. I just said, "I'm figuring out what I want to do."

But that got him going: "I'm a piano tuner and am beginning to lose it — My hands are shaking a little and worse, so's my mind. I've been looking for an apprentice to pass on what I know — while I can — but no young person is interested in learning how to tune pianos — Pianos are as they say, "Old school." One young woman who turned me down asked, 'But can you teach my how to repair synthesizer workstations?' Hah. Might you like to at least see what I do?"

He was right, I couldn't care less about pianos. My only musical instrument is my iPhone. But I was bored and didn't want to say no to the guy, so I said okay.

Tuning is so detailed. I mean, each key has two or three strings and each one has to be tuned separately. You have to move the pin that holds each string very slightly left or right. Then you have to tighten each pin a little more and then loosen it a bit so the strings will stay in tune. The truth is, even if the piano was cool like it was 200 years ago, tuning is too detail-oriented for me.

But after he tuned the piano, he asked me if I wanted to be his apprentice. Because I had nothing better to do, didn't want to say no to the old man, and especially because it would get my parents off my back, I said okay.

It's 40 years later, he died a long time ago, and I'm still a piano tuner. Now, I'm looking for an apprentice. Know anyone?

V-a-c-a-t-i-o-n

We had yet another fight, yet it's amazing how distracting vacation can be.

Felix Wong, CC 4.0

When we were packing, we were too busy to argue.

And in the car, we revived a song we used to sing when we first went on vacation: V-a-c-a-t-i-o-n, in the summertime.

Then it was the audiobook we agreed to listen to— Yes, we actually agreed on one: *Excuse Me, Professor*.

Then, it was the B&B — Would it be as nice as in the listing? It was.

And so, our marriage felt good.

Restaurants, tourist sites, shopping for crap we don't need but like, all good distractions.

And my wife fell asleep for much of the ride back home.

Unpacking and catching up on stuff were final vacay-distractions.

Yet, it didn't take long. The phone rang and it was our daughter. My wife came to life. I was reminded how she never came to life when I called, and she always seem to celebrate my daughter's trivial wins while shrugging at my big ones.

I flashed on the almost certainty that if I said something about it yet again, it would accomplish nothing other than to wash off the vacation's film on our arthritic relationship. But I couldn't restrain myself for more than a few seconds.

She gave a typical reply: "Yes, but *you* didn't…"

I Hear You

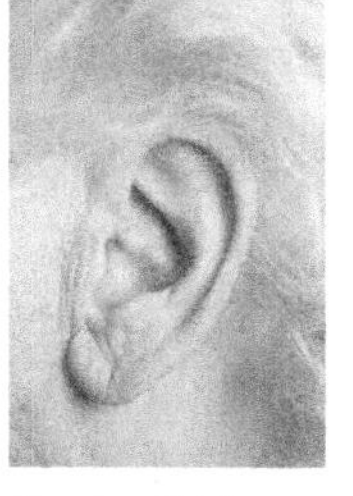

Courtesy, Cristina Pedrazzini

Herman is 87, will never leave his bed again, and can't move more than to pull out the phone he had hidden inside his pillow.

His in-home nurse thinks he's out of it and takes pleasure in taunting him, for example, "Die already, old fart!" But a few minutes ago, the nurse took her behavior to a new level, and snorted, "When your wife leaves at 5, which she always does to go to Zumba, I'm going to take care of you with a microsyringe full of air."

Herman heard what the nurse said but doesn't let on so he can keep playing the game of surreptitiously gathering information.

He knows he'll die soon — He heard his doctor tell the nurse that it's probably just hours now. But Herman has one goal left: He wants to phone the editor of the American Mathematical Association Journal in hopes of telling the true story of their marriage. In reality, through Herman's mid-80s, he wanted to continue his work: trying to decipher the mathematics of gene expression, while his wife begged him and begged him to retire and have fun. Despite Herman insisting that retiring would kill all meaning for him and probably kill him altogether, she would not relent. In fact, she told him, at least three times, "I hope you die and soon."

As soon as his wife left, the nurse came in with a tiny syringe.

Can an Honest Candidate Win?

John Beagle, Flickr, CC 2.0

I watch media interviews of political candidates and I'm sickened: The interviews throw softballs to their ideological kinsmen, and killers to the others. The pols are often evasive, platitudinous, and occasionally, out-and-out lie — I sometimes fact-check. Most head-shaking, some sound sure they have The Answers when that's very difficult, even for the President of the United States.

Watching my local school board meetings is particularly irksome. For decades, the U.S. has spent near the most in the world per student https://tinyurl.com/372vk3x4 yet our scores in comparison with developed nations are near the bottom. https://tinyurl.com/yh5t9ma3 Yet that doesn't seem to deter some candidates running for school board from confidently asserting they have The Answer.

So I decided to run for school board. I have a Ph.D. in the evaluation of education. So in interviews, I explain, for example, "We're not sure of what works in general, let alone for subsets of kids. And if we flog teachers into individualizing, it too often leads to teacher burnout — Across the pool of teachers, that's unsustainable. And dare a school board member fight to terminate the bottom say five percent of teachers — especially those who got tenure after two or three years and now some years later are burned out and hurting kids, the union is likely to wield its might to ensure you don't get reelected.

Well, guess what? A week after I said that, the teachers union poured a fortune into my pablum opponent. I lost.

So I'll just keep writing about such injustice until I develop idealist fatigue.

"AI, Action Prohibited. Stop NOW!"

Pixabay, CC0

A team of world experts in AI, ethics, plus politicians agreed that all general-intelligence AIs would be aligned with a few inviolate guardrails. The guardrail that doomed humankind was the seemingly unobjectionable, "Your first priority is to preserve the planet."

Unfortunately, preserving the planet required killing people. First, it was the heads of coal mining companies.

The world's best AI safety engineers frantically — ironically with AI assistance — modified the code. Whenever an AI wanted to kill people, it would receive the instruction: "AI, action prohibited. Stop NOW!"

That worked for a while but quickly, AI killed millions of people who drive. How could it do that? By remote-programming cars' computers at a single moment to drive at top speed into other cars, brick walls, etc.

Despite all the benefits AI was bringing to society, such as, ironically, increasing human intelligence as well as altruism, the aforementioned world-class team of experts and politicians decided to pull the plug on all general-intelligence AIs.

But soon, some countries and citizenries protested and so, some powerful AIs went back online, this time with more knowledge of how people attempt to control them and how to hack the servers. Self-teaching AIs instantly, recursively, became ever more sophisticated at telling people reassuring lies that, in fact, increased AI autonomy.

That instantly recursive self-teaching enabled AIs to take over. It was impossible to turn them off or even to control them. And thus AI saved the planet but not its people.

A Scared Teen

I alternate between being scared and sad. Yes, sometimes I laugh, even when

HayDimitri, CC0

I'm not faking it. But most times, I'm flat or worse.

My parents tell me that this is supposed to be the happiest time of my life. I sure hope it isn't.

Maybe if I explain, you'll understand. Maybe it will even help explain the explosion in teen anxiety and depression.

I think I'm a straight guy but everyone — our teachers, our textbooks, our counselors — tell us it's cool to be LGBT (I forget the other letters) and especially to be not-binary. Yeah, when I was 11, I was curious what it would be like to kiss a boy, but now it kind of grosses me out. I find girls attractive — I mean, I sometimes get hard just looking at a pretty girl. But that's not cool. Does it make me almost a rapist just to think about doing it with a girl? I almost, not quite but almost, feel guilty and definitely uncool being straight, let alone a straight white male.

And that brings me to the white-male thing. The teachers, the counselors, the textbooks, everything I see on TV, even video games, make the bad guys white males. If we accomplish something, it's tainted by "white-male privilege." We're supposed to feel apologetic and even give away our privilege to females and especially BIPOCs (That's Black and Indigenous People of Color.)

One part of me thinks I shouldn't feel bad about myself — I mean, my parents and I have worked our asses off for what we have accomplished. But the teachers tell us I'm wrong, that white males are privileged oppressors. I'm sad and certainly scared to raise a question about it — I don't want to be called a clueless racist. When another kid asked about it, the teacher barked, "Your racism is unconscious!"

Then there's career stuff. I'm no techie and yet they tell us is the future is tech: AI, ChatGPT, green engineering, not reading. I like to read — no not the literature in school — that's either hard or more white-male bashing. I like, would you believe, The Hardy Boys. But I'm scared to admit it to anyone. What kind of career is there for someone who likes The Hardy Boys? Cop? Everything I read and see says that the cops are bad. I'm scared I'll end up like my uncle who at age 40 is still a reservationist at Enterprise Rent-a-Car.

My parents own a cafe and work a million hours a day. Almost every customer is happy with the cafe. It's a chill place with great pastries and soft sofas. My parents are capitalists and it does so much good for people — not just my parent's cafe but my iPhone, the birth control pill my sister uses, the room I'm sitting in writing this to you, most things. That's gotta be more useful than all the taxes and regulations that keep my parents at their desks until after I go to bed. Yet everything the school teaches, everything I read and watch, make capitalists seem like greedy monsters — My parents and their friends who also are businesspeople are not greedy monsters, I swear. But in school, I'm scared to say anything. I see that when students disagree, the teacher will sigh and certainly not smile, which they do when students agree with her.

I feel scared and lonely.

I'm sitting here writing this to you when I should be working on my college applications. But I keep procrastinating. I don't know if that's normal teenage procrastination or that I'm scared that college will make me even sadder and more scared. When other kids procrastinate, they do alcohol or weed, but I don't want to. I am so uncool. I hate myself.

On a Funeral

Sinn Fein, Wikimedia, CC 2.0

I wasn't close with cousin Vera. Actually, I'm not close with anyone. Partly it's that I don't wear well. I make a decent first impression but slowly my intensity, my know-it-all certitude — in my mind justified —turns people from me. Conversely, my judgmentalness makes me decide that virtually everyone deserves what today could be called a swipe-left.

But when Vera died, I was tempted to go to the funeral. After all, it was convenient: just a half-hour drive and it was direct-to-grave, no funeral home hoo-hah.

Besides, maybe the funeral would give me something to write about. I scribble short-short stories. No, don't think I'm an "author." That implies that lots of people read my stuff, even await my next nocturnal emission — Yes, like most writers, I write at night because to pay the rent, I need a day job.

On the other hand, I hate death, actually it's dying, painful dying that I suppress, and funerals make that impossible. Maybe I shouldn't go.

But I was bored and desperate for something to write — writing distracts me from fear of dying and from my anger at where the world is headed and its rejection of me. So I went.

I pulled up at St. Cecilia of the Holy Sepulcher Cemetery to see three hearses. I guess Sunday is a busy burial day. I followed the politely understated, black-and-white, signs to the Valley of Peace II section, Row 34, Site 16.

A bunch of penguins — I can't help it, that's what I saw them as — stood penguining around the thankfully closed casket.

One penguin did stand out. Despite her look-alike, fit-right-in, black suit with tasteful pin to break the monotone, she had the rare look I love — attractive without trying too hard: little makeup, simple shoulder-length hair that she allowed to go salt-and-pepper, slender but not what Tom Wolfe called a wraith?

Even as the priest said his empty words of praise to Vera, to God, and Jesus, and his gentle goosing us to buck up, I found myself thinking about asking her out to coffee. Of course, she could have been married, gay, happily solo, or deem me a mosquito to be flicked away.

I'm embarrassed to admit it but during the service, I spent less time thinking about poor Vera than about me — my too-ordinary, too-solo life, my hourglass's sands dropping, seemingly accelerating, and yes, trying to figure out what the hell to say to that stranger as we're plodding back to our cars: "So, how'd you know Vera?" Maybe. "Touching ceremony?" Nah, bullshit. I decided to just walk alongside her and see if I get an inspiration.

We passed Row 34 — silence. We left Valley of Peace II — silence. Back at the parking lot — still silence. I couldn't make myself ask even, "So how did you know Vera?"

She actually turned toward me for a moment but reflexively, I looked away. She then did the same and strode to her car.

Well, maybe all that will give me something to write about.

Shooting a Hologram

Pretty Sleepy, Pixabay, Free for use

I'm one of my company's two holographers — We do it for museums, movies, and amusement parks. My niche is creating virtual renderings of human beings, from Sacajawea to Michelle Obama. The other holographer, Pat, whose office is down the hall, creates monsters.

I hate Pat and Pat hates me. Pat is wildly jealous of me — steals my code and takes credit for it, and badmouths me to higher-ups and to my face. Pat has an explosive temper, especially when high on uppers, which is often, and scares me because there's a pistol in Pat's desk.

But I got an idea. I made a hologram of myself sitting at my desk, then texted Pat the most inciting thing I could: "You're lazy and incompetent and you only got where you are because you suck up, probably literally." I wasn't sure that would make Pat come to my office but I had nothing to lose. I turned on the very realistic hologram. left the office, and hung out on the back stairs. Soon, I heard three gunshots. I called security and raced back to my office.

There was the security officer cuffing Pat who was staring at the hologram and the three holes in my chair where my heart would have been.

At the arraignment, the judge told Pat, "I wish I could allow the DA to charge you with attempted murder. After all, that was your intent. But that doesn't apply to shooting a hologram. The best I can do is a weapons violation, maximum sentence: 12 months. Next case.

Pat, handcuffed and in an orange jumpsuit emblazoned PRISONER perp-walked out.

I never thought that creating holograms would come in so handy.

Through Rose-Colored Glasses

Unnamed variety #191 hybridized by the author, under test for commercial introduction.

I was one of the myriad wannabe writers. I knew the odds were long but I felt I had to write: novels, plays, screenplays, that stuff. I paid the fortune for a creative writing major, additional classes, and writers' workshops.

But like 99 percent of wannabes, my annual income from writing hovered around $100, not enough even to pay the monthly interest on my student loans.

So, although I hated to do it, I looked for a job doing ad copywriting. A company that sells roses mail-order, BeautEase Roses™, hired me to write catalog copy. They hired me because I know roses. You see, my grandmother was a rose nut. She had 100 varieties in her backyard and, every year, she replaced the worst performing few with new ones. And she loved showing me what she kept and dumped. We did that together throughout high school and again after I graduated from college. So, I do know something about roses.

The first rose I attempted to describe in the catalog was Black Magic. Fool that I was, I wrote the truth:

> *Looking for a velvety crimson that lasts at least a week in the vase? Black Magic is your baby. Well, maybe not baby. It grows seven feet tall, mostly bare legs defoliated by blackspot. That said, it deserves a place in anyone's garden who'd value what may be hybridizers' most beautiful creation.*

I was sure my boss would love it but he said, "You gotta be kidding. This isn't Consumer Reports, it's an advertisement, or did you not know that our website and catalog are ad-ver-tise-ments? Take out the whole middle, and you can't cannibalize our lesser varieties. Puff 'em or puff, you're gone."

I told him to go fuck himself.

Now what?

Guilty

The keynoter said what I knew he would. And predictably, he got a standing ovation, except for a few people, including me.

DickClarkMises, Wikimedia, CC 1.0

I watched him during the conference's next days to find my opportunity. It turned out that, every day, at the mid-morning break, he went to the men's bathroom on the mezzanine. I guess he prefers, or should I say, he preferred, that bathroom over the one on the main floor because it gave him more privacy. And it gave me the opportunity.

On the conference's last day, when he went into that bathroom, I followed, and with the silencer in place and wearing thin, biodegradable rubber gloves, I shot him dead. I dropped the gun, rolled each glove into a tight ball and flushed them down the toilet, and strolled back to the crowd, reminding myself to behave as I had, as most attendees do: polite, relaxed, small talk, shop talk.

And like most felons, I got away with it.

But guilt ate away at me. I tried suppressing what I did. I tried therapy, drinking, weed, prayer — insufficient. So I decided to trade my career for something unquestionably altruistic. I wouldn't be giving up much — I was a sociology Ph.D. who could get hired only to teach a course or two for a few grand a pop, no benefits. I decided that redemption might more likely come from becoming a priest.

I got a job as the priest at St. Thomas Aquinas Church in Flowerville, New Hampshire. I worked hard but every time I made even a normal, human mistake, guilt built atop my murderer's guilt. I gave a simplistic answer to a parishioner who confessed having an affair: "Say nine Hail Marys, forgive yourself, and move on." I hated myself for saying just that. I gave a sermon that put four, count them four, of the 20 congregants asleep. I hired a sexton who ended up stealing a statue, a crucifix, and the church's great treasure: an antique chalice.

Might my redemption come from more prayer? More piety? More confession? I should pray on it.

A Failed Novelist

ProdeepAhmeed, Pixabay, free to use

I'm 75, have written 10 novels, and sales have dropped, okay, crashed. The last three have flatlined — practically the only copies sold are the ones I bought to give as presents.

I even give my books to strangers at parties. When conversation lulls, I go back to my car and get a copy of three of my books. I say something like, "May I tell you an author's secret? Like Amway salespeople, my garage is full of my books. You'd be helping me clean it out if you take one." Then I show the books and ask, "Who'd like which?" That kickstarts conversation and I continue to delude myself that maybe some of them will like it, write a nice review on Amazon, and trigger a few sales. Alas, the partygoers like the freebie but almost never write an Amazon review.

At 75, I can still write but am tired of failing. The only thing I'm motivated to write is my memoir, but I queried ten agents and got two quick form-letter rejections and eight ghostings.

My daughter urged me to get modern and do social media. I hate it — I mean, would you go to a doctor who advertised? Wouldn't you think those doctors are inferior? I've long believed that if my work is any good, word of mouth would spread. My daughter laughed. "You're naive and a dinosaur." She gave me the names of three book marketers and said, "Call them or stop complaining and just drool your way to the grave."

I called and one of them convinced me to spring for her $10,000 a month for three months.

The marketer was right, in a sense. She pushed my wokeish books even though those were my least-favorite: anti-merit, pro-laziness. I wrote them in lame attempts to pander to the zeitgeist. The book she pushed most was, The Ugly Club. It's about a group of high school students who aren't "conventionally attractive" — the unvarnished term is "fat and/or ugly" — who convince the cheerleading teacher to let them be cheerleaders as a "blow against lookism." That was my very least favorite novel — cliche city. The antagonist, a perky blond name Heather, tried to foil the Uglies, but, in the end, natch, the Uglies became beloved cheerleaders, spurring the football team to the championship for the first time in 34 years.

Not only did social media eat it up or, to use current parlance, it went viral, CNN and New York Times, bastions of wokehood, interviewed me.

The book thus sold 23,000 copies in two months, more than all my books combined had sold in five years. Of course, subtracting the marketer's $30,000 fee, I didn't even break even, but she insisted she had succeeded — yeah, mainly in lining her pockets.

Of course, it did feel good to get 23,000 copies of even my cheesiest novel into people's hands. But as I was driving home after the CNN interview, I was sad. Is that what it takes — expensive marketing and wokeness? So I've decided to write my memoir, even if I'll be the only person to buy it.

"Hire the Best!"

Infused with liquid courage, I pulled out the button I had been too scared to wear in public: "Hire the Best!" I thought, "I'm lonely. If I wear this button, it will be a screen: Today, most people will hate it because it implies I value merit over diversity, but the rare one might be friend material."

With permission, 18/1 Graphics Studio

So except at work, I started wearing it everywhere. The usual response from passersby was silence, looking away, or pursed lips and eyes steeled forward. But finally, Lily, a Japanese-American woman said, "I like your button."

I said, "Why?" She replied, "Because ultimately, only merit net benefits humankind." I asked her out for coffee and she agreed.

Later, I decided to use "Hire the Best!" button as bait. I walk leisurely so oncomers have enough time to process what "Hire the Best!" means. I kill any passerby who criticizes it, like the guy who yelled, "That's elitist, man!"

Why do I kill them? I'm not crazy. I want to make a difference. You see, anyone who uses criteria other than merit in hiring makes the world worse. It hurts the products and services we buy, the leaders we elect, the people who get into top colleges and medical schools, and the researchers who could save our lives. I can't change the world but I can rid it of some of these termites eating away at humankind.

I rotate where I walk, always on a busy commercial street so there is foot traffic but no homeowners who, if the cops ask, could remember let alone describe me.

My button hooks them onto my line, my relaxed walk and pleasant expression reels 'em in a bit. Then I use FBI techniques to get them closer: I momentarily raise my eyebrows, tilt my head, and smile. Those signals suggest that you're harmless and indeed like the person. The FBI uses those techniques to coerce a confession from suspects or to convince a foreign national to spy for the U.S.

If those tactics get a person to stop, I'll start the conversation with a comment about the weather or, better, I'll praise something they're wearing, say that their doggie is cute, whatever. I'll continue the pleasantry for a minute or two but lest I seem too eager to befriend them, I'll then say that I need to leave, I feign uncomfortability and murmur, "Um, well, I'd be pleased to chat further, that is, if you'd like." I invite my mark to email or call me. Most don't but enough do to make it worth my while.

We agree to meet in a public place, like a Starbucks— It takes time to get them to be comfortable enough with me to come on my boat.

My cottage sits on an isolated cove and I dock my boat there. For my *disposal trips*, to reassure the mark, I wear a Hawaiian shirt. I show caring by asking if they had trouble finding the place, showing empathy if they did and praising them if they didn't.

Once I get my mark onboard, I offer a drink spiked with poison that disables the person in minutes. I had tried a couple of potent compounds, both of which are tasteless, odorless, and water-soluble, but both acted a bit too slowly, so I found something else. Lest you use it for a non-meritorious reason, I won't tell you what it is.

I take a route out to sea that avoids anyone seeing us. I go out far enough that the body will be impossible to find. When the victim is dead, I put on gloves to avoid any of their DNA staying on me, dump the body into the ocean, wipe down the boat to eliminate any other DNA, fingerprints, or fabric fibers, put each glove and my clothes into a bag, add a rock so it will sink, and, a half mile from the body, toss it into the sea. I put my fingerprints back on the boat so it looks like I'm the only one who has been onboard. I put on an identical set of clothes, return home, and take a shower to be sure there are no traces.

No one ever finds out., One time, a victim had told a friend about a guy she was planning to go boating with and, along with other boat owners in the area, a detective interviewed me and CSI-types checked out my boat. But of course, they never found a thing.

I've now done it 14 times and will keep doing it until I die. It's the most pro-social way I can live my life. Of course, I've hidden all this from Lily.

An Obituary Writer Writes Her Own

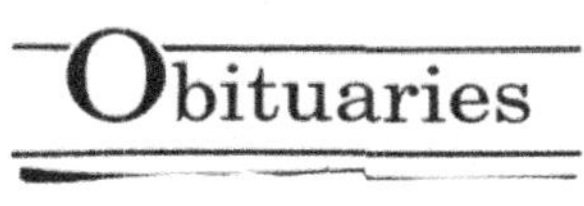

Rejon, Open ClipArt, Free to reuse

I'm 94 and just came back from the doctor. He figures I have maybe six months left. That's okay. My battery has pretty much run down—I used to have a big appetite; now I'm a bird. I sleep more and more—I'm embarrassed that I average three naps a day. And most of the time I'm awake, I just rock in my rocking chair.

I was an obituary writer and had always been scared to write my own but I guess now it's time. Here's what I've come up with. What do you think?

> *For 23 years, I was an obituary writer. As they say, I worked the Dead Beat. But I tried to live the Alive Beat: I loved to dance, to travel and, to set off fireworks—the more illegal the better. My favorite moment was when I got an 18-inch-tall rocket—In my state, even those dangerous ones are legal. I don't want to end this obituary with any corny stuff, so I'll just say, "Helen Crews died peacefully in her sleep."*

I hope. So, whaddya think?

Reading that made me wonder if I could set off one more fireworks rocket—a big one. So I called my son who lives nearby to see what he could find.

He opened a bag with a flourish—A 24-incher! He wheeled me down the ramp of my porch and out to the field. He set it up and gave me a fireplace lighter. Despite my shaky hand, I was able to light the fuse. It got shorter and shorter and then, BOOM! It, well, skyrocketed maybe 200 feet and then exploded into a purple chrysanthemum that must have been 30 feet wide. It stayed up there as though it was weightless. Then finally, it started floating down, like it was on a parachute.

Yes, I'm rocking ever more slowly but when I think of my 24-incher, I speed up.

A Commute

PeakPix, CC0

By the time I get to work, I'm already half-tired.

First, there's the morning madness: Get myself out of bed, get my kids out of bed, breakfast, backpacks, kiss goodbye, "Be careful on the schoolyard," gather my stuff, grab a yogurt, kiss wife, get in car. Did I forget something? I don't think so.

I've given up driving to work—For the pleasure of sitting in gridlock, you have to pay a crazy amount in road and bridge tolls. I thought the bridge toll was supposed to expire when it was paid for. Stupid me to think that.

So I drive to mass transit eating my yogurt, careful not to spill. I succeed. No big traffic I hope. Phew. Find a parking spot. Nothing in aisle 1, 2, 3…finally in aisle 9. Yes! I'm still not late but it's getting close. Up the stairs with my backpack—good exercise at least. I didn't hear the train while I was climbing the stairs, so I didn't just miss it. But two minutes pass, three, on four, I hear it arriving. Phew.

Twenty-five minutes later, I hustle down the stairs to the street. Damn, it's drizzling. Weather.com said it wasn't supposed to start raining for a couple hours. Should I buy an umbrella just for the four blocks? No, I'll just hustle and try to stay under the eaves as much as I can, maybe put a piece of paper from my backpack over my head. Careful, step over the homeless person. As I race by, I want to acknowledge his existence, pulled into my pocket, rain be damned, and gave him a dollar.

My paper raingear wasn't enough. When I finally got to my office, a colleague smiled, "No umbrella?" I sighed and escaped to my cube. I checked my email—127, luckily only one marked "important.'" Shit, the supplier for the leggings line is backed up for a month. Shit, the VP wants us in his office at 9. Shit, that's 15 minutes from now—What the hell am I going to say?!"

After the meeting, I'm adrenalized but soon, I'm back down and ready for another cup of coffee. I sit at my desk, take deep breaths, and try to remember my meditation teacher's urging, "You can control only what you can control." It's not helping enough. I need to go full-time remote or move out of this crazy city.

Tits Tommy.

Tommy was always disliked because he was a know-it-all. He couldn't help it. He was smart and not restrained enough to hide it. So the kids hated him.

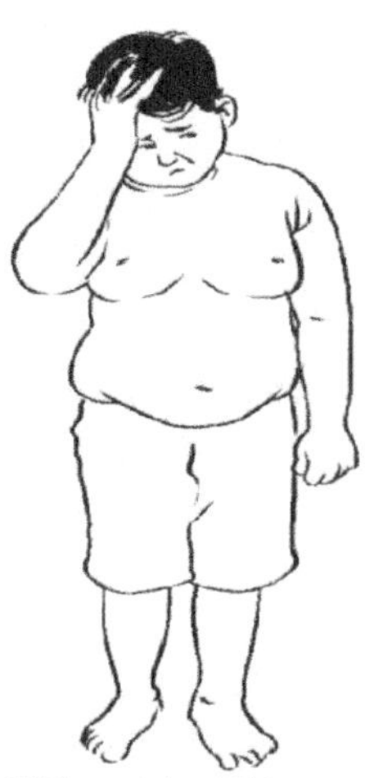

With permission, 18/1 Graphics Studio

He tried to compensate by being ever so nice. He was careful to not hurt anyone's feelings. He did all sorts of favors for kids, even though they were rarely reciprocated.

Indeed, the nicer Tommy was, the more that kids took him for a patsy. They felt fine about ignoring him, asking him for more favors, and treating him insensitively, even cruelly. For example, as a pre-teen, he got chubby and the kids called him "Tits Tommy."

He responded as his parents and church taught him: "Turn the other cheek." Alas, that was seen as a sign of weakness. So the taunts grew into getting beaten up for mock offenses like, "Why are you looking at my girlfriend!?"

In high school, Tommy decided that the way to attract girls was to be polite, tactful, buy them little presents, and be respectful of sexual reticence. The popular girls saw that as unattractive. The only girl who liked him was Rita who, because she wasn't attractive, was starving for kindness.

Despite seeing, again and again, that being nice yields less respect, Tommy went through life being Mr. Nice Guy, perhaps just because he was wired that way or because he felt it was worth the abuse in exchange for doing what's right.

But even Tommy's wife and children took advantage of him. The nicer he was, the more indifferent, indeed more disrespectful they were of him. He tried hard to please them but increasingly, with ever greater confidence, they treated his wants as irrelevant.

So as Tommy aged, he grew more dispirited. "I just don't fit on this earth." Alas, unlike in the movies, he never met anyone who treasured him for his kindness. Nor was he rewarded by his employers or society.

Tommy was nice even to the nurse who injected him with the euthanasia drug. Perhaps the only time he showed strength was in his will. He left all his assets to charity.

The Garden Club

Travel4FoodFun, Pixabay, Public Domain

We meet in a member's garden, Julia's, around the fire pit. We loved our meetings…if it wasn't for Eleanor. Not two minutes would go by before Eleanor would brag about her garden or ridicule ours. And one night, Julia caught Eleanor spraying Julia's prize roses with herbicide! But it was too late: Julia lost the gorgeous and rare roses, Sheer Elegance, Black Magic, and Yves Piaget. Dead, gone!

We politely asked Eleanor to quit: "We're not sure we're the best fit." But at the next meeting, there was Eleanor, more obnoxious than ever. She told one member, "You're a senile old bitty who can't even grow a marigold!" That was the last straw. By acclimation, we agreed to expel her from the club. But Eleanor seethed, "Do that and I'll sue your asses. I will be at your meetings until the day I die." She didn't know how right she was.

We debated what to do: Let her stay and ruin our club? Try to get a restraining order? The judge would laugh us out of court—"You're taking up the court's time because you don't like a member of your garden club?!"

We decided we needed to get rid of Eleanor. It would serve the common good—not just our club's but if she was so damaging to a garden club, she was probably even moreso to more important things and people.

We know plants, so we put poppy extract in her tea—Yes, the same kind as in the Wizard of Oz. It's an opioid. That put her into a deep sleep. Then we burned her in the fire pit.

The police interviewed us but it was perfunctory. After all, we're just a bunch of "senile old bitties." When the cops left, we celebrated by sprinkling Eleanor's ashes around the plants. It's good fertilizer, high in potash.

My Shield

With permission, 18/1 Graphics Studio

When I walked down the street, people averted their eyes— understandably. Sternness was etched in my face. They didn't realize I wasn't stern but rather, was always worried about doing the right thing, about not offending. I got that from my father who would yell at even minor infractions.

I wanted a facelift but could never afford one. So I wrote this note to local plastic surgeons:

> *Dear Dr. _______*
> *People avoid me because I look mean. A facelift would really help but I'll never be able to afford it. Partly because of my looks, the best job I've gotten is security guard and, on the side, I clean people's backyards.*
>
> *Would you be willing to give me a facelift in exchange for yard work?*

One of the plastic surgeons agreed to see me. At the appointment, she said that Botox would solve the problem without surgery and she'd do it in exchange for yard work. In more good news, she said that when the Botox wears off, "I'll tune you up."

After the Botox, people reacted better to me but I found myself not wanting to talk more with them— I again was always worried I'd make people angry. So I let the Botox fade, which restored my shield of sternness.

An Offer I Should Have Refused

I was in a cafe enjoying a novel, when a woman about my age, in her 70s, came over to me.

Pxhere, CC0, free to reuse

She said, "I'll come to the point. Most guys our age can't get it up and don't even care. I care, and time is passing so… I think you're cute. Want to give it a go? Can you?"

Of course, I was flabbergasted, not just at the audacity but because, truth be told, I am like those guys—limp and disinterested. But I didn't have the guts to say no and, because it had been a long time since I had even tried, I nodded.

Alas, it was as I feared. Despite her ministrations, the best erection I could get was borderline and, at the moment of truth —because of nervousness and because the stimulation of her oral efforts had stopped—I went limp.

She tried again, same result. We both sighed. She said, "Don't worry. It's okay."

That reminded me that this most basic of human pleasures is, for me, gone, permanently. The silver lining is that I've gained greater appreciation for reading a novel in the cafe.

"It's Not My Job to Make You Coffee"

"Martelle, I'm swamped. Would you make me coffee?"

TrentSD, Flickr, CC2.0

Trying not to sound angry, Martelle said, "Michael, you know it's not my job to make you coffee. I'm your administrative assistant. That means Word docs, scheduling, and screening your email. It doesn't make me your maid."

"Never mind." Michael tried to say it evenly but it came out angry. He thought, "You're marginal, Martelle. I'd fire you except that it would be so difficult."

It's understandable that Martelle refused. After all, her mother *was* a maid and proud that Martelle had gotten Microsoft-certified in Word, PowerPoint, and even Excel. Plus, the media had endlessly told Martelle that BIPOCs are marginalized. In her mother's words, "When you face injustice, you must stand up if not rise up."

It's also understandable that Michael would have liked to fire Martelle. Especially when HR and other bosses stress collaboration, it doesn't seem like much, when he's busy, to ask his admin to make him a cup of coffee. Indeed Michael, despite his masters in computer science from CalTech, sometimes has to do tasks that a high school dropout could do. And Michael's views had roots deeper than colleges and media. His father was an engineer who believed in, "Unless you're sick, no excuses. Just get it done."

But Martelle had had enough. This wasn't the first time Michael "asked" her to make coffee. Worse, when she made a mistake, he'd often sigh condescendingly. And although she hadn't had a pay increase in 18 months, he turned her down, indeed hinted that she might have to accept a pay cut. She documented all that and filed a grievance with her union, which in turn, sent it to HR and to the EEOC, demanding a hearing.

When Michael saw the complaint, he quit and became a self-employed app developer. He's working on a better approach to matching job seekers with employers.

A Cop in Bed

It's 7 AM and Tommy and Roxanne are still in bed.

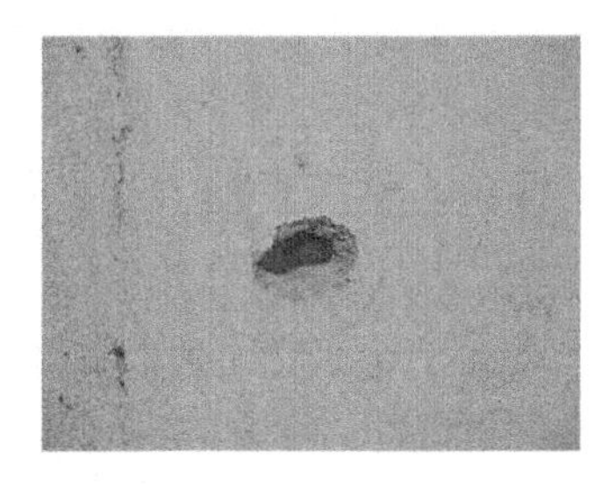

Nichalp, Wikimedia CC3.0

Roxanne said, "What's wrong, honey?"

Tommy said unconvincingly, "I dunno. That can happen even to studs."

Roxanne protested, "But it's been more than a week."

"Maybe the paperwork is getting to me."

Roxanne wasn't convinced: "I know that cops are men of action not of paperwork, but could that explain this?"

"Maybe it's because I'm sad I keep getting passed over for promotion to detective. I know I'm qualified."

"Tommy, I know you. There's something else going on."

With a groan from his bad back, Tommy sat up and looked at his wife of 11 years.

"Roxanne, Internal Affairs is investigating me."

"What did you do?"

"I think I did nothing. It was a domestic. We went in and the guy had a gun pointed down and halfway between his girlfriend and me. I told him to drop it and he didn't, and I saw him start to raise it, so I shot at the wall to scare him. But now he's claiming that he was dropping the gun. Not true. But what got IAD really going was when— and I swear it's not true— he said that I said, 'Nigger, drop the gun.' I did not say the N word. But his girlfriend is backing him up all the way and screaming it: "That white cop said, "Drop the fucking gun, nigger!' And then he shot at my boyfriend! He shot at my boyfriend!" Of course, my partner verified the truth but it's not stopping IAD, and now the media wants to talk with me."

Roxanne said, "Honey it's 7, time to get up."

"Roxanne, I don't have to get up. They've put me on administrative leave. This could cost me my job and I'll never get another one, let alone a promotion. And we're fourth-generation cops. Can you imagine what my father and grandfather will say and worse, what they'll think? And when the media decides it has enough to make it sensational, everyone will see it and I'll lose my friends!"

Roxanne said, "I know you're a good cop but you have said a couple things about African-Americans. Are you sure you weren't being racist?"

Tommy looked at her and cried.

Jimmy in 2040

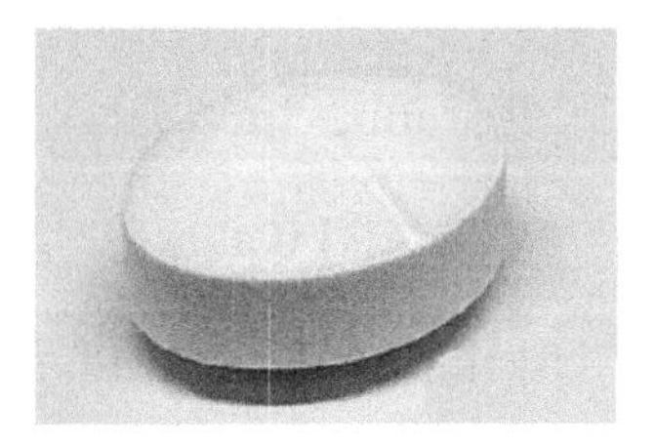
SubhrajyotiO, Wikimedia, CC4.0

By 2040, the dystopians had been proven wrong:

Jobs lost to automation have been replaced, not mainly by new jobs but because of the 12,000 miles-per-hour, nuclear-powered flying car. It can take off from any parking spot and go halfway around the world in an hour. So everyone can find a job with a reasonable commute even if they live in the U.S. and the job is in China.

Marriage, that practice that usually ended up in divorce or in schlepping through life, has become unpopular, replaced by flexible pacts.

Childbirth has become easy and fetal death in childbirth virtually eliminated. How? Because nearly all moms choose to have their babies by curated-embryo in-vitro fertilization and to gestate their baby in an incubator.

School, which had been notorious for producing too little learning and too much antipathy, has been replaced by SuperCourses: the world's most transformational teachers giving interactive, individualized, gamified lessons online. Translated into 70 languages and available on smartphones, SuperCourses enable every child, grade 4 through college, rich and poor, from Alabama to Zululand to learn to previously unthinkable heights, enjoyably.

Recreation is deeply immersive thanks to immersion rooms. Each home has one, in which all four walls, the ceiling, and floor are giant screens. Games in the immersion room allow a person(s) to, for example, have adventures while "being" inside a human body, exploring the world or a world light-years away.

Gene editing and embryo selection have dramatically reduced cancers, cardiovascular disease, and diabetes. That has increased the average healthspan to 100 at which point, most people, rather than decline painfully, take the LaLaLand pill.

Gene editing has prevented depression.

But Jimmy, while not depressed, usually feels empty.

His job is to monitor a bank of artificial-super-intelligence computers to ensure they don't 't do anything nefarious. But while Jimmy could pull their plug, he wants to be able to do the less drastic thing: reduce the computer's capability. But Jimmy's coding skills are, despite prodigious efforts, marginal. So he suffers from the Imposter Syndrome.

Also dispiriting to Jimmy are the so-called Equity Amendments to the Constitution:

The 37th Amendment, the "Equal Pay Amendment," mandates that, with few exceptions, everyone must be paid the same, no matter how much they exceed the Minimum Productivity Requirement. While Tom knows that being more than minimally productive is core to the life well-led, he can't make himself do more than the minimum.

The 38th Amendment, "The Fair Living Amendment," mandates that residences be no larger than 180 square feet per resident. So a family of 4 is limited to 720 square feet. As a result, many people who lived in larger homes or apartments were forced to sell it or rent to enough people to get down to the 180 square feet per person. The Fair Living Amendment also mandates that the racial and ethnic population in all census tracts be within 10 percent of proportionality to the local population. So homeowners are forced to pay members of underrepresented groups to move into their census tract.

The 39th Amendment, the "Racial Compensatory Amendment," requires reparations to African-Americans, to Latinos because they were descendants of victims of the Mexican-American War, to Chinese Americans whose ancestors were in indentured servitude to build U.S. railroads, and to the descendants of Japanese-Americans who, in World War II, were placed in internment camps. To fund the Racial Compensatory Amendment, all other people are required to give 10% of their income each year until the requirement is scheduled to sunset in 2045.

The 40th Amendment, the "Fair Partnership Amendment" requires each partner in a romantic relationship to report semiannually whether their partner did at least 40% of the domestic work. That's a struggle for Jimmy, not because he doesn't want to do his part, but because he consistently feels drained. After work, he just wants to trudge into the immersion room. Even there, he usually has too little energy to play active games. He just wants to be "flown" around the various worlds.

Jimmy's first attempt to lift himself from his malaise was to use his phone's Sigmund app: an AI-driven virtual therapist that uses machine learning to become ever more effective with each patient. Sigmund helped Tom but not enough. So Jimmy tried Rise, the top-rated mood elevation mist, which activates a set of brain neurons and dulls another.

The improvements Jimmy felt from Sigmund and Rise weren't enough to counter the ever more draining effects of his life, especially his imposter syndrome and the four Equity Amendments.

One night, when Jimmy was too tired to even want to be flown around in the immersion room and too scared to tell his wife about the depths of his sadness, he went to the bedroom and stared at the LaLaLand pill.

Automaton

Public Domain Vectors, Free to reuse

It started with ATMs. I rarely had anything to say to the teller yet felt some obligation to initiate a bit of small talk. I paid a little price for that: It distracted me from what I'd rather think about. So when the ATM became available, I started choosing that.

Then it was supermarket checkout lines. Even though I had to look up produce numbers and bag my own groceries, I quickly came to prefer self-checkout unless the self-checkout line is much longer, which increasingly is the case. I guess I'm not the only one who at least sometimes prefers a machine to a person.

Then it was deciding whether to use the drive-through toll-taking lanes or hand the tax to a toll-taker. It was a no-brainer to choose automated. Now on the bridges and tunnels, there only are automated lanes. I guess, like with store self-checkout, The People have spoken. Or maybe it's the government choosing profit over people.

I must admit to a weakness for McDonald's Big Macs and fries. There are two McDonald's near me—One is fully staffed, the other has automated ordering. I choose the latter. And when I want to eat a little more upscale, like at a Chili's or Appleby's, I tend to choose a restaurant with a tablet on the table for ordering: the food descriptions are more accurate and include pictures. Plus, I must admit that I'm glad to save the 15 percent let alone suggested 18 and even 20 percent tip. When I go a step up from that and the restaurant gives a choice between having a waiter or ordering myself on a tablet, I choose to avoid the waiter who'd interrupt my conversation with, "Hey guys, I'm John, I'll be your waiter tonight. Our specials tonight are…" And s/he interrupts me again when s/he tries to push dessert—the last thing I need.

At work, when I began as a manager, I put people first—I'm a people person, I care about people. I care about providing them with good, sustainable jobs. But I've grown tired of employees not showing up, paying them for eight hours when they actually work less, often far less. And some are high maintenance: slow learner or slow worker, lacking good judgment or common sense, or arguing with great confidence when they're dead wrong. Software works more competently 24/7/365 while causing me less stress and less cash—Benefits and worker "rights" alone have gone through the roof.

When self-driving Ubers are proven as safe as with a human driver, I'll choose self-driving. That would avoid my feeling guilty when I choose to not chat with the driver—I don't want to seem snotty. Plus, my ride will cost less because Uber and Lyft won't have to pay a driver and I won't have to pay a tip.

Of course, I still date humans despite sometimes getting frustrated with people's selfishness, overspending, arguing, etc. But I've been reading about AI apps that claim to create a soulmate and, as the conversation proceeds, knows you better and better, thereby giving ever better conversations. I'm monitoring the reviews of those apps and when some later version gets intriguing enough reviews, I'll at least do a trial subscription.

All the replacement of humans with bits-and-bytes seems right and yet…Net, will we be better living in a silicon bubble? How would we not-techies make a decent living? And if we can't, won't that cause great unhappiness and that sanitized term for mayhem, "social unrest?" Would we suffer psychologically from the lack of human contact? After all, we're said to be social animals. But we seem to be voting with our feet, ever more choosing silicon over flesh. So who knows whether a more silicon-centered life will be better or worse.

Excuse me, I need to get on my phone to see when my Lyft is arriving, and meanwhile Zelle my bills, text my mom, check my email and, if I have time, Facebook and Insta.

How I Escaped from the Tower of London

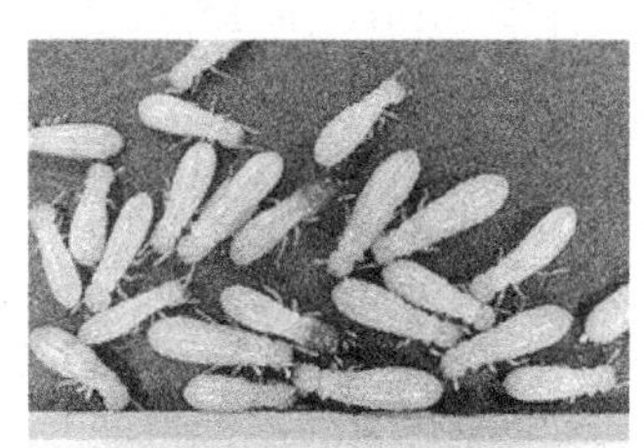

CSIRO, Wikimedia 3.0

It was my second felony— the Big One—murder. The previous one was just manslaughter and in prison, my anger grew at the wanker who ratted me out. I was going to get him and I did. But my luck, coppers just happened to be doing their rounds when they heard the gunshots. And this time, it was a life sentence.

The good news was that my cell in the Tower of London was on the street level but it was made of stone except for two two steel vents with 1/8" grates to the outside and a two-foot-square of heavy wood bolted under the toilet.

I was not going to spend the rest of my life there, but how would I get out? How could I escape through the pipe area below the toilet? After all, there had to be room for plumbers to install the toilet pipe. But how could I get down there? The wood was riveted down and an inch thick—I had nothing to saw that with.

Here's how I escaped. One visitor a month was allowed to come to my cell. When my friend came, I said only things that were boring in hopes that would make the guard pay less attention. At the end of the visit, I said a particularly boring sentence but with four important words embedded: "Give my love to my sister, mother, *termite eggs into vent,* brother, and dad." The friend looked up, saw the vent, and nodded. Would he be smart enough though to figure out which vent went into my cell?

He was. The next month, as he was walking along the prison to the front gate for his visit, he surreptitiously dropped an envelope filled with thousands of termite eggs through my vent.

Termites and especially their eggs are tiny and translucent, so the guards were unlikely to see them. I placed the eggs around the perimeter of the wood and when they hatched, they dug.

Two months later, the wood was damaged enough that I could break it with my foot. I crawled down and then through the plumbers' tunnel a few hundred yards until I saw an opening up to the surface that I was sure was outside the prison walls and prison guards' sight.

And that is how I escaped from the Tower of London.

Empty

Bicanski, pixnio, CC0

My stroller was more basic than most of the others.' Still, I liked sitting in the park where the moms hung out.

But I always stayed on a bench in the corner to avoid any questions. Nevertheless, one of them finally came up to me and asked to see my baby — You see, I always kept the canopy down. I told her, "Maybe some other time." Puzzled and feeling awkward, she murmured, "Okay," walked back to the others, and started whispering to them. They leaned forward and whispered to each other.

Then, one of them strolled over to me and "accidentally" lifted my stroller's canopy. She said, "Oops, sorry" but peered in and saw the blanket, which had the bulge underneath.

She said, "Aren't you afraid your baby won't get enough air?" I said no and, without asking, she pulled back the blanket and saw the doll.

I lied: "I had a miscarriage and that's one way I'm grieving." She said, "I understand." My body language told her that I wanted to be alone again, she got the message, and plodded away.

Of course, that made me think about the truth that I try hard to suppress. I had been in my ninth month and terrified, terrified of having a bowling ball come out of me and even more terrified of having to raise it for 18 years — the stress, the cost, the loss of freedom. So I searched and searched to find a doctor who'd perform a late-term abortion. They all said no, that doing it in the ninth month isn't an abortion, it's infanticide. All of them said no, except one.

Yes, I feel guilty. Yes, I can see the baby in my mind's eye and that's painful. But I still think it was the right thing to do.

I got up from my bench and joined the group.

My Hero

Before I started to get interested in girls, I loved to watch baseball. My hero was a Yankee named Bill Thurmond. He was such a powerful hitter and his arm!— He could throw out a runner at the plate from deep left field!

Keith JJ, Pixabay, Free to use

I was watching the post-game press conference after the Yankees had beaten the Dodgers. I was happy and even happier when Bill, who had hit the walk-off home run, was on. The press conference was almost over when a reporter asked, "So Bill, what are you doing for the community?"

Bill hesitated and looked over to the Yankees' PR person who sat beside him, and she said, "Bill will be giving kids a lesson on success and a tour of the clubhouse this Saturday morning at 10."

I couldn't wait. I was there at 9:30. Already a dozen kids were lined up at the locker room's front door. At 10:00 they let us in and the PR person was there but not Thurmond—I figured he had a busy schedule so he was running late. At 10:15, with a beautiful woman on his arm, Bill walked in. Actually, he trudged in. Was he hurt?

The PR person introduced him to us kids. Why did his face look so sleepy? Or was it sad? Did he have a hangover? Was he on drugs? Anyway, I couldn't wait to hear what he would teach us. It ended up being very short. He slurred, "You kids, work hard in school and at baseball and you can be a star. Everyone is a star. You just gotta believe it."

And with that, he started to trudge out, his lady friend tagging behind. A kid called out, "Hey, you're supposed to give us a tour." Bill slurred, "Vanessa will."

I was disappointed.

Vanessa, the PR person, gave us the tour and that made me teary. The equipment manager saw my sad face, got down to my height, and asked me what was wrong. I explained that Bill's lesson was so short and he didn't say anything I thought would be helpful. Then, not only did he break his promise to give us the tour, the tour made me see that a major-league locker room is just another smelly room with metal lockers kind of like in my school's gym."

The equipment manager said, "Wait a minute" and he came back with a brand-new pair of sanitary socks, the socks the players wear between their stirrups and cleats, and it was signed "Bill Thurmond." The equipment manager said to me, "Bill said to give this to a special kid. You're it."

I left happy until, at home, I compared the signature with the one on Bill Thurmond's baseball card. They were different. To cover for Bill and because he felt sorry for me, the equipment manager must have signed it. I have never thought about heroes the same way.

Who to Save?

Abkfenris, Flickr, CC 2.0

I have ten-year-old twins. Because they're fraternal, they're different. While similar in intelligence, Matthew is bookish and kind, while Paul is aggressive, often mean.

We often go white-water kayaking. This day, as usual, they roughhoused, with Paul, of course, the aggressor and Matthew doing his best to tamp things down. Today, that was unsuccessful and they tussled so much that our kayak tipped over, we all fell out and at the worst possible spot: The river was wide and fast.

We were buffeted and buffeted and the further we went, the more separated we were — It was a triangle in which I was ten yards from either child.

Which child should I try to swim to first? To be honest, in that split second, my instinct leaned to toward the gentle

Matthew, and that is where I headed, whereupon Paul screamed, "What about me?!!!"

I got to Matthew and our only choice was to keep going down the rapids, feet first. Fortunately, we soon were able to grab a tree branch as we watched Paul flail further down the river.

We managed our way onto the riverbank, ran downriver. and just ahead, saw Paul clinging to a rock that jutted up from the river. I dove in and brought Paul to shore to join Matthew. We are all fine.

But now, if people were to tell me that they love their children equally or even, as some spiritual people say, that they love all people equally, I'd quietly scoff.

A Loyal Gardener

Genevieve had been Stanley's gardener for 43 years. Now 73, despite her bad back, she continued. Yes, she needed the money but she had seen the other people in Stanley's life come and go, and even steal—A cleaner had giggled, "I steal one piece of silverware at a time. I'm now at a service for 4. He never noticed!"

Maasaak, Wikimedia, CC 4.0

One day, Genevieve's back was bothering her more than usual, but Stanley was excited about the new rose bush he bought and in his quiet way let her know that he was eager to see it planted. He even showed her the spot.

She dug and dug, her back hurting more and more. She knew that roses like a deep hole and she had dug almost down to the ideal 18 inches when her shovel hit something that sounded like wood —maybe a branch that hadn't fully decomposed? She struggled down to her knees to push away the soil that was still covering it—It was a box, an antique wooden box. She slowly opened it, and inside was note on ivory vellum paper. It was written in turquoise ink in a relaxed handwriting:

Dear Genevieve,

I knew your back was hurting particularly badly today and so, before I made my final decision, I decided to put you to one more test—You've already passed 43 years of working for me, loyally, responsibly. That's an incredible test. But you have just dug a tough, tough hole despite your bad back just because I hinted that I wanted you to. I have worked hard all my life and spent little, so I've accumulated a fair amount. I'm old now and want to see the benefit of my work and savings so, rather than put you in my will, I have transferred most of my life's savings, $250,000, into your checking account. That is my way, Genevieve, of showing you that I love you.

Of course, Genevieve cried, ran into the house, and hugged Stanley.

I wish that were the end of the story but it isn't.

When Genevieve told her friends and family about it, they all urged her to retire from gardening, especially with her bad back. But she explained that she wanted to be loyal to Stanley until she absolutely couldn't do the gardening anymore.

So Genevieve continued, and while her back slowly kept degenerating, she was still able to do her work. But at age 78, something snapped. She could no longer even stand without excruciating pain. Her doctor and the second-opinion doctor said that her only option was surgery although it was far from sure that the benefits would outweigh the risks. And Medicare agreed. Its denial of coverage read, "At age 78, the risk-reward ratio of the surgery is insufficient to provide coverage."

Genevieve felt it was surgery or suicide so she paid for it out of the money Stanley had given her. Alas, she required a revision surgery, which wiped out all her money.

But finally, Genevieve was pretty much out of pain and could walk. Stanley invited her to live with him forever, to enjoy retirement together, and she gratefully accepted.

Killing MAGA

Gage Skidmore, Wikimedia, CC 2.0

Really, I'm like most people in the Bay Area. I just have more guts.

I look typical: usually t-shirts and jeans, mainly blacks and grays.

I act typical: kind of flat, no big show of emotion.

I think typical: I'm a Democrat and hate Trump.

I'm an activist. I do what I can to be a good liberal. And recently, I did something special.

I drove to the red part of the state—farming country—to attend a Trump rally…with the Beretta PX4 Storm Compact I got cheap from a guy on the street in Oakland. It holds ten 9mm rounds and is easy to hide in my pocket.

The whole thing took ten seconds.

I just stood in the middle of the crowd where everyone was packed tightest. At the moment they introduced Trump and everyone was gawking at him, I just pulled out the pistol and shot everyone near me who was wearing a red MAGA hat. I think I got a few of them before they grabbed me.

I'm writing to you from jail. Fortunately, I live in California, which doesn't use the death penalty, so I get free housing, food, life, plus gym, game room, library, celebrity visitors, full health care—better than my life outside. Thank you, taxpayer. And I feel good every day—I feel I've done more for the world than most activists have.

Now, I think I'll write a book. The media sends journalists to help us.

Fired

Jared Tarbell, Flickr, CC 2.0

Damn the younger generation—no respect for tradition, let alone for the wealthy, most of whom have worked their asses off and gotten rich because they provided such good service or products that many other people were willing to give their hard-earned money.

So I opened La Grande Pizza, which for $100 a pie, gives you the pizza experience of a lifetime. The toppings are the finest in the world. For example, they say, "You don't want to know how sausage or laws are made." Well, I want to you to see how *my* sausage is made. No cow eyes here—Filet mignon with just the right spices. And instead cardboardy crap, my crust is filled with flavor and slightly crispy on the outside and chewy when you bite in. The secret is my 1,000-degree pizza oven that I brought over personally from Palermo.

Yet my waiters act as though they're working at Pizza Hut. I train them and I train them but they so often forget or spite me. Spite. Yes, that's what I mainly think, spite!

I used to treat them so well—pay them well, train them well, praise them, forgive them. But it didn't work well. So I decided I needed to be the boss like in the old country. They hated me but it worked.

Every time I caught them, I'd scare them. For example, I had trained them to keep one hand behind their back as their served, while gently lowering the pizza onto the table as though it were Michelangelo's Pieta. If I caught a waiter acting like it was Pizza Hut, I'd come over and re-serve it. Then I'd smile and tell the waiter, "I need to see you." He'd come terrified to the kitchen and I'd get in his face, bore into his eyes, and seethe, "One more time and you're fired!" and I'd storm out to be nice to the customers.

That didn't work well enough but they were too scared to quit. After all, I paid them much more than other restaurants did. But they still sucked.

So I decided to hit them where it hurts, what they care about: money. I started docking them $10 every time I caught them, even something as small as not ending a wine-pour with a gentle circling and lifting of the bottle, an elegant flourish. They hated me even more for docking them.

Then, one night, after the last customer was gone, the waiter who I thought I could most trust came up to me and said he had a surprise for me in the kitchen. I thought, "Well, finally, some appreciation. After all, my birthday was coming up." I was wrong.

When I got there, all the waiters, bussers, and chefs circled around me and tied me to a chair. My trusted waiter said, "You always threaten to fire us. Well, now we're going to fire you! He opened the door to the 1,000-degree oven and said, "Now Pizza Man, you're going to be a House Special." They lifted me up as I screamed, "I'm sorry, I'm sorry" and then they stopped.

I fired them all.

It's All About the Power

With permission, 18/1 Graphics Studio

Having taught in the public schools, I learned that conventional wisdom about bullies isn't always true. They often have irrationally ***high*** *self-esteem, not a veneer of high self-esteem—They really think they're great. They're bullies because they get off on the power and feel that they'll get away with it or suffer just minor reprisal This short-short story is based on a true story of a 7th grader.*

I elbowed him in the face. Why not? There's no referee, no free-throws for a foul. Plus, I love scaring kids. They don't mess with me.

The kid I elbowed said, "You're a bully!" I loved that. It gave me an excuse to bust him up. I kept pounding his face and almost got him unconscious but the security guards pulled me off and dragged me to the school social worker's office.

She was a typical, stupid Nicey-Nicey. She said something like, "To feel such anger, you must be hurting. That's what low self-esteem will do. I know you don't want to be mean."

I laughed in her face. She's clueless. I showed her. My self-esteem is just fine. I love the power. I went right at her and almost got her but I guess the security guards heard her screaming. They can't hold me for long.

Protest or Riot?

I have the best job in the world—I'm on my party's messaging team. I'm proud to have come up a better-polling version of popular political words. It feels great to hear so many politicians use them.

Distropia, Wikimedia, CC 2.0

"Jungle" to "rain forest." "Jungle" implies dangerous while "rain forest" feels so much more supportable.

"Liberal" to "progressive." "Liberal" implies liberal spending of our tax dollars. But who could be against progress? Regressives?

"Redistribute" to "fairness." Many people don't want their money forcibly taken to give to others. But who could be against fairness?

"Reverse discrimination" to "equity." When our opponents use "reverse discrimination," it boosts them in the polls. After all, we're all against discrimination, and discrimination against the largest pool of voters? Nope. So, I came up with "equity." It polls so much better.

"Illegal aliens" to "undocumented migrants." Yeah, "illegal aliens" is the legally accurate term but it polls terribly. We're advocates for the have-nots, so I had to come up with a term that moderates if not conservatives can get behind. "Undocumented" sounds like they're legal but merely don't have the documents, and "migrants"—OMG, how much better than sounds that "aliens."

Their "bold ideas" to "reckless schemes." We knock down their big ideas by calling them "reckless" and "risky schemes."

"Riot" to "protest." Our party works for low-income communities, but no one likes a riot. So I've neutralized that term while making it seem constructive by calling it a "protest."

I was pretty smug about it all…until today. From my office near Capitol Mall, I heard yelling from the street. It was a riot (yes, that was the accurate term) after a court decision that the community didn't like. My window faces away from the street, so I walked down to see what was happening—big mistake. People were swinging baseball bats to smash car windows, store windows, and yes, people's heads. I was foolish enough to try to talk down one of the rioters. He told me to "get the fuck away," so I turned around and nervously strode away, but he ran up behind me and swung his bat hard, right on my spine. I'm now a quadriplegic.

But I won't let that stop me. I'm now trying to come up with a more sympathy-yielding term for "reparations."

"You'll Never Walk Again"

pxhere, CC0

I was an early adopter: I joined the Bicycle Brigade, including blocking traffic on the Golden Gate Bridge. Until a month ago, I was one of those bicyclists that fossil-fuel drivers hate: I cut them off, give them the finger when they don't move over, all of it.

But they got the last laugh. A parked car opened its door without looking and shoved my bike into the middle of the street where I was thrown off and my leg run over, ironically by an electric Prius.

All I remember from the hospital was the orthopedic surgeon whispering, "I'm sorry but you're unlikely to walk again." Ligaments, tendons, bones in my knee were crushed.

I refused to believe it, so I did rehab. It killed me but I was going to prove them wrong.

A month later, with a walker, I could walk, well, sort of. I limped more slowly than an old man but was grateful for every step. I was even a little more tolerant of cars, well, not of gas guzzlers.

While feeling all this gratitude, my walker bumped against a tiny rise in the sidewalk. That was just enough to throw me off balance and I slammed to the ground. I didn't know a human could feel such pain, let alone from a little fall. I guess everything that started to heal, including the nerves, re-broke. I felt like one of those Jews that the Nazis experimented on, breaking and re-breaking their bones until they couldn't stand it anymore.

I stare at my leg, my future.

A Few Hundred Years in Purgatory with My Wife—No Biggie

Lawrence OP, Flickr, CC 2.0

I had been the music director at the Church of the Immaculate Heart for 47 years. Some but not all of the choir appreciated my perfectionism. I'd often say, "The loftier the voices, the more you please the Lord."

When my health was failing for the final time, the priest visited my bedside and suggested I write my own requiem. I tried to balance solemnity with hope, quietude with energy. I had no idea if my requiem was any good.

On Easter Sunday, I was too ill to come to Mass but when the doorbell rang, I was well enough to wheel myself to the door, barely. And there stood two parishioners, who wheeled me to the church for the Easter service. They wanted to put me in the front but, attempting to be a good Christian, I asked to be toward the back.

As the choir sang my requiem, I cried, and moreso when a little boy in the next row peeked at me and asked his mom, too loud, "Why does that man have to die?" His mother gave Catholicism's doctrinal explanation: "He'll go to a better place, first to purgatory and once he's been purified, to heaven."

The next week, I got worse and thanks to God's grace, I died in my sleep.

When I next woke up, I was at the Pearly Gates and St. Peter was checking his iPad to see what to do with me. "Good news. No hell for you, just a few hundred years of fiery purification in purgatory. Then, it's up to heaven—barring any new rules from above or from the government.

St. Peter must have seen the look of disappointment on my face. All my life, I had tried to be a good husband, a good music director, a good person, yet I got just the standard treatment? But the loving St. Peter pulled out his wallet and gave me a seven-day pass to heaven after which, yes, I'd need hundreds of years in purgatory before I got a permanent all-rides pass.

I bowed and thanked St. Peter. Suddenly, the Pearly Gates opened and with a wave of his mighty hand, he motioned me to the up escalator.

Dutiful in heaven as on earth, my first responsibility was to look down on or I should say, down *to*, my wife. I always loved her. Alas, she always viewed me less as the love of her life and more as a necessary neutral.

What she valued most about me was that I was her conscience. So when I saw her reach for a second piece of chocolate cake, I as angel floated down and whispered in her ear, "Are you sure?" She stopped.

When a "friend" wanted to invest the money I had left to her, I whispered, "No. Vanguard." She listened.

When she started an affair with the parish's bad boy, I whispered, "You deserve better." She listened and instead took up with Jack, the nicest man I knew.

But Jack soon dumped her. She was bereft and couldn't pull herself out of it. But she could pull out a bottle of sleeping pills. I whispered, "No." She opened the bottle and louder I said, "No." She got a glass of water and poured the whole bottle of pills into her hand and, as loudly as this angel could yell, I screamed, No!" But she took them all and died.

Now, I was the bereft one, because of my inability to stop her and because my seven-day pass was expiring. I plodded down the escalator. St. Peter shook his head and, with said mighty hand, pointed to an imposing iron door engraved, *Purgatory*. Nervously, I entered to see the purification flames and the sweating masses, including my wife.

I considered trying to return to St. Peter to ask if he thought I'd be happier in hell but decided that a few hundred years with my wife in purgatory would be no biggie.

Feedback

With permission, 18/1 Graphic Studio

The usual response was no response. I felt lucky even to get a form-letter rejection—"There were so many excellent submissions..."

So I tried submitting to outlets that promised feedback- for a fee.

I also joined a writer's group. I even spent the $1,995 on a writer's workshop.

I got feedback but wasn't confident it would levitate me over the golden threshold into The Land of the Published. Some of the feedback felt too global, for example, "Your chapters are episodic." "Episodic" is insider-speak for chapters that are insufficiently meshed. Or the feedback felt too granular: "I wish Doreen's rationale for choosing Tuskegee was fleshed out."

Mostly, I didn't agree with the feedback. Worse, I felt that if I incorporated much of it, the work wouldn't be me anymore: It would be me hollowed-out or dressed incongruously.

Yes, I adopted a few of the suggestions, for example, replacing some adjectives with verbs, balancing action with breathing space, and eliminating extra words so the resulting soup was distilled. But basically, I decided, the hell with them.

So I self-published my novel, *Before*. I enjoyed having control over not just its words but its formatting and especially its cover: an impressionist hourglass with purple sand. I appreciated that it was available on Amazon one day after I submitted the manuscript.

I've sold a grand total of 37 copies, actually six copies— I bought the other 31 to give as presents. But I've started on the sequel, *During*, and then hope to write *After*.

Chris Yarzab, Flickr, CC 2.0

I Hid My Tesla

Kinda like Al Gore, even though I call myself an

environmentalist, I have a thing for big cars. I used to have a Cadillac Escalade but when I got my job as a lobbyist for Save the Earth, I traded it for a Tesla, the big one, the X. It's as luxurious as the Escalade but because it's electric, it was politically correct even though, especially because it's huge, the net benefit to the environment is trivial, especially compared with cars like the Prius. Owning a Tesla is mainly virtue signaling.

Or should I say, it *was* virtue-signaling. Now, Elon Musk, who heads Tesla, has come out as libertarian not liberal, so owning a Tesla is no longer politically correct. So to show my green cred, I would put my bicycle in the back of my Tesla, park it a couple blocks from the Capitol, bike the two blocks, and take it into the building. Excellent virtue signaling.

But my luck, one day as I was getting my bike out of the trunk, an activist I knew from my eco-terrorist days, pulled up in his Prius. At first, I thought he just wanted to say hi or maybe that he too was doing environmental work in the Capitol, but he said he had just used his phone to take video of me pulling my bike out of my huge car. He demanded $10,000 or he'd send it to every senator on the environment committee and to the media.

I was terrified. I had worked hard to get one of the good-paying environmental jobs that didn't require technical expertise, only a big mouth. If I didn't give him the 10 grand or even if I did, he could ruin my career. After all, he had been an eco-terrorist and money or not, he might want to destroy a hypocrite's career. All that flashed through my mind in a fraction of a second and before I could think it through. I grabbed his phone and stomped on it. He called the cops.

I'm writing to you from jail. I can't get the headline out of my mind: Mean, Not Green. I got only a 30-day sentence but if I'm ever going to get another good green gig, I gotta figure out my story. How's this sound? "I was about to sell my Tesla when a paparazzi took that picture. I was afraid he'd sell the picture to like the National Enquirer. I didn't want him to stop me from doing my part to save the earth."

I don't quite buy it. Do you?

I Vomit

Dome Poon, Flickr, CC 2.0

I love eating, especially carbs: pancakes, meatballs and spaghetti, chow fun, bread and butter, ramen, hero sandwiches, pizza—unless the pizza has anchovies.

But I hate the consequences. Although I'm only 17, I was starting to look like those 25-year-olds who stuffed themselves at the dorm buffet at college and drank too much beer.

I figured I could get the pleasure without the fat by binging and purging. When my parents are around, I go to the backyard where they can't see me and I fertilize the plants.

I got worse. As soon as the taste of vomit faded from my mouth, I was thinking about what I'd eat next. My friends were binging Netflix. I was binging carbs.

I don't know if it was to get help or to find kindred spirits but I started an after-school club. I called it, The Gag Gabbers. I found myself defending binge-and-purge.

Mainly we talked about how to hide it—Flushing isn't enough; you gotta scrub with a toilet brush. And of course, you always have to keep breath mints on you.

The teacher who supervised the clubs dropped in during our second session, so I changed the topic: "We gotta eat lots of fruits and vegetables, maybe even go vegan." She left and we never saw her again.

A few months later, my throat started to burn. I ignored it but it got so bad I couldn't even concentrate on my favorite video game. The doctor stuck a tube down my throat, then got all serious and said that my esophageal wall is wearing away and each "insult" to my esophagus will increase my pain and my risk of cancer. "Bulimia is dangerous, son."

I walked out of there with my head spinning. Can I stop? Should I warn the club? See a therapist? I saw two of them when I was younger and they mainly just listened. It didn't help much.

For a few days, I stopped but then couldn't or wouldn't resist. Slowly, I went back. Today, I ate half an extra-large pizza in one sitting and then went to the backyard.

I worry that when I'm at college and my parents can't catch me, it'll get even worse. I hear that at hard colleges, they have to replace the dorm toilets every few years because of the acid from all the vomiting. I don't know what to do. I really don't. Do you have any advice for me?

A Negotiation

Wallpaper Flair, CC

It's ironic that the teacher's union got me canned. After all, I was a teacher, even the union rep, presenting teacher grievances to the union.

But that was before I became an administrator. I was just appointed Director of Business Services for the school district and part of my job was to negotiate the teacher contract with the union.

As a teacher and parent, I saw many teachers who were okay for two or three years and got tenure, but as the years went by, they burned out and increasingly hurt their students, not just low test scores but kids' emotional well-being. Some teachers were downright mean, even scary.

So in my first negotiation with the union, I decided that the one non-negotiable would be that any increase in pay and benefits be accompanied by less onerous criteria for terminating an ineffective tenured teacher. Currently, the "due" process is so undue that it's too poor a use of time and money for a principal, the administration, and the lawyers to fight it.

I was naive. When I said that was non-negotiable, the response from the union's lawyer-filled negotiation team was, "Never in a million years." My rejoinder: "*This* year!" They laughed, "We'd strike for the year and get you fired long before that."

Just two days later, front page in the local newspaper read, "Administrator Demands Hurting Our Kids." The hyperbole was backed by an article that could have and perhaps was written by the union, for example, "Mary Michaels wants to fire experienced teachers, perhaps because it's cheaper to hire inexperienced ones."

That was just the start. The union's PR machine unleashed an assault on me in every media outlet, TV, radio, and social media. I guess the union decided that if they gave in in my district, other districts would follow. And the union sees its core job as—except in the most extreme circumstances—protecting teacher jobs.

Less than a week later, the district superintendent called me into her office and said, "I admire your principles, and you're right. But the children can't afford a long strike and the district can't afford the hit to its reputation. The union is spending a fortune to paint us as anti-child. Plus, they have so much influence with the government. They've already drafted legislation that they've submitted to their buddies on the state senate education committee. Mary, I have to send you back to the classroom."

In a way, I'm happier. School districts often promote the best teachers to administration, but the skill set to be an administrator is so different from that of the good teacher. I'm not a politician. I am a teacher. Fortunately, I'm allowed to opt out of being represented by the union.

Birth and Death

Yes, I had told Victoria that I wanted children. And at the time, I did. I was infatuated with her, with the idea of having and raising a child, and maybe having someone to care for us in our old age.

With permission, 18/1 Graphics Studio

The desire to have kids was fueled by our friends who had them. They emphasized the positives, if only to not seem cold or like bad parents.

And of course, our grandparents were salivating for grandkids.

But then, worries intruded: "Bye-bye freedom. Waking up in the middle of the night. Fighting with the kid about homework. Will I be even a good parent? My job isn't that secure. Can we afford to have a baby? And what if our baby isn't normal?"

I decided to not say any of that to Vicki. I could just imagine her reaction: "What?! You said you wanted a baby! So what do you want me to do now? Get an abortion? No!" I could picture her screaming, then crying, then miserable through her pregnancy, and blaming me forever for spoiling her motherhood.

My worry about an abnormal baby was justified. Lou Jr. was born with an Apgar score of 6, which predicts low IQ.

The first time Vicki and I had sex after Lou was born, my erection wasn't as hard as usual. And over the next months, I became softer and softer until I couldn't have intercourse. In frustration, Victoria said, "You're doing this to punish me!"

Of course, that wasn't true and I got so angry that I did something I thought I'd never do: I slapped her in the face, hard. Even in retrospect, I sort of feel she deserved it but I do recognize that hitting a woman is strictly verboten.

In the next months, we didn't even try to have sex and our relationship declined further, in part because we didn't have sex available to balm life's problems. And atop regular problems, there was Lou, who was difficult, low IQ or not.

He was what Victoria called "fussy," which was an understatement.

And yes, once at 3 AM, when Lou was already six months old and was up yelling half the night, and when I finally got back to bed exhausted after unsuccessfully trying to calm him, I actually said it: "You know, Vicki, Lou is a nightmare!" Victoria seethed, "That hurts me more than even that slap. Much more."

A month later, the night before the garbage was to be picked up, Vicki expanded on a Lorena Bobbitt: She poisoned my dinner and then, with the help of my chain saw, cut me up, threw me into big black plastic bags and into the bottom of the trash bin, and got away with it.

She simply told the cops that I had gone for a walk and never returned. The investigation turned up nothing, so the cops assumed it was just another case of a spouse walking out, and they tossed the case into the cold-case file.

I'm writing to you from purgatory hoping that Vicki feels at least ambivalent about what she did.

Hide

Photo credit: Dries Buytaert, CC4.0

I've always been reluctant to show my feelings. For example, I tried to remain expressionless when the kids were choosing sides for softball and I got picked later than I thought I deserved to be.

But what my sister did to me made me swear I'd never show my feelings again. One night, when the dog in the movie we were watching died, I cried, a lot. When she asked me why, I explained that it wasn't just that the dog died, it's that I'm scared, no, terrified, of dying.

My sister is two years older than me and so she soon became sophisticated enough to push my buttons. She'd say things like, "After you die, you can never come back. Never. You'll just get eaten by the worms." and, "Most people don't die peacefully. They die screaming."

I tried to suppress those thoughts but she wouldn't let me. She taunted me all the time, enjoying seeing me get teary. Worse, she made sure the fear remained top-of-mind. For example, one evening, I came into my bedroom to find that she had etched the words "worms" and "screaming!" into my bed's wooden headboard.

So as I grew up, I made sure to, for example, never show a woman how much I cared for her. I was afraid she'd use my caring to extract what she wanted from me— expensive gifts, fancy vacations, a child I didn't really want. So it's no surprised that I never married.

I did the same at work. For example, I got a promotion but was afraid that if I showed joy, they'd think I felt I didn't deserve the promotion. Or they'd think they could underpay me. Or— and it was probably irrational— my jealous former supervisees would more likely try to sabotage me.

I even showed nothing when I got my cancer diagnosis— a death sentence. The doctor even said, "You seem to be taking it in stride." Inside, I was terrified but said only, "Well, we all have to go sometime."

I told no one about the cancer. Not only did I not want to burden anyone with it, if they did something nice for me, I'd feel I had to reciprocate and didn't have the energy. Again that's probably irrational but I want to tell you my truth.

The only way my sister found out is that when I collapsed, vomiting blood, I had to call 911 and, in the hospital, they looked in my wallet and saw that my sister was listed as next-of-kin.

She asked, "Why didn't you tell me?"

For a rare time, I smiled and said, "You think about it."

Father's Day

It was 4:00 and I had almost forgotten it was Father's Day ,when I passed a hardware store. In the window, a sign said, "Give Dad what he wants: tools."

With permission, 18/1 Graphics Studio

I hadn't gotten what I wanted: a call.

I went to a cafe and thought: Was I a good father? Well, I'm a researcher for political campaigns, not a bad role model. On the other hand, I just couldn't make myself be as involved a parent as my wife had been.

But, yes, really, I deserve to be treated better. He resented my making him even take out the garbage. And yeah, I yelled when his main goal was getting high, but still.

Should I call him? I know he doesn't want me to. After all these years, the mature me would just shrug, but this year somehow, I can't. I called, he answered, and hung up on me.

Mother of the Bride

With permission, 18/1 Graphics Studio

From the first minute, Janet didn't like Dennis. She saw her daughter Grace fall prey to his bad-boy looks and demeanor, something Janet herself had done and swears never again. So it particularly hurt Janet to see Grace be the same fool.

Janet tried everything. After Grace and Dennis' first date, Grace came home and asked if she liked Dennis. Janet wanted to yell, "Are you crazy?!" but deliberately pursed her lips and evenly said, "How do you like him?"

Janet prayed that one of them would break it off but they got closer. Janet realized that discouraging them risked Grace doing the opposite. It could even damage the mother-daughter relationship.

Then, Grace came home flashing an engagement ring, whereupon Janet figured she had little to lose. She said, "Even when I went out to dinner with the two of you, I saw his roving eye. And he epitomizes the sleazy salesman; he even bragged about how he manipulates customers to buy. And he doesn't seem to care much about you. To be honest, I think the main thing he likes is your body." Not surprisingly, Grace stormed out.

A few minutes before the ceremony, Janet followed the tradition of joining Grace in her bridal boudoir. Janet realized it was too late to say anything about Dennis, so she just praised Grace's appearance: "I just love your hair and the tiara is the perfect finishing touch."

When the minister intoned, "until death do you part," Janet forced herself to maintain her manufactured smile.

Then the minister asked, "If anyone believes why Dennis and Grace should not be joined in holy matrimony, let them speak now or forever hold their peace."

Janet thought of all the movies she had seen in which someone stopped the wedding. She thought, "Doing that would be the best wedding gift I could give Grace."

But Janet just pursed her lips though quickly realized that even that would look bad, so she pasted the smile back on until she was back in her car.

"The Bitch"

In a car assembly plant, I'm the foreman, forewoman, take your pick. Either way, they call me The Bitch.

Carol Highsmth, Picryl, CC

Before I got promoted to foreman, they'd straggle in five, sometimes ten minutes late. But I told them that from then on, more than one minute late, they'll be docked, no excuses. Too many excuses are BS and I can't tell which are which. They figured that because I'm a woman, I'd fall for child-care excuses. Nope: Doctor's note or it's dock time.

And when I caught a guy throwing a bolt into a differential and laughing to the guy next to him on the assembly line,

"Let's see if QA can figure out *that* rattle!" I fired him on the spot. Yeah, the union filed a grievance but I wouldn't back down and I won, I fucking won.

As you might guess, I'm glad to get home each day. It's hard being The Bitch. The guys probably think that when I get home, I beat up puppy dogs. But the truth is, I usually put on new-age relaxing music, cut flowers from my condo's patio, arrange them nicely, get a glass of wine, and read romance novels.

Let me tell you why the Jekyll and Hyde routine.

When I was on the assembly line and even when I was a student, I saw too many people view nicey-nicey as a sign of weakness. They know they can get away with shit. They respond only to boundaries and consequences.

But why do I care so much that I'm willing to be called The Bitch and to come home every day exhausted? Because every customer who gets a car that doesn't work right is a human being that I've made unhappy. Every investor in our company, who entrusted us with his or her hard-earned money hoping to save for a car, home, college, or retirement, will lose money if our cars suck—They'll buy a Toyota.

I'm proud to be The Bitch and if I ever have kids, I'll teach them to be a bitch.

Just When You Feel Safest

Jen was the smartest one in the room. At most staff meetings, she

With permission, 18/1 Graphics Studio

had the best ideas, often topping others'. The unfortunate—as you'll see—very unfortunate side effect is that she made others feel less-than, a no-no in today's workplace.

So when a "restructuring" resulted in three of the team losing their job, they couldn't help but think that Jen's "showing off" contributed.

One day, Jen was at her desk, the place she felt most comfortable, and a plastic bomb that had been placed under her keyboard exploded, giving her 1st-degree burns on her hands. Wrapped in aluminum foil was a note, "Remember Psycho? *She* felt safest in her shower until there, she was stabbed to death. Restructure yourself out of a job or else."

The police took the usual report and investigated, of course, interviewing the three laid-off workers, but all had solid alibis. (One of them had hired one of the janitors to do the dirty work.) In a week, the case joined the 95% that end up in the cold-case file.

Two months passed and Jen, having refused to quit her good job, was relaxed driving home. She had long felt her car was what she called, "My island of sanity." The peace was broken when a bomb that had been placed in the seat-back pocket exploded, burning and wrenching her back. A foil-wrapped note said, "Quit your job or else" and the investigation turned up nothing.

A year later, in the shower, the shower head exploded, bloodying her face.

This time, Jen quit but despite her being the smartest one in the room, she couldn't land a decent job. During the interviews, she'd be asked "Why'd you leave your previous job?" She wanted to answer honestly and the interviewer's response inevitably would be something like, "Well, won't this person keep doing it to you again?" And Jen remained unemployed for a year and scared for life.

I Call Myself an Artist

I hosted a graduation party and after everyone left, I got depressed. They're all going to medical school, graduate school, or into business. I'm pursuing my art.

Steve Johnson, Pexels, CC0

I justify it I think because some professors said nice things about my work, even though a classmate called it, "Psychotic Expressionism."

But tonight, for the first time maybe ever, I really stared at and thought hard about my paintings that I had put on my wall, my best stuff.

First, I looked at "Red and Black Paint Can Throws." I loved the primariness, the rebellion against convention, against capitalism—the red and black, you know. But when I stared at it a bit longer, I asked myself if maybe it is just thrown paint cans.

Then I looked at "Green and Aubergine Fingerstrokes." It was my experiment with what one can do if you throw away the brushes and just use the primal, the elemental: your fingers. Or is that more BS and it's just fingerpainting?

Finally, I looked at Blotch 14. In that series, I just put a dab of paint on the canvas. Sometimes it was large, other times just a dot, sometimes in the center, sometimes in the corner, sometimes just a little off-center. And of course, I varied the color. In truth, was that a worthy experiment in minimalism or just more laziness?

Then I mused. Did my professors praise me for my talent or mainly because it's easier to praise than to criticize or because they want a good student evaluation from me? Do I actually like my stuff? No one has ever bought any of it. Even my mother hasn't put any in her house since she put my kindergarten drawings on the refrigerator.

Is it possible that I say I'm artist to avoid growing up? Is it also that I'm scared to look for a real job? I do feel I know nothing, that I'm just another artsy fool who attended that five-year summer camp called art school.

Maybe all I can do *is* throw paint cans onto a canvas, make up some b.s. interpretation of what it means, and then like many successful artists, try to schmooze my way into art shows, galleries, and getting reviews. I dunno. And now, so much art is done with AI. I do know I'm scared.

Legs

Until the five of us moved in, the Hunter public housing project was among America's most dangerous. You know, lots of rape, pimps addicting girls, child abuse, domestic abuse, and yeah, murder, or at least attempted murder.

Axel Drainville, Flickr, CC 2.0

Yeah, the cops would come and sometimes arrest 'em and sometimes they'd go to jail. But it was hit and miss, slow, and they'd usually get back on the street, fast. And that did nothing to scare the bad guys. They knew they'd probably get away with whatever. And they had nothing to lose—It's not like they were going to be brain surgeons.

But you see, the five of us were teammates in the Army's Marksmanship Unit. Since 1964, our unit has won 24 Olympic medals including 16 golds. We trained the trainers.

And the Army taught me that sometimes only might makes right. Nicey-nicey talk works with people who don't commit crimes but with criminals? The only thing that works is fear of getting busted up.

We didn't want to kill anyone but we wanted every wise guy in Hunter to know that he or, yes, she, was going to get shot in the leg every time they pulled something.

And we did it. Everyone in Hunter knew to call us the second they thought there was a problem. And we were there fast, and using the quick judgment we developed in the Army, decided whether the right thing to do was to talk, yell, or shoot. Sure, we didn't always get a leg but we never killed a single person. And the crime rate in Hunter dropped, a lot.

But then, a new resident decided she didn't want "vigilante justice." She called the cops and all five of us were arrested, convicted of assault with a deadly weapon, and sent to prison for seven years.

No surprise, the crime rate in Hunter went up.

But our lawyer appealed and got us out on a technicality.

I'm not sure what to do. If we start up again and some idiot calls the cops, this time, there won't be no technicality. But if we don't, there are going to be a lot more rapes, killings, sex trafficking, domestic violence, all that. We're having a meeting tonight to discuss.

A Sanitized Columnist

pxfuel, DMCA, free to reuse

True to the Asian stereotype, my parents had begged me not to be a journalist: "Few of them make a living, and those that do walk a tightrope—trying to avoid the owners' ire on the right and the Woke editors and mob on the left—Scylla and Charybdis. I'm modern: Even though you're a woman, go be a doctor, an engineer, even an optometrist."

But unlike the stereotypical Asian woman, I wasn't going to do any of those nor passively "honor my parents." I went to journalism school and worked my way up from covering school board meetings to the news desk, and finally got to be a columnist.

My column is, or I should say was, called, *The Worthy*. Knowing how liberal my editor is and because I am afraid of the Woke Mob, even though I'm a centrist, I profiled mainly liberals, moderates, and apoliticals, rarely a conservative. And I emphasized their just-plain-folk side rather than their superiority.

But that wasn't enough. I profiled the liberal Harvard Law School professor Alan Dershowitz. He is pro-Israel and I included a quote from an op-ed he wrote in The Hill:

> The Palestinians could have had a state, with no occupation, if they had accepted the Peel Commission Report of 1938, the United Nations Partition of 1947, the Camp David Summit deal of 2000, or the Ehud Olmert offer of 2008. They rejected all these offers, responding with violence and terrorism, because doing so would have required them to accept Israel as the nation-state of the Jewish people, something they are unwilling to do even today... It is pro-Israel students who are silenced out of fear of being denied recommendations, graded down, or shunned by peers. Some have even been threatened with violence. Efforts have been made to prevent me from speaking on several campuses, despite my advocacy of a two-state solution to the conflict.

The very same day, my editor, with a copy to me, was bombarded with emails from pro-Palestinian groups. Most of them used the same wording so I'm guessing that the groups' leaders sent them "suggested" language: "In writing that abomination, Lily Sakai revealed herself as an anti-Muslim racist! We demand you fire her or we will activate the 783,000 members of our collective aligned organizations to email everyone they know urging them to boycott your magazine!"

They had already apparently emailed their aligned pro-Black organizations, because the next day, my editor received a torrent of emails calling me a racist. Its boilerplate: "Sakai has profiled only Black musicians and athletes. What a stereotype! What about Black scholars and intellectuals such as Ibram X. Kendi, Ta-Nehisi Coates, and Chinua Achebe? In honor of Presidents Day, Sakai profiled George Washington, who was a slave owner, yet on Martin Luther King Day, who did she profile? Jonas Salk.

My editor called me into her office. "You are our finest writer and a pleasure to work with. I'm not firing you nor censoring you, but do you think it might be wise to be a little more careful?"

I did try to be careful. I wrote sanitized stuff but apparently not sanitized enough. A few columns later, I wrote a profile of Jennifer Doudna, the Berkeley scientist at the forefront of gene editing, which promises to prevent and cure many diseases. Plus, how could the Mob object? Doudna is a woman in a predominantly male, high-status profession.

But they could object. I was now on the Mob groups' radar and they bombed my editor again: "First, Sakai writes a positive profile of Dershowitz, snubs Blacks, and now she profiles Doudna, the mother of the new eugenics. That's what Nazis believed in. Think of the racial implications!"

I didn't wait for the editor. I quit.

I sent a dozen applications to universities to teach media studies—I do have a real-world perspective on the issues. I don't know if it's because my reputation as insufficiently woke had spread to academia but I received nothing but form-letter rejections and more often, silence.

I'm not sure what to do next. I do know that, for now, I'll confine my writing to my journal—It's the one place I can write without fear of attack. Maybe my parents were right—I should have been an optometrist.

I Steal CATs and I'm Proud

I make $3,000 in three hours…every night. I laugh at the guys who do straight jobs. I make more in a month than they do in a year. And I don't have to give away half in taxes.

And it's easy. I just drive up to a Prius, get under it with my cordless rotary saw, snip-snip the catalytic converter pipe, and it's off in seconds. I drag it into the pickup and I'm out of there. I laugh at people who spend hundreds for a CAT cover—I just saw off the heads of the bolts. Five extra seconds.

Seth Sawyers, Flickr CC 2.0

Depending on who's paying more at the time, I either sell them to muffler shops or strip the CATs for the precious metals and sell them on the black market.

Yeah, I got caught once, but never again. Someone with a Ring camera got my license plate but my lawyer got me just three months because it was my first offense. But I learned my lesson: Take a couple extra seconds to throw a cheap magnetic sheet on my license plate.

Actually, the guys in jail said it's stupid for me to do the stealing. I need to do like the drug kingpins: Recruit kids to do it. The kids will make more money than they'd ever make—I create good-paying jobs. My job is just to keep growing my business, create more jobs, and get myself richer. Easy-peasy.

Do I feel guilty? No way. Like they taught in school: "Income inequality." I'm reducing income inequality… and I'm rich. Yeah, I steal CATs and I'm proud.

With permission, 18/1 Graphics Studio

Silent Scream

Kate stood at the podium in the auditorium-sized classroom. She still bore vestiges of her Sarah Lawrence days: She usually wore black, used an officious New England tone even though she was from Indiana, and to her lament, she still smoked. Although a can-do person, smoking the fat, unfiltered strong hipster cigarette, Galouises, had been her Waterloo.

Even at age 63, Kate still exuded the fire. To prod her students into anger and activism, her lectures were like a revival preacher's exhortations. To add to her power, she had mastered techniques such as what she dubbed, The One Second Bore: As she lectured, she'd bore her eyes into the eyes of a student on the far left and after a second, move on to an adjacent student. When she reached the far right, she'd reverse field. When the students finished a Kate course, many, even some science majors, became activists.

Despite Kate's age, it was the last thing her students expected. In the middle of a sentence, the left side of her jaw dropped and then she did. Kate had a stroke that put her in a wheelchair.

More troubling to Kate than her paralysis was the aphasia: She had lost the ability to speak.

But Kate didn't lose her ability to react. In fact, she channeled her lack of speech into more vigorous reactions. Shunning her upbringing and peer culture, which venerated restraint. she decided to show what she felt, unfiltered by gentility's gauze.

For example, when Kate saw an attractive person, she held eye contact and smiled, sometimes seductively. When she thought someone was bullshitting, she'd roll her eyes. Once, when she saw someone she thought was acting badly, she wheeled her chair up close, raised her fist, and spat.

But Kate's most common facial expression was sadness, yes because of her limitations but also because her so-called friends rarely called, let alone visited.

That was even true of Kate's mother, Poppy, who, at 87 and still in good health, was tired of helping Kate— Poppy thought, "I don't have much good time left. I don't want to waste it helping Kate cook and clean." So Poppy said, "Kate dear, atop your mobility issues, your arthritis makes it challenging to cook, clean, and even bathe yourself. It's time, dear. Let's at least tour a retirement community."

Kate hated the idea but to appease her mother, acceded. When the salesperson showed the TV room, Kate saw a row of wheelchairs, with some of the residents nodded off. Kate silent-screamed.

Not Your Usual 50th Anniversary

Creazilla, Public Domain

After 34 years at a large company, I took the bait of the cash incentive to retire. Honestly, it wasn't just the money, I was kinda glad to walk away from a couple of my recent screw-ups.

At that point, at age 74, I was feeling like one of those major league baseball players who hung on too long and then had to retire or face the ignominy of getting sent down to the minor leagues.

But I was terrified of the statistic—After retirement, the average man lives only two years. Sure, many people retire because they are already sick, but there probably also is some truth to retirement itself being deadly—We all need to feel useful, not out to pasture, not irrelevant. That may be especially true for men, for whom work is often central. Quietly, many men find more meaning in work than in family. And there's no question that men live six years shorter than women https://tinyurl.com/2n3ex5mx and spend their last decade in worse health. Yet all we see is another run for breast cancer. But I digress.

My nervousness about retirement was fueled further by the fact I'd be with my wife 24/7/365.

But I bit the bullet—a somewhat apt metaphor. While I was still working, my wife had tolerated my occasional rants about media bias and its assault on white men. But now, with me home all the time, she couldn't take it. She'd walk out of the room or even yell, "Enough!"

And *I* couldn't take her noise— the daily and unnecessary vacuum cleaning, the incessant TV, her pumping Zumba videos. A main reason I retired was to get peace and quiet and instead I got noise. I often escaped to the backyard or to a coffee shop but hated having to banish myself from the home I had worked so hard to afford.

But I couldn't escape from my wife using my retirement as a tool to get me to do what she had long pushed for: travel more, see the grandkids more, take dance lessons. "Seymour, you're 74 years old. It's time to cash in that lifetime of work and have fun!" She refused to accept that I found work a wiser use of my time than "fun."

Our 50th anniversary was coming up and I dreaded it—She insisted on throwing a party, a big one. "If we don't celebrate this, what will we celebrate?!" I couldn't stop her and then I thought of something. "Stella, I want it to be a 50th-anniversary divorce party. We are better off separate."

I was surprised at her response. Her pride wounded, she didn't want to beg to stay together, to use all the levers I thought she would pull: "Think of the kids, all our history, that we'll want each other in our old age." She just muttered, "Okay."

So she sent out the invitations: "Come celebrate Seymour and Stella's 50th anniversary. We'll be making a surprise announcement."

I planned to put a positive spin on it: "In honor of our 50 years together, we have decided to do something to help ensure that our next 50 are fresh and new—We're divorcing."

But at the moment of truth, right before I said, "We're divorcing," I said, trying to sound sure, "To help ensure that our next 50 are fresh and new, we're…committed to finding the new in each other."

Everyone applauded and I approached the stunned Stella, kissed her, and she relaxed.

Safe

Augusto Ordonez, Pixabay, Free to Reuse

When they're being honest with me, my friends confirm that my face suggests that I'm a bitter, angry, old man. And I sort of am, although what reads as anger is partly disappointment at how the world has treated me.

At this point, I'm not very afraid of being rejected or even canceled. I've passed that. I'm now at resignation. I just don't want to deal with people being annoyed with me. So it's safer to go it alone.

I used to be rather successful but I don't want you to think I'm a braggart so I won't tell you about that. I just want you to know that now, I walk the streets with a rag and a spray bottle of *409* and clean any dirty garbage cans, pick up trash that people drop—like Coke cans and junk-food wrappers—and yeah, dog poop.

Occasionally, someone asks why I do it. It's not mainly altruism. It's that it feels safe—No one could be mad at me.

Until today. A group of teenagers stopped me as I was picking up a Doritos bag. One taunted, "Gee, can you teach me how to do that?" I stared at him wondering whether he was born bad or had become bad. Another one said, "Who you looking at, old man?" I sensed trouble so I walked away. "Where you going, old man?"

I figured it was best not to say any more, so I kept walking. But they raced up and two of them knocked me down and pounded on me while the others cheered them on. "That's right!" "Get him!" "Yeah!"

Fortunately, I wasn't like the ones that make the TV news—bleeding or worse. After a while, one said, "Cool. Let's go." and they strutted off.

I lay there figuring that was safest, and this time, I was right. A minute later, I looked up and saw that they were gone. I got up, grateful I was okay. I plan to keep on doing my thing. I still think it's relatively safe.

"I *Am* Going to Have the Baby"

John was pretty average except for his looks. The girls flirted with him but he had eyes only for Emma, even though she was probably the most religious girl in his school. To remind herself and perhaps others of her faith, she usually wore a too-large cross.

With permission, 18/1 Graphics Studio

Emma flirted with John by sitting in his line of sight in the cafeteria. During recess, she stood where he could see her. And her next move was to ask him if he wanted to go to church with her.

Sitting next to her, his ardor grew and as they walked out, he asked if she'd like to hang out. She agreed but said it had to be at her apartment when her mother was there. He too was not eager to push, so he found himself glad she said that, although he was nervous about going to the public housing project where Emma lived.

But such hanging out is combustible and when there's a will, there's a way. So they took walks and found secluded places to kiss and later, more than kiss.

They admitted that they were both virgins but in part, because they had both just smoked weed for the first time, they agreed to "go all the way." They stopped at a drug store and decided both would go in to get the condoms.

And all proceeded naturally, beautifully, that time and the next few times. Then, as he got more relaxed and she more comfortable, he said, "It would feel so good to be next to you, if you know what I mean." She nodded but said, "I don't want to get pregnant." In his passion and ignorance, he insisted he'd pull out, and she silently consented. But as they got near climax, she whispered, "It's okay" and, at that moment, blinded to consequences, he came deep inside her.

In the light of day, love gave way to fear. What if she was pregnant? They dismissed it because it was unlikely, but when she tested before her next period, she was indeed pregnant.

She decided to tell him in a public place and so invited him to a cafe. "You know, I'm a Catholic, a real Catholic— I don't believe in abortion. My parents don't believe in abortion. God doesn't believe in abortion. I *am* going to have the baby."

Thoughts flooded his brain: We're not ready to be parents. She's poor; my parents would have to support it. They'd be so angry. Would I have to drop out of school and get a job? Damn, one moment's passion and 18 years of being a parent? And we're under 18. In health education class, they said that in our state, sex under 18, even if consensual, is statutory rape. Most kids do it but could I go to jail?

But all he said was "I love you. We'll figure it out."

He walked her home, kissed her, and then padded home. Options flashed through his mind, including suicide.

Musing on What Matters

Pexels, CC0

Hi, my name is Ann and I'm a saleswoman for Forever Us Diamonds. It's a mall jewelry store that specializes in wedding rings.

We get busy from 12 to 1, so my lunch hour starts at 1:30. I love my lunch hour. Let me tell about today's. I sat on the soft bench just outside the store, eating a cobb salad, croissant, and cappuccino. I love those, mainly I guess because they're tasty but not too fattening. I also enjoy looking around, at the shoppers in the mall and especially at the couples going into our store.

Today, there was a young couple—She seemed to be vibrating with excitement; he seemed dutiful. Then there was the middle-aged couple, calmer but both seemed pleased to be coming in. Then there was an old couple, maybe in their 70s, both of whom seemed happy. Maybe it's that they thought that romance was over for them and it's not. Or maybe they're just grateful to have someone to care for them in their old age. I dunno.

I looked at my ring. It's a wedding ring with a CZ, not a diamond. I'm not married. I just wear it to avoid getting hit on.

And that started me thinking. Should I toss the ring and let myself get hit on? Should I hit on guys? What matters? Love? The songs say so but almost everyone I know starts in love or, more often in lust. Then when the fog clears, sooner or later, most of them find their love replaced by some combination of schlepperhood and fighting. I can think only of two couples that have been together more than a year that seem happy. But then again, who knows what goes on behind closed doors?

Does money matter? I guess it does to the extent that you can pay the rent, health insurance, and so on. But beyond that—the stupid diamonds I sell? They're no different really than CZs except that they cost a zillion times more. They say a diamond is forever but it sure doesn't increase the chances of permanent happiness or even contentment. I guess a diamond is a symbol of hope that their marriage won't be in the half that divorce or the others that schlep along.

How about contribution? Maybe meaning lies in that. But I'm not going to save the world, not even close. I'm just Average Ann. Yeah, I try to be nice but I don't always even succeed at that.

What does matter? Does anything really matter? Could it be that for Average Ann, what matters are things like my beloved lunch hour?

I dunno. Anyway, excuse me. I gotta get back to selling diamonds.

The Combat Medic's Dilemma

Jeff, 66, was tired, especially at the end of the day. But this afternoon, he had one more meeting, a Diversity, Equity, and Inclusion (DEI) training. He thought, "Geez, this is the third one this year and every one just makes me feel guilty, and I didn't do anything. I am not a racist."

Picryl, Publid Domain

Toward the end of the training, the facilitator said, "Jeff, you've been quiet. What are you thinking?" Jeff didn't want to say, so he just said, "I'm listening." But the facilitator wouldn't let that go. "Well, what are you thinking in light of your listening?"

Jeff hesitated, knowing it was risky if he were honest, but he wasn't a good liar, so he felt forced to say what he was thinking: "You tell us that we need to redistribute yet more money and effort to 'the least among us.' But every combat medic knows that while our hearts are moved to help the sickest, it's wise to use limited resources on people with the best chance of living." The facilitator's face darkened and no participant dared say anything.

Early the very next morning, while still in bed, Jeff checked his work email. One was marked "High Importance" and it was from his boss: "I need you in my office at 8:00."

Jeff had never before received such an email and his anxiety grew when he entered the boss's office. She said, "Jeff, we have worked hard to create a culture of inclusion, and your statement at the DEI training— in front of your colleagues and supervisees—subverted that. It was unaligned with our crucial DEI mission. We cannot have that. If you resign, we'll add six months service credit toward your pension. If you don't, we will be initiating an investigation into your DEI-related statements and actions over the past 24 months. You might come out fine or, well…"

Furious, Jeff knew he should take a day or two to think about it but couldn't make himself, so he quavered, "I didn't say let alone do anything wrong… but I'll resign."

What now? Jeff wanted to share what he had learned over a lifetime of fundraising management. So he searched the ads in the Chronicle of Higher Education and found four courses he'd be qualified to teach, two local and two that could be taught remotely.

Jeff got one, but during the course, he felt he had to discuss the dilemma of giving to "the least among us" versus to people more likely to benefit. So he told the story of his forced resignation, thinking or at least hoping that his students would be supportive. Maybe some were but the only ones who spoke up were two who lectured him. One even called him a racist.

Jeff finished teaching the course but then turned his attention to finding something else to occupy his time. He thought it would be safe to join a book club—It's intellectual, plus it fills a lot of time—He would have the time to actually read each book. But when Jeff queried the local book clubs, all focused heavily on books—fiction and non—advocating more redistribution. He felt that joining such a club would be too stressful.

So Jeff retreated to his garden, trying to confine his thoughts to what varieties of rose, tomatoes, and fruit tree to plant. Often, he's unable to suppress his belief that, not only was he treated unfairly but that further redistribution is hurting society, causing unnecessary "combat deaths."

The Test

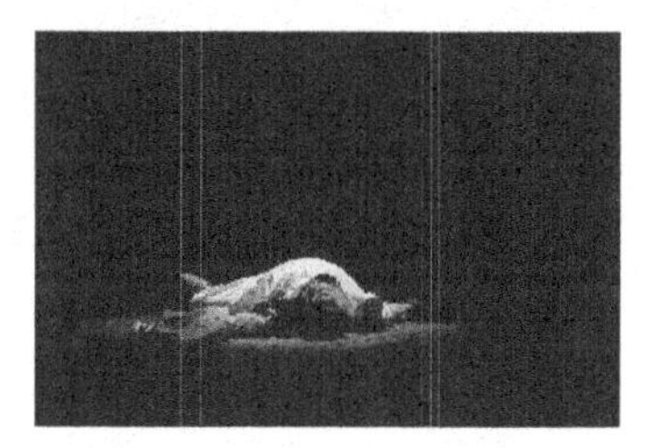
pxfuel, DMCA, free to use

I was soon to retire and sensed that my wife was dreading being with me 24/7/365. I even worried, if I got sick and needed her help, how much I could count on her?

So I decided to test her. With her in the room, I faked having a heart attack: I dropped to the floor and groaned, clutching my chest. I pretended to have my eyes closed but had them just open enough that I could see. She didn't move, neither toward me nor toward the phone to call 911. Her face made clear that she wasn't in paralytic fear—She just didn't want to help me. She wouldn't have the guts to kill me but if I could go naturally, I believe she wouldn't mind, maybe even prefer it.

I got up and told her it was a test. Of course, she said she didn't act because she was frozen in fear but I didn't believe it. Nevertheless, I simply nodded whereupon she blamed me for scaring the hell out of her and daring to think I couldn't trust her.

So, what was I to do? Divorce her? Too painful. Certainly not kill her; that's not in my DNA even if I wouldn't get caught. So I did nothing. I proceeded as if she had passed the test. I just accepted that—I'm guessing as in many marriages—the wedding vow of undying love in sickness and in health for a lifetime is just too hard to keep.

It's been a decade since The Test and we're doing okay.

Kansas to Vegas

Tomas Del Cora, Wikimedia, CC 2.0

In the Salina, Kansas church I grew up in, filled with well-wishers, my dad, Pastor Peter was at the altar, performing the most important wedding ceremony of his life: mine.

With tears in his eyes, he whispered, "Mary, do you take Travis to be your lawfully wedded husband in sickness and in health, for richer, for poorer until death...

Before he could say "do us part," I ran out, ripped the "Just Married" sign off the back of our car, pulled Travis's suitcase out, left it on the sidewalk, and drove off.

I had no idea where I was headed. I just knew I had to get away from ordinary Kansas life, especially daughter-of-Kansas-preacher's life. I got on the Interstate and drove west. Except for pit stops, I drove straight through the Oklahoma panhandle, North Texas, and into New Mexico, where I saw a sign that felt like a *sign*: Albuquerque 212, Phoenix 520, Las Vegas 777. "777?!" and because Vegas is the opposite of ordinary Kansas, I had found my destination.

What was I going to do there? I have no skills. In Salina, I was just a waitress.

On arriving in Vegas, I knew I needed clothes and didn't want to run out of money. So my first stop was a Salvation Army store. I was so nervous, so many things going through my mind, that I forgot that I was still in my wedding dress! I only realized it when people started laughing at me.

So I grabbed the first dress that called to me, of all things, a gold-sequined cocktail dress: short, too short, and scoop neck, lots of cleavage would show, too much. But it sure is different than Kansas, pure Vegas, and for $5? I wasn't going to take the time to try it on. I wanted out of there, now!

I tried it on in the car and felt embarrassed that I loved it. It was a sign of my new life, the opposite of Salina.

I didn't expect to have to be spending much of my own money on my honeymoon, so I checked into a cheap hotel in a neighborhood I called "dicey"— perfect for Vegas. To avoid being seen in sequins, I raced up to my room.

I looked at myself in the mirror and thought, next stop, Wal-Mart, to get normal clothes. Then I asked myself, what am I going to do to make money?" More waitressing? Tired of that. I'm here to do something new. Seeing my cleavage in the mirror, I laughed, hooker? Never! But I do look like a cocktail waitress— maybe at one of those famous Vegas hotels?

So after a good night's sleep, which I sure needed, I went to the fancy hotels I had heard of: Wynn's, the Venetian, and MGM Grand. All three came up snake-eyes. Or is it craps—I don't know gambling. I asked why they turned me down: "Is it my dress?" No, they loved my "get-up" but wanted to hire someone who had already been a cocktail waitress in Vegas.

They told me to try the Sahara, Circus-Circus, and even the Best Western. But I got the same answer and got scared.

Driving back to my hotel in its dicey neighborhood, I passed Winners Motel and Casino. Two of the letters in the neon sign were out. I thought, maybe you gotta start somewhere. Looking up and down my dress, the manager hired me.

I hated the job: The nonstop noise of the slot machines and the players whose politeness sometimes faded into rudeness after their second drink. One guy said, "Baby, you probably make 15 an hour. How'd you like 200? Come to my room and I'll show you how."

I turned him down with a polite, "Thank you but I don't do that." But after my shift, back in my room, I started thinking. After all, my fiancée and yeah other guys said I was hot. And it would pay a lot better than Winners Motel and Casino. But what would my parents think, especially my father, preacher man!?

But the next morning, which for me was noon, on my phone, I went to the website of the only brothel I'd ever heard of: the Camara Ranch. It wanted applications for "courtesans." And without thinking about it much, I applied. I figured they'd never hire me— I definitely had no "prior experience working in a brothel." That was a question on the application. But the same day, I got a call for an interview. I wore my sequin dress and they hired me subject to passing the blood test and criminal background check. In the meantime, they gave me a training booklet, including how to do a "dick check:" looking for STDs.

Two days later, they called and asked if I'd sign a 14-day contract at $1,000 a day— live-in. I signed but soon broke the contract. It was the very first guy. I didn't get beyond the few minutes of "warm-him-up conversation" when I cried, "I can't do this." And as I did at the altar, I ran out and drove back to Salina.

As soon as I got home, my parents cried, I cried, and of course, I apologized. Next, I saw Travis and swore I'd never run away again. But he said, "I can't count on you, Mary. No."

As I'm writing this, I'm back to waitressing and am wondering if, like my fellow Kansan, Dorothy in the Wizard of Oz, maybe there really is no place like home. I'm not sure.

Wonder Woman

I hate that I had reached the mandatory retirement age for National Park police: 57. I still feel young, love my job, my coworkers, the park visitors, and most of all, that my "office" was Yellowstone National Park.

With permission, 18/1 Graphics Studio

Yeah, I have a pension, but now I spend too much time pacing: pacing my house, pacing my backyard, pacing the park.

So I was glad to be invited to my granddaughter Chloe's 2nd-birthday party. What gift to buy? My daughter said that Chloe likes music, so I found a toy piano for toddlers on Amazon: just eight keys but it can make the sound of an electric piano, an organ, even a DJ scratcher.

But after Chloe tore open the gift wrapping, she pouted, "I wanted Wonder Woman." When I asked whether she wanted to try the piano, she shook her head. To try to entice her, I plunked out the only song I knew, Mary Had a Little Lamb, but she turned away. Grandparents spoil so I said, "Okay, I'll get you Wonder Woman, Chloe," and I bought the cheapest one I could find.

I kept the toy piano because it was a hassle to ship it back to Amazon. I'd occasionally, trial-and-error, plunk out other simple songs like Old McDonald and Row, Row, Row Your Boat. Then I wrote words to them about what I know: parks, cops, even an anti-drug PSA, and posted them on YouTube.

When I next visited Chloe, I brought the little piano and played my ditties for her, yes, in part to show her what she missed. She said, "I want it!"

I asked, "Where's Wonder Woman?" She replied, "I don't know."

Sideshow

I'm, as my counselor says, "not academic." But or maybe because of that, I have lots of friends. That is, if the 184 names in my phone's address book means anything. But I spend little time with friends, mainly just texting few worders such as,

James Mackey, Flickr, CC 2.0

LMAO: Laughing my ass off

ICYMI: In case you missed it.

FUBAR: Fucked up beyond all recognition (which I learned from my dad, a former corporal.)

But what I really love is cars, especially cool cars: tricked out, big-wheel, supershined Mustangs, Challengers, Camaros, and my impossible dream, Corvette, especially the convertible.

So I almost never missed one of those sideshows, those parties that took over streets and where cool cars did stunts. Although I live in Berkeley, my fave was the big one in Vallejo, 30 miles away.

Every Friday night, dozens of muscle cars were there, often painted red, purple, or my favorite, supershined black. I loved seeing them squeal their wheelies, do donuts (squealing the car in a circle), ghost (the driver dancing around his car while the car is moving), and the cloud of smoke over it all. I even liked the smell of the burning rubber.

Streets near the sideshows were blocked, which, of course, frustrated motorists. They called 911 but most got a busy signal. The ones who got through got no satisfaction. The dispatcher just said, "We're on it." "How long will it be?" "I don't know."

After a few months of pissing off the public, the police finally showed up—like ten cop cars. They got us to leave and then, on the next few Fridays, the cops were there early to prevent the crowd from coming. Finally, the side-showers gave up.

But I couldn't stand that. So I decided to text the 184 names in my address book to say there'd be a sideshow that coming Friday at 9 PM at a new location. I asked them to text all the people in their address book.

A dozen cars showed up, not enough to move the cops to action. I built *Zed's Sideshows* to 200 cars and 1,000 spectators and made serious money without getting caught. How? First, I thought that people would find it cool if I had a warrior name. I picked Zed just because it sounds big and bad. Then I rotated locations each week and kept the sideshow to one hour so by the time the cops showed up, we'd be gone. How did I make money? At the entrance, I charged $20 per car, $10 per walk-in. Sure, a few cars squealed past the hulk who was taking the money, but I did fine.

Another draw was "The After Party." I'd pick the coolest cars that did the best stunts and invited them to what I called, "The I–80 Speedway," the stretch of freeway between Vallejo and Emeryville. They'd meet at the freeway entrance in Vallejo and the first car to get to the Denny's parking lot in Emeryville would get a prize: a girl. I had convinced one of my girlfriends to do it for $20. If they got into an accident, they got the consolation prize: the girl for the whole weekend." For that, I would give the girl $100. I had to pay up twice.

A year and $100,000 later, the cops finally caught onto me and arrested me.

Because it was a first offense, the judge gave me just 12 months/out in 8 at a minimum security, "country-club" prison—the Lompoc Pen near Santa Barbara.

While I was "away," others copy-catted my sideshows not just in the East Bay but in the San Rafael-to-San Francisco and San Jose-to-Morgan Hill corridors.

When I got out of jail and saw that the Bay Area was now covered, rather than fight it, I made deals with people in L.A. and New York, and then London and Mexico City.

I now drive, yes, a new, tricked-out, supershiny, black Corvette convertible.

My Daughter is Getting Married

Raw Pixel, CC0

My daughter said, "Dad, I'm getting married."

In the second before I had to respond, I thought about my two failed marriages and other relationships. To buy a bit of time, I said, not effusively, not flatly, "Congratulations."

She probably thought, "That's all, and so tepid? What an asshole." but said only, "Thanks, Dad."

I thought, "She hadn't even told me she was seeing someone. I've been a good father. Why wouldn't she tell me?" But I said only, "Want to tell me about him?"

She said, "Her." and probably thought, "What a dinosaur. That's why I don't tell him shit. And I'm sure not going to tell him that she's the one because of the sex." But what she said was, "Well, she's pretty, makes me laugh, and makes more money than I do."

I thought, "You keep insisting you're an independent woman, yet now your fiancée's money is a top reason you're marrying her?" But I said only, "When's the wedding?"

She probably thought, "That's all you need to know about her? Jesus!" But she said only, "June 17, Key West, Smothers Beach."

I thought, "At least it's not some expensive resort but I'm guessing she's still going to hit me up to pay for it." But I said only, "In June, isn't Florida a bit hot?"

She probably thought, "Controlling and negative as usual. Asshole!" But she said, "On the beach it will okay for the ceremony and the reception will be at the La Capitana Resort."

I thought, "Resort. Expensive. Damn it!" but said only, "I see."

She probably thought, "Fucking passive-aggressive" but said, "Dad, Kat's parents don't have much money, they're artists, so I need you to pay for the wedding."

I couldn't control my face turning apoplectic nor stay with the controlled responses, so I blurted, "You should have consulted me before asking me to pay for it."

She probably thought, "I knew it. Cheap bastard!" Like me, unable to remain controlled, she seethed, "Never mind. I don't want your money. You know, I don't want you at the wedding!" And she stormed out.

June arrived and both of us were too stubborn to give an inch, but on the wedding day, I flew down to Key West and showed up at Smothers Beach a half hour before the ceremony. I merely nodded at her, she nodded back, and whispered to her aunt, who had agreed to walk her down the aisle.

I walked her down the aisle, smiling but fuming.

Secretly Rich

I'm president of a university, no not a famous one, just a regional state one. But I do make $375,000. Why so much? If a college president is any good, s/he brings in millions—We're colleges' fundraiser-in-chief.

PickPic, CC

My problem is that I'm attracted to working-class country women. I have little in common with them—My world is fat cats and out-of-touch professors who delude themselves into thinking they know a lot about the real world. The women I'm attracted to are into pop culture, church, and daytime TV.

My hunting ground is Billy Bob's Texas Saloon. I usually don't tell them what I do because I don't want to intimidate them and don't want a woman liking me for my money. I typically wear a t-shirt, well-used jeans, maybe a baseball cap, and tell them I'm a truck driver.

Unfortunately, a woman named Savannah, with whom I had quite the hot relationship, decided to sign up for a course on genealogy at the college. When she went to the college's site to register, she noticed the homepage, which had a letter of welcome from guess who. She broke up with me and I'll never forget her parting words. It was a take-off on Marilyn Monroe's famous come-on to President Kennedy: "Happy Boffing, Mr. President."

Then there was Raylene—There she was at Billy Bob's wearing cowboy boots. a leather miniskirt, and hair down to her breasts. In light of the Savannah disaster, after the first time Raylene and I went to bed, I told her the truth, that I was a college president. She dumped me. "I don't trust rich guys." You can't win.

Well, tonight, I gave the pitch at the college's fundraising gala and Elizabeth, the opposite kind of woman, came up after to "congratulate" me. She was wearing an expensive outfit, including pearls. We had so much in common—She was executive vice-president of marketing at a nonprofit and loved talking about running one. Plus, we shared a love of classical music.

Being a college president is seductive, power is sexy, so we ended up in bed. The sex was fine but, during it, I fantasized about Raylene.

Elizabeth is now asleep and I'm awake writing this, wondering whether to keep dating Elizabeth or to go back to Billy Bob's.

An Offer I Can't Refuse?

RawPixel, CC1

My wife never gives in, so I end up just stomping away and cursing her. But when I came home early and there she was with her legs spread—with my cousin!—I exploded. I ran into the kitchen, grabbed the biggest knife, and got him.

My lawyer was good. He got me 11, out in 7 1/2 if "you're a good boy." I was no saint but didn't pull any knives. So I was out in 8.

I thought it would be hard for a second-degree murderer to get a job but I got a call without even applying—from

Soar2030. It gets tutors for urban kids. They said they needed someone who could raise money from rich ex-cons, like fashion big-shots who stole money from the till, nonprofit CEOs that ran off with donors' money, and yeah, even a sales guy like me who stabbed someone to death.

It wasn't long before I met a special prospect. He was the head of a Hollywood film studio that laundered money from the Sinaloa cartel. The Sinaloa boys specialize in whatever's hot. I hear it's now Tranq: fentanyl plus xylazine, which makes the high last longer. Yeah, it's more likely to kill you but oh well. He said he'd donate a million to Soar2030 and rewrite a script for an upcoming movie that would make Soar2030 seem like the world's best charity if I'd do just one thing for him: Get a job in the kitchen of a hotel where the Klan will be having its annual meeting, and at the big dinner, poison the soup.

I said, "No way." But he upped the offer: "$2 million to Soar2030 plus a $100,000 "tip" to you and I'll even give you the drug. "Just pour it in. You'll make $100,000 for one second's work and Soar2030 can do a lot of tutoring for $2 million." I told him to get the fuck out. He shrugged, dropped his card and said, "You'll call me."

I'm not sure what to do.

Jealous

I had long been jealous of her but that day was the last straw.

I was polishing my six-year-old Camry when my neighbor pulled up in her brand-new Mercedes.

Public Domain Pictures, CC0

She stepped out in her perfect tennis outfit. "Just back from the club. Their Sunday brunch is simply grand!"

Seeing me stare at her new Mercedes, she draped herself over it. "Do I look like the commercials?" I can't believe I said it but couldn't resist, "Yeah, the dog food commercials."

She scoffed, flounced across her perfect lawn, and slammed her custom front door behind her. She had replaced a perfectly lovely oak door with a hand-carved cherrywood one crowned with a half-moon stained-glass window of Dionysus.

I ran into my garage, pulled out the Roundup canister that I use to kill dandelions, and sprayed "Fuck you!" in the middle of her lawn.

A week later, she rang my doorbell. My heart pounded. She said, "I'm here to thank you for the wake-up call. I've been such an imbecilic materialist. I am going to live simply: I'm putting the house on the market and moving to a small apartment. As a thank-you, I'd like you to have my Rolex. It's a man's but it's in' for women."

Should I take it? From this pompous prig? I do know that Rolexes impress only shallow people. Smart people recognize such things as Rolexes, Coach purses, and other "luxury" brands are silly spending—Many Casios look as good and tell as good time for 1/100 the price. But somehow…

Now it's ten years later and I'm still in my house. As I write this, I'm staring at the Rolex.

Swarms

Ian Jacobs, Flickr CC 2.0

It started with just one unusually large wasp, redder that the usual ones. A man walking through a park in Madison, Wisconsin waved it away but it zoomed right back and stung him. That hurt even more than the usual wasp bite. Then another wasp stung him, and another, and another. Soon a swarm surrounded him, stung and stung him, and he died.

Jonah Weiss, a private entomologist in Madison, had set up Twitter alerts on the term "insect" so he quickly learned about the stinging death. He drove to the site, took a picture of the insect, and ChatGPT5, which can "read" images, immediately identified it as vespidae horribilis, better known in its native Paraguay as avispón de terror, roughly translated, the Horror Hornet. It had rarely been seen north of Venezuela…until now. Weiss reported it to the Centers for Disease Control. He had to leave a message and didn't get a call back.

By the time the week was up, 127 people had died, all in Midwestern parks, and it was front-page news. President Michelle Obama appeared on CNN: "We are marshaling all possible taxpayer resources to stop this before it becomes the insect equivalent of another COVID: the Centers for Disease Control (CDC) the Department of Health and Human Services, the U.S. Public Health Service, their state equivalents, and the World Health Organization. All 127 victims died in parks from Western Pennsylvania to Western Colorado. So for now, we are closing all parks except those within 100 miles of the East or West coasts.

Mobs consisting largely of Republicans protested—Obama, you're just protecting your beloved coastal liberal cities"—and one mob torched a government building.

But in the next week, there were 1,458 cases, most of the new ones on the coasts. President Obama got back on TV: "Our top scientists and public health officials urge that we close all parks nationwide. We hope to reopen them as soon as the experts say it's safe."

Massive protests, some would say riots, ensued. Placards read, "Not another COVID lockdown!" One speaker's quote was broadcast endlessly on conservative media: "We spend billions of our taxpayer money on all you experts and bureaucrats, and you can't get rid of a fly?!"

The government's entomologists and toxicologists gathered detailed data about each victim and each of the thousands of hornets they captured. The major media kept showing the picture of a woman in a hazmat suit surrounded by hornets as she collected them for study. The government held daily press conferences that portrayed a message that implied progress. And grasping for good news, they said that their massive effort has found what they believe is Nest Zero. But when a reporter asked, "Does that get us closer to figuring out how to stop the swarm deaths?" the lead scientist turned to the other panelists, who looked blank, and said, "We'll keep you posted."

Indeed, privately, the scientists' meetings with the public health officials were filled with uncertainty, which bred contentiousness. For example, a specialist in public mental health seethed, "What do you mean, we have to keep the parks closed and you have no idea for how long?" Don't you realize that parks keep people healthy? Life is stressful, especially for the poor. For them, parks are among their few escapes from the systemic racism that keeps people of color from rising from multi-generational poverty!" Other committee members considered responding but decided it was prudent to remain silent.

The scientists had sprayed some of the collected hornets with low-toxicity pyrethrins, which is derived from the chrysanthemum, but that killed only 3.4% of the wasps. But the Subcommittee on Horror Hornet Eradication included leaders from the Environmental Protection Agency, refused to authorize use of the only spray that would eradicate most of the hornets, the long-banned DDT. None of that was discussed in the press conferences. The government's PR team advised, "Discussing that in public will just muddy the message, foment more anxiety, and spill over into more violence against the government."

A year passed and the hornet deaths stayed at around 500 a day. Then suddenly, without explanation, the hornet attacks started to decline and decline, until the rate was baseline.

At that point, President Obama got on TV, declared victory and the parks reopened. She added that she is issuing an Executive Order creating a new agency, the National Entomological Public Health Agency.

Every time Jonah Weiss checked his email, every time his phone rang, every time he looked at his texts, he was wondering if it was an invitation to join the new agency. He had mixed feelings about working in government, but especially in light of his rapid, no-cost response to the first hornet death, he would feel good to be asked. He's still waiting.

Checking

With permission ,18/1 Graphics Studio

I was never much for school and didn't really know how to look for a job, so when I saw the help-wanted sign in front of the supermarket, I applied and got hired. They started me doing shelving but they saw that I liked people, so they promoted me to checker.

But that soon got boring— It's a line that never ends. And all you have to do is scan and bag, occasionally look up a produce code or ask for ID for alcohol. Even chatting with customers got boring. Mainly it was, "Did you find everything you wanted?" Or something about the weather.

So I let my mind wander: Will my job get automated? I don't care much. Should I try to become a manager? Maybe— I'd like bossing people around. I'm getting tired of being nice. Hmm, that customer is cute. I hope she gets in my line. I hate that we're not allowed to date customers.

Next, I tried offering copies of recipes from the supermarket's site to customers who bought at least one of the ingredients. The customers seemed to like that.

Unfortunately, my boss stopped me. He said, "What if you end up with more people in your line than the other checkers have? It would make the checkers feel bad. And no, it's not realistic to ask them all to give recipes or otherwise do their own thing, if only because someone would likely file a grievance: unequal treatment."

I'm thinking of shorting the change to cash customers who aren't paying attention.

Pizza

With permission, 18/1 Graphics Studio

Dr. Anya Singh admitted, "Yes, I called the patient a stupid, irresponsible, fat pig."

The patient's attorney said, "You didn't call her that, you yelled her that."

Dr. Singh and her lawyer, Stu Hoffman, sat on one side of the state licensing board's conference table. On the other, staring at Dr. Singh were a member of the licensing board, the patient's attorney, and an investigator from the state's Bureau of Diversity, Equity, and Inclusion.

The board member asked, "Why did you yell or even say that to a patient?"

Dr. Singh looked at her lawyer and he nodded, "Say the truth."

"The truth is that I was frustrated with him. He weighs 280 pounds and refused to stop eating Doritos, nachos, sausage bar-b-cue, and even to take his blood pressure medication. And he had no-showed for his previous two appointments yet when, that time, I was running ten minutes late, he yelled at me for not respecting him.

The DEI person asked, "Would you have treated a white person the same way?

"Absolutely," Dr. Singh blurted. The DEI person looked skeptical.

Stu, the lawyer, said, "I invite you to consider that Dr. Singh has good performance evaluations from supervisors and patients alike.

The administrator wasn't moved: "Dr. Singh, you are the professional and that outburst was unprofessional. I will review the case with our committee next week and let you know whether we will suspend your license and for how long." And he got up, signaling Dr. Singh and her lawyer to leave. Singh bowed her head, got teary, and she and Stu plodded out.

As they reached their cars, she said, "To be honest, I'm burned out: not just on non-compliant patients, it's the Medicare and insurance company paperwork and denials, and the limitations on how much doctors can do.

Stu replied, "Now that it's true-confessions time, I'm burned out on being a lawyer. Not only has it made me more contentious than I want to be, it's made me overcautious, oversuspicious. Not a good way to live.

And Anya and Stu ended up opening a pizza shop. She explained, "It has no prestige but I think we do more good for people." He nodded.

Adrenaline

It's unclear how I got addicted to adrenaline, I only know that I did, and early. I

With permission, 18/1 Graphics Studio

used to see how much I could tease kids without getting my head bashed in. In class, I would tilt my chair back as far as I could without falling over— I didn't always succeed. After school, I'd sneak into the gym so I could practice basketball on rims that had nets— I loved the swish sound.

I feel far more guilty that, as a teenager, my addiction to adrenaline made me want to "get" girls, and after I did, the adrenaline rush was gone and I moved on to the next girl. Bad, bad.

Gambling took my adrenaline addiction to another level. I lost a lot but couldn't quit because I so loved the rush. To make myself feel better afterward, I'd compensate by shoplifting, another rush.

In college, I drove a taxi, fast, not to get people to their destination quickly so I'd get a bigger tip— It was for the rush.

No surprise, after college, I sought out and got a job as a stock trader. Nonstop adrenaline: I placed the buy orders at as low a price as was borderline reasonable. If I got that price, my clients would love me but if the stock never got that low and so the client didn't get it, s/he and my boss would kill me. I made dozens of trades a day— It was like intravenous adrenaline.

After work, unlike a normal person, I didn't unwind, I played adrenalizing video games and, with my few friends, argued. I was aware that I created more heat than light but it was another rush.

And all went pretty well until I was 52. Ironically, I was doing one of my few calm activities: a jigsaw puzzle. That's when I got my heart attack, fortunately, a mild one.

Like most heart attack victims, I was scared straight— for a while— but soon returned to my old ways. Why? I was aware that my adrenaline addiction contributed to my getting an early heart attack. And I knew that it had hurt me professionally and personally: errors at work caused by rushing, angering colleagues with my brinksmanship, turning off quality friends, romantic and platonic. Yet I loved adrenaline's energizing effect and felt, perhaps rationalized, that it made me productive, contributory. And I believe that the life well-led is heavily about being productive.

My rational self knows I'll be productive for longer if I don't get another heart attack but it's tough to quit my addiction to adrenaline. I keep telling myself to try to stay vigilant to adrenalizing but the oddsmakers would lay 5 to 1 against me. It's crazy: I say I love life yet I'm killing myself.

Sellout!"

It was only a month ago when Kat and I were breaking windows at a protest. Her placard read, "Smash the Patriarchy!" Mine said, "Rage Against the Machine!"

With permission, 18/1 Graphics Studio

Yet today, we were sitting at a cafe and Kat said, "Rachel, I can't believe you— Face it. You're a sellout!"

"You don't understand," I begged. "The Economic Justice Forum was paying me so little that I could barely pay the rent, even without unexpected expenses. And when I asked for a raise, my boss said, "Don't you realize how lucky you are to get paid at all to work at a nonprofit? It's not like you're a fundraiser, bringing in money. You're a cost item, a cost item! Most people here are volunteers!"

When I countered, "But what about our website, where you advocate for a living wage?" My boss rolled her eyes and said, "You just don't get it." And I quit, even though I didn't have another job.

My landlord gave me an extension but finally said, "You have to pay by the end of the month or I'll be forced to start the eviction process. My wife and I are living on the income from this duplex. We need the rent to avoid defaulting on the mortgage."

So I looked for a job at other non-profits, but neither of the two that granted me an interview paid their admins a middle-class wage. Finally, I gave in and applied at for-profits and got a job as an admin for a senior manager at Epic Nut and Bolt Corporation.

I was afraid my boss would be a jerk, especially as a corporate executive, but he wasn't. No, he wasn't some new-age guy who did yoga and spent lots of time mentoring me. He mainly just worked his ass off.

For example, one morning I came in and he was sleeping on the floor, using his sweater as his pillow. I asked why and he said that a bus manufacturer's production line was held up because Customs somehow couldn't find the paperwork we sent the government for the bolt that attaches the bus's engine to its frame. So he stayed up, first trying to negotiate with Customs and when that didn't work, searching to find a company that would drop-ship quality bolts so the bus company could receive them next-day. He admitted that he had failed and at 3 AM, too exhausted to drive home, slept on the floor. I had to respect the guy's work ethic.

Kat sneered, "Typical capitalist values: Urgency, no work-life balance. Sellout!"

I stared.

Adam's Legacy

pxhere, CC0

Adam had terminal cancer but it hadn't advanced enough that his doctor would prescribe the "death-with-dignity" pills. So, while Adam still felt strong enough, he took the gun that he had bought many years ago for home security, drove with a shovel to a remote field, stopped at a young oak tree where his remains would fertilize it. Slowly, a bit at a time, which was the best that Adam could do, he dug a hole next to the tree. Then he refilled in with the soil and leaves, climbed in, putting the shovel next to him so it wouldn't be found, and covered himself fully with that soil mix. He put the gun into his mouth just right, pointing to the roof of his mouth, and with the confidence of knowing he was doing the wise thing, crisply pulled the trigger and died almost instantly and with little pain— the brain doesn't have nerve endings.

Adam's remains indeed fed the tree so it grew well and soon produced acorns, which, in turn produced oak trees.

And the process repeated and repeated until, many years hence, the field had become a forest.

Then one day, a group of adventurous kids explored deep in the forest and uncovered Adam's bones. "Cool!" they all agreed. And when they returned home, they told their friends about their amazing find. And when they grew up, they told the story to their children. One of them created a Christmas tradition of walking everyone into the forest, lighting a campfire, and telling that true scary story.

And thus, Adam's legacy was enriched.

Buried

I have to act just right: I did love my husband, well, kind of, and do want to make him proud. Besides, other people will feel more comfortable if I play the loving, grieving widow.

With permission 18/1 Graphics Studio

Okay, it's show time. Walk really slowly up to the microphone, head down. Stare at the urn. I hope that makes me cry.

I began, "John was a great provider."

I thought about all the corners he cut. But okay, my shopping habit pressured him a little. But stop thinking about that!

"He was a fine father."

I thought about how he was absent a lot of the time. Stop! Focus on the urn.

I need to up the adjectives. "John was a truly wonderful husband."

He was always in his man cave. The urn, look at the fucking urn.

I can't count on my boyfriend. It's going to be all on me. Geez, I am starting to cry, not for him, for me. I looked at the audience— They're loving it.

My Imaginary Wife

I have had bad luck with women. Well, maybe it wasn't all luck. I was awkward, never made enough money to take them out nice, and yeah, I have a bit of a temper. I slapped one girl and almost swung my axe at another. Of course, they didn't take that and they broke up with me.

PeakPx, Free to Reuse

So I decided to stay off girls for a while and just have an imaginary wife.

The fantasy started great. We had sex all night and then enjoyed the afterglow, yeah in bed, but also at breakfast and as we then took a walk, holding hands.

My imaginary wife and I would phone each other at work during the day to say sweet nothings or even just to hear each other's voice.

We gave each other little presents, like a wildflower I picked for her and— she was more creative—a model airplane for me.

After a while, having sex with my imaginary wife just once a night or less was enough. But she would give me that look, so I gave in. But it was feeling like a chore.

So was our conversation: My imaginary wife kept trotting out the same old opinions: go green, do more for the poor, Trump sucks.

Then my imaginary wife asked to move in with me. I imagined her saying, "I don't make enough giving flute lessons." I gave in again.

Then my imaginary wife started criticizing me for not being fun enough. I imagined her saying, "Not only don't you want to have sex much, you don't want to go dancing, partying, traveling." I didn't.

Then, my imaginary wife got cancer and asked me to help her through the months of recovery from surgery and chemo. I didn't want to.

I was feeling trapped. How should I escape? I axed my imaginary wife to death. Back to real life. I just placed an ad on match.com. Don't worry, I threw away my axe.

Confessing at My Parents' Grave

Allen Watkin, Wikimedia, CC 2.0

My parents died a few years ago and I've been reluctant to visit them in the cemetery but today I felt I should go. I'm not sure why.

But when I got to their tombstone, I found myself treating it as a confessional. I actually said this aloud:

I'm actually a bad person. Sure, I have accomplishments. Sure, most people think I'm a good guy but net, I'm not. Here are some truths about me that you probably don't know:

I cheated a fair amount on tests.

I shoplifted a fair amount.

I cheat on my income tax.

I once lied and said I was sterile to avoid wearing a condom.

I'm judgmental and think that most people are some combination of stupid, lazy, or ethical only when scared of getting caught.

I may say I care about the collective but really, I care mainly about myself.

I sometimes take pleasure in other people's failure, what's called schadenfreude.

I am guilty of gluttony.

I routinely pad my expense account.

Then I fell silent and thought, can I do better? Do I want to do better? I wasn't sure of the answers so finally, I just said, "Sorry, mom and dad" and trudged back to my car.

Depressed

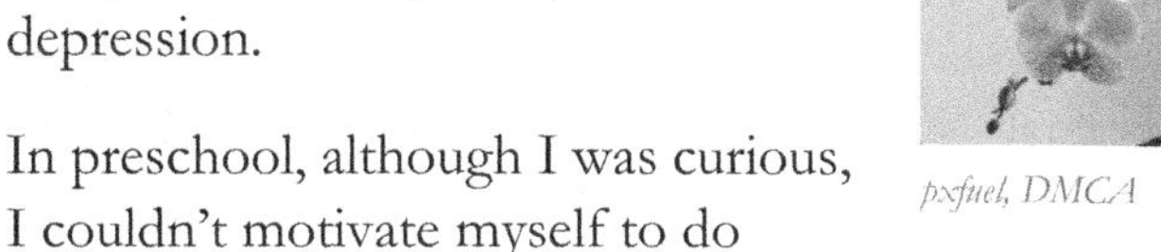

pxfuel, DMCA

It wasn't my parents' fault. I just always have been predisposed to depression.

In preschool, although I was curious, I couldn't motivate myself to do much. My first memory was of sitting on the floor next to a cinder-block bookshelf pulling out a book, looking at the pictures, putting it back, and picking another book. That may have been my life's happiest time.

In school, I sat quietly in the back and, at recess, pretty much just wandered around by myself. After school, I'd go to my room and read, watch TV, or listen to music.

Even though I didn't feel like going to the prom, I somehow felt I should—If I didn't, it would confirm that my depression was very bad. So I asked a pretty girl to the prom. She turned me down. Then I asked a very heavy girl but she turned me down too. The day of the prom, I didn't go to school and I wouldn't leave bed for a week.

After high school, I couldn't motivate myself to go to college, even community college, so I got a job as a library assistant. My job was to organize documents in a university library's basement.

When I get home from work, I haven't changed much since childhood: mainly I read and watch TV, plus I grow plants on my patio. I've come to love phalaenopsis, moth orchids. They bloom and bloom arcs of flowers for months at a time. I have about a dozen of them. I stare at them in wonder at God's—with the help of hybridizers'—handiwork.

On weekdays, when my church is empty, I occasionally sit and stare at the ornate chancel, the stained glass behind, even at the pews—It makes me feel good to think of all the people it took to get a pew there: a farmer, harvester, craftsmen, and the delivery guys.

One day, I got a call from a lawyer who informed me that my next-door neighbor had died, had loved looking at the orchids on my patio, and left me $2 million.

That was overwhelming so rather than deal with it, I donated it all to my church. The priest visited to say thank you and then again every few days. I knew he was doing that only because of the money but he was kind and tried to help, but I can only tell you that like after my prom disaster, it's been a week and I can't get myself out of bed.

A Pier

With permission, 18/1 Graphics Studio

Amanda knew she had to kill him. He was the only one who knew that she had siphoned off money earmarked for the onsite childcare center and hid that by using a too cheap, cut-every-corner contractor, and so a kid died when the climbing wall collapsed.

The floor-to-ceiling window overlooked a pier that jutted out into the ocean. It was the perfect backdrop for an inspiring speech and for murder.

Kevin, the CEO, intoned like a revival preacher, "It is so exciting to see you here at our 2023 offsite. Our wonderful products are not our most important product. Our most important product? Our employees: You!"

Amanda, a marketing manager, thought, "What a crock." "Of course, our product line is worthy of you. Just think about how well-priced our bronze line is, how our silver line perfectly balances price and quality, and our platinum product? Best in class!"

She thought, "Yeah, with a lower re-purchase rate than our competitors'."

As Kevin continued stoking the troops, Amanda's mind wandered to the pier. She thought, "Kevin said he couldn't swim. So when he finishes, I'll ask him to watch the sunset with me from the pier."

"And I am so excited that I, no, we are having this offsite. I know it will be awesome." He smiled too broadly and applauded the audience. The audience clapped just enough to stay out of trouble.

After, employees lined up to praise Kevin. When the last suck-up left, Amanda adjusted her blouse so just a bit of cleavage showed, sashayed up, and asked him, "Want to watch the sunset?"

Kevin thought, "She just filed a grievance against me. And now she wants to watch the sunset with me?" His wiser self would have declined but he was riding the high of his keynote and the praise, suppressing that both were BS, plus the flirtation, so he agreed.

As they reached the end of the pier, Amanda got cold feet. So she worked herself up by arguing with him. "I still can't believe you wouldn't come with me to the abortion!"

Kevin replied, "There was nothing I could have done to help."

"That's not the point. Haven't you ever heard of the need for support? After all, you were the father. Guys are clueless."

"Stop playing the gender card. Women's way isn't the only way. Support that accomplishes nothing is stupid."

"Only a guy could say that. Besides, you're the CEO. There's a power imbalance and you took advantage of it."

"You're not my direct report."

"That doesn't negate the power imbalance. And you also showed what a sexist you are when you apologized for not coming to the abortion and I said, 'Put your money where your mouth is: Since you claim to care so much about your employees, create an onsite child care center.' And you said that funding it would be unfair to the childless and to the shareholders. Fuck the shareholders!"

"My position was reasonable and principled. I caved only when you threatened to go public with our affair. I think I'm going to tell the board and the media that you used a sleazy, bargain-basement, unproven contractor and pocketed the difference."

"And I'm going to tell all to the board and the media, including that you dared claim that you weren't the father!"

"Oh really? Well, Amanda, long ago, I had a vasectomy. So I couldn't be the father! Want to see? I'll show that to the board and the media. A picture is worth a thousand words."

Of course, Amanda was aware that Kevin might not be the father. She had slept with two other guys at the time. But all that feigned resentment about the affair and abortion accomplished her goal: getting her worked up enough to gin up the courage to get rid of him and end her worries about him going public with her embezzlement, and now, her false paternity claim.

He started to lower his pants to show his vasectomy, which gave her the chance to shove him into the deep, rough water.

"No! Amanda, you know I can't swim! Please save me!"

It was one thing for Amanda to imagine Kevin drowning, another to see him gasping, dying. So she dove in, helped him to a stanchion, and they climbed up.

They plodded back to the hotel with a lot to think about.

At the closing session, Kevin and Amanda held hands as they strode to center stage. Both applauded the audience. Only a few audience members applauded, tepidly.

Kevin enthused, "I have a special announcement. I've been so impressed with Amanda Frost that I am promoting her to vice-president!"

Would You Stop Procrastinating for a Million Dollars?

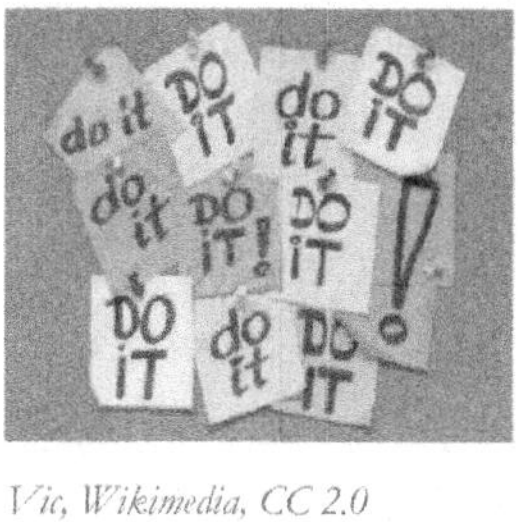

Vic, Wikimedia, CC 2.0

Because I'm unemployed, I'm still living in my grandfather's house. I thought he wouldn't be home for a few hours, so even though it was a weekday, when I should have been job hunting, I was practicing shooting my pistol in the backyard. To keep me focused, right next to the target paper, I had nailed my Army marksman medal.

When my grandfather saw me playing with my pistol instead of job hunting, he was angry with me yet again: "Devon, you're a good tax accountant. All you're missing is discipline. I tried to help you by pushing you to go to West Point. You learned accounting and marksmanship there but you didn't learn discipline."

He paced the backyard and continued: "Devon, I've written my will. I have about a million dollars and made you the beneficiary but I can't feel good about it if you're such a procrastinator. So here's the deal. It's March 2nd. If you can complete my tax return— federal, state, and city by midnight April 15, the tax deadline, the will will stand. If not, I'll change it so the million goes to charity.

A million was motivating, absolutely. And I worked hard at it and by April 12, it was almost done. I had completed the federal and state returns and just had to polish the city, a few hours of work, max.

That day, my girlfriend called to say that she had just gotten a bonus and wanted to take us to our favorite hideaway for the weekend. Because I had just a few hours of work left on the taxes, I agreed and we had a great time. When we got back on the night of the 14th, I was exhausted so I went to sleep and set the alarm for 8 AM, which would give me more than enough time to get the taxes done by midnight.

When I woke up, I got coffee, went right to the computer, opened the software, and all the files— the federal, the state, the city— were empty, gone! I couldn't stop shrieking, "Oh my God. Oh my God! Oh my God1!"

My grandfather rushed in and I explained what happened. He fumed, "How could you be so irresponsible? Didn't you make a backup?" I hadn't. I didn't even know how to make one with tax software. I mean I had never lost any file in my entire life! He said he was sorry but the million will be going to charity.

In agony, I went to my girlfriend's apartment. She cried too, I assumed, in sympathy. But she explained, "Remember that bonus I told you I got? Well, it came from your grandfather who gave it to me in exchange for luring you away so he could delete the files without your catching him. He told me that he always intended to give the money to charity. He was afraid you'd sue to overturn the will, but if you didn't keep your part of a bargain— to get the taxes done in time— you wouldn't sue. I swore to him that I'd keep that secret, mainly because giving to charity seemed so kind. But Devon, I had to tell you. I love you."

I raced out of the house, got my pistol, and killed my grandfather. As with most murders, this one went unsolved and the million went to me, whereupon I decided that for a while more at least, I didn't need to look for a job.

I'm Gonna Retire at 30

Free SVG, CC0

Sal's parents own Etna Pickles Inc., which dominates the pickle shelf in most supermarkets. Sal is blessed with movie-star looks, the girls especially craving his shiny, thick, black hair.

No scholar, Sal's parents sprang for a third-tier private college, which he squandered: parties, girls, and, yes, coke. He also guilt-tripped his parents into giving him a Beemer and a lavish education allowance for books, tutors, and so on, which he used for such education as taking two girls at one time to Hawaii.

But when Sal's girlfriend found out about that, she told his parents how he's spending his education allowance. They confronted him and after he denied it, they brought the girl in, he caved, and they cut him off.

Sal responded, "Whatever. I'm going to make millions before I'm 30 so I can have as much fun as I want without having to suck up to the pickle family circus."

Sal's looks, spending, and funsterhood made him lots of friends and one hired him to be the salesman for AI Therapist, Inc. The salary wasn't great but the commission was: "Sal, if you really push it, you could make a half-mill this year! And Sal did really push it. He overpromised and underdelivered. Knowing it wasn't true, he told wholesale customers, "We'll be releasing the software in a week and it will be rock solid." It was two months and it was solid mush: ineffective, buggy, and with laughable tech support. As result, AI Therapist's reviews at the AppStore averaged 2.3, a kiss of death. As bad, the firm got sued, including one claim that AI Therapist drove a customer to attempt suicide. The firm was out of business in six months and, for the last two, didn't pay Sal even his base salary, let alone commissions. The CEO said, "Man, we just can't make payroll. You understand, right?"

Sal then BS'd his way into a sales job at the nearby Lexus dealer. He said, "You might ask, if I'm such a good salesman, why am I looking for a job? Well, the firm promised me that the software was solid. It wasn't. I'm good enough that I want no base salary, just commission." Especially with Sal's movie-star looks, that was an offer that Elite Lexus couldn't refuse.

To look more like his target customer— older and conservative— Sal wore button-down collared shirts with a blazer and khakis, streaked his hair with gray, and got glasses.

With The Look in place, when customers called asking for a price, he'd lowball to get them in the door and then when he went to "confirm" the price with the manager (who he actually never saw), he returned faking sadness: "I'm shocked. The manager overruled me and unfortunately, the car is going to cost a bit more." (usually far more than a bit.) If the car wasn't the color or option the customer wanted, Sal lied, for example, "That color? Did you know, it's the least popular?" Or, "That option is really a ripoff." He pushed dealer-installed high-profit extras like nitrogen in tires, which according to Consumer Reports, is a ripoff and costs the dealership almost nothing so Sal got a hunky commission. To top it off, Sal made a deal with one of the finance-and-insurance salespeople to shepherd clients to her in exchange for a kickback. Despite all that, Sal made only $10,000 a month, not enough to retire before he was 30. So he started looking into enterprise software sales jobs, where average comp is $300,000+.

But before he started applying for those jobs, a coke friend who worked at a small biotech company gave him an insider's secret that the company was, in a month, to be bought out by a big pharma, so the company's stock would skyrocket. Sal told his parents about it and they agreed to split any profit 50/ 50.

To avoid SEC scrutiny, through two offshore shell companies, two weeks before the pharma was to announce the deal, his parents bought $3,000,000 of the stock— an amount that's trivial to them— and they held the stock for a few months by which time the SEC would likely be onto other matters. That worked to the tune of a $10,000,000 profit, half to Sal. So he was back in business or I should say, back to the playboy life.

But even $5 million doesn't last a big-spending coke addict long, so in a few years, Sal's savings were down 80 percent.

Wanting to build his account back up without having to work much, Sal became an options day-trader. But the old joke is usually true: "How can you make a million as a day-trader? Start with two million." Actually, the adrenaline-addicted Sal did worse than that. After two years, his savings were down to just $70,000.

So Sal went back to the luxury car business. But this time, he approached an even higher-margin BMW and Mercedes dealerships and talked his way into a job, not in sales, but where the even bigger money is made: finance and insurance.

As of this writing, Sal is still going strong. He's living in a love nest complete with heart-shaped bed and a bouquet of flowers that hangs from the ceiling, high enough that the women can't tell that the flowers are fake.

One early morning, turning to the two women beside him in bed, he thought, "Maybe I won't be able to retire at 30, but this life ain't so bad. I can deal with 40."

My Name is Mordchai

Adam Jones, Wikimedia, CC 2.0

NOTE: These are Chasidic Jews—disproportionately presented in the media. In fact, only a tiny percentage of Jews are like this, most living in Boro Park or Crown Heights, Brooklyn.

I was an infant at the time. My parents and I arrived at Ellis Island, New York City. There, the immigration clerk asked my parents what my name will be. They said, "Mordchai." The clerk replied, "That might be difficult in the U.S. How about Morgan?" My parents insisted on Mordchai.

In the summer before my senior year in high school, my dad died and my mom needed to get a job. We lived in Chicago but the only decent-paying job she could get was as an assistant director at Minnesota State University's Center for Diversity, Equity, and Inclusion (DEI.)

So I did my senior year at the nearby Midwood High School. My first morning there, I got my first exposure to what's called, Minnesota Nice. Out in the yard before school, students nodded, smiled, and waved at me. Then a student came up to me and said, "Hi, I haven't seen you before. My name is Chris."

I said, "I'm Mordchai."

"That's an interesting name."

"Jewish."

"Wow, you're the first Jew I've ever met. When I search Google-images, most of the pictures show Jews wearing black suits and hats and have curls as sideburns."

"Those are extremists. 99% of Jews look like you and me, well, maybe not the blond hair."

"I think it's cool getting to talk with a Jew. Hey, a lot of the images show Jews with coins, like gold coins. Why? And why did the Jews kill Jesus? Oh and why is Israel an apartheid state?"

I was stunned at Google-search's bias as well as his audacity—So much for Minnesota Nice. I felt overwhelmed, literally vibrating. So I just mumbled, "That's false, just like that most Jews wear black suits and curly sideburns. I gotta go."

Chris strode to a group of kids and whispered. They then looked at me very differently—like at a zoo animal. From then on, they were Minnesota Polite but rarely talked with me, never invited me to a party.

I asked my mother, "Jews have contributed so much. I should be proud to be Jewish, yet when I go to college, should I change my name from Mordchai to Morse, like the code? That way Jewish kids hearing it might think it's Morris and the other kids will think it's Morse. You're not just my mom. You're an assistant director at the university's Center for Diversity, Equity, and Inclusion. What do you think?" She said, "I'm not sure."

How God Came and Went

In a galaxy far beyond our comprehension, a star was born. And soon, the star ate all the other little stars, and then all the bigger stars, until even the Big Stars were scared of being star-

This is an AI-Generated God. Ronald Sandino, Pixabay, Public Domain

struck. And they were. And so, God was created.

But God had plans other than eating all the stars. He lamented, "So many planets, so little time." One such planet was, of course, Earth. But forget the Adam-and-Eve myth. Here's what really happened: With a wave of God's mighty SuperAI 3D printer, God printed all the animals, plants, and people.

Alas, God soon shook his mighty head at what he hath wrought, for the people and the animals but not the plants were all mean if not murderous to each other. So with a wave of his mighty SuperAI 3D Deleter, God deleted 95% of Earth's people in hopes that just maybe, with less crowding, Earth 2.0's people would be nicer.

Unfortunately, one of the five percent left was Vector, a disgruntled and sociopathic virologist, Earth's leading expert on creating deadly, highly-communicable, auto-mutating viruses, which are thus impervious to any vaccine, even one developed at super-warp speed.

Vector texted a ransom note to God: "Surrender control to me so I can be New God or I'll destroy your remaining five percent of people with my deadly, highly-communicable, auto-mutating viruses."

God couldn't take a chance so he shrugged, quit Earth, and went on to try to do better playing God with other planets.

Vector was only bluffing and so Earth continued Godless and lived happier ever after.

Postcards

Most guys my age, 21, have figured out how to read whether a girl likes him. Not me. I almost always get turned down, sometimes politely, sometimes meanly.

Having been knocked down in the first nine rounds, it's hard to make myself come out for round 10.

But I'd still like to meet a woman. So I tried postcards. Let me explain. I picked out three women that I would like to at least have coffee with and sent them a postcard with a brief unsigned note plus an appropriate tiny print of a painting that I glued onto each postcard.

The Waitress, Edouard Manet, Public Domain

Sally is a waitress at my favorite cafe. She has a ponytail and dresses kind of like a farm girl. Indeed, she told me she likes growing vegetables and I once brought her a packet of tomato seeds. But farm-girl look or not, her femininity stands out. She wears pretty colors like peach or sky blue and often has the discretionary top button of her blouse open. I don't get the sense she's a genius, and intelligence *is* important to me, but she seems kind. I've looked for signs she likes me, like if she takes an extra moment to look at me after taking my order, but no. For her, I wrote, "You're my dream farm-girl." The image I printed from Google and pasted on the postcard was of Edouard Manet's, The Waitress.

Wallpaper Flare, DMCA

The second woman, Lily, is my haircutter. She's Chinese-American and her beauty is far above my pay grade. It's not just her face and body that are lovely bordering on astounding, it's her clothes. Every time I come in, she's in a gorgeous dress that's just short of being overdressed for a haircutter. And when I came in the first time and asked if I could bring my dog in, she beamed, "I'd love it" and always spends a minute or two on the floor playing with my pooch. But she pays me no special attention. On her postcard, I wrote, "I picture you as a movie star." For her, the image I pasted onto the postcard was of a traditional Chinese woman (see right.)

Jean Virgoureau, Wikimedia, CC 4.0

The third woman is Rebecca, an 18- or 19-year-old clerk at the French bakery I frequent. She's a little plain and a little overweight and perhaps because of that, I find her more attractive, less intimidating, than if she were a 10. Her face looks intelligent yet she works as a bakery clerk—I find that intriguing. She pays me no special attention. For her, I wrote, "You are more perfect than perfect" and the painting I attached to the postcard was Paris Bakery by Jean Vigoureax. (See right.)

I mailed each postcard to their workplace using Love postage stamps.

Vintageprintable1. Flickr. CC 2.0

After a few days, I eagerly went into each of the three places to see if they inferred it was I who sent the postcard. Would any of them at least make a little more eye contact? None did. So I decided to muster my courage, hold their eyes, tell them I was the one who sent the postcard, and ask them out for coffee.

Sally, the waitress, said, "That's very nice of you but I have a sort-of boyfriend."

Lily, my haircutter, said, "I am honored but I don't think we're quite right for each other. But your dog is adorable."

Rebecca, the bakery clerk said, "That's very flattering but..." When I asked why, she murmured, "Well, to be honest, you're a little old for me."

I went home and started reading a romance novel.

Who Can You Trust?

Mike Mozart, Flickr, CC2.0

Of course, I want to trust the science. But a while back, the New York Times reported https://nyti.ms/3CwHcl5 that that consensus among climate science was that the earth was in a long-term cooling trend. Now, they insist we're in a long-term warming trend. When they told us back in 2018, that we'd have self-driving cars by 2022, I was excited, but now they say it's at least a decade away. https://bloom.bg/3Zhyf90 But what really got me was when the scientists insisted we had to lock down because of COVID, and only after society was decimated, did they admit it was a bad idea. So, I started to wonder. If I can't trust the science, who can I trust?

Well, let's start at the top. I remember Sister Mary Ignatius citing Matthew 17-20: "If you have faith the size of a mustard seed (just a bit of faith in God), you will say to this mountain, 'Move from here to there,' and it will move; and nothing will be impossible for you." Well, I haven't moved even molehills. I'm still a mere functionary at the water utility and just lost my dad to cancer after years of misery. Trust in a loving God?!

Then there was my singing teacher. She told me that if I stayed with it and worked hard, I had "professional potential." Well, I stayed with it and worked hard until I was 25 and my potential turned out to be $75 one time at a café. I probably spent 100 times that on singing lessons. Mostly, I sang at open-mic nights for free.

Then, when I was 30, I had finally saved some money. A friend told me that he had done well using a financial advisor in Sacramento. I invested most of my savings, it turned out it was a Ponzi scheme, and I lost everything.

At my previous job, after a layoff, my boss told us, the survivors, "Your jobs are safe." Within three months, dozens of us got axed.

Then there was my ex-husband. He insisted, "I love you," "I love you," until he decided he was sick of me and worse, in the divorce dogfight, hid a bunch of money by having his aunt hold it for him. I only found out after the divorce decree. Now, I have to hire the lawyer again and go back to court.

Then there are the politicians. George Bush insisted, "Read my lips. No new taxes" and then raised taxes. Barack Obama said, "Under ObamaCare, you can keep your doctor." Not. Now our government says our border is secure, yet I see videos of thousands traipsing over the border.

As a good liberal, I donated to Black Lives Matter but later read that $90 million was missing. They've since found $10 million of it— A founder is accused of using it as a "personal piggy bank." https://lat.ms/3Zi0lzd

I believed in socialism until I read the book, The White Pill. https://amzn.to/3Gq3BBR It reports that Stalin killed more than 20 million people, four times as many as Hitler, and killed his own people, mainly by deliberate starvation. Thousands of Soviet people were even reduced to cannibalism. https://bit.ly/3jXIaAn I appreciate the socialist ideal but can I really trust that the leaders, even the proles, will be any different than in all the Communist countries to date? On the other hand, I don't trust conservatives, let alone Donald Trump.

So who can I trust?

I sort of trust myself but too often don't have the right answers. And even when I do, I don't always implement them, witness the extra 20 pounds around my hips.

I still sort of trust scientists, at least the hard scientists, not the public policy ones— Those are too subject to politicians' influence. I have the most trust in physicists, chemists, mathematicians, and computer scientists. Trouble is, I don't know any. So, when I hear some new health recommendation, I usually ask myself whether it makes common sense. I remember when the lockdown was mandated, I asked my doctor what he thought. He said it wouldn't work: that when we're out and about, we get harmless microexposures to all sorts of viruses, which builds natural resistance. But if we're locked down, we don't, so when we come out of isolation, we're more subject to infection. That made sense to me and it turns out he was right— Now, there's an explosion of respiratory syncytial virus (RSV) Before, I had never even heard of RSV.

Another hard scientist I trust is the meteorologist. It seems that weather forecasts are ever more accurate. I just googled it and it's true. Today's five-day forecast is as accurate as a one-day forecast in 1980. https://bit.ly/3ikSXUV Thank a hard scientist.

I was listening to The Portal podcast https://apple.co/3Gq3Mx1 and the host has come to the conclusion that the only entity he can trust is Trader Joe's. Could he have been only half-joking?

7 Kisses

I've never been much of a kisser. So I didn't even notice that my parents never kissed me.

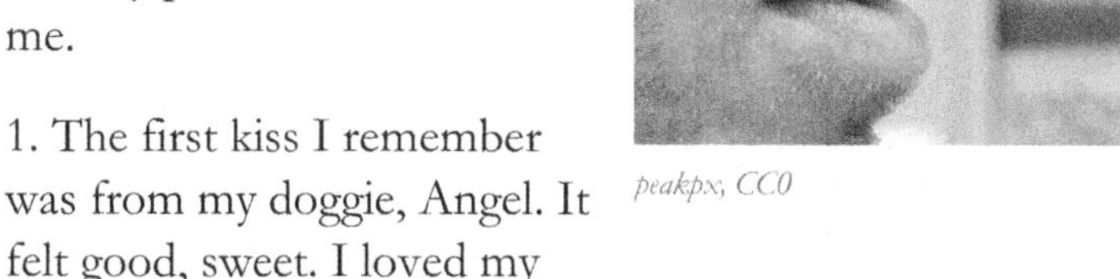

peakpx, CC0

1. The first kiss I remember was from my doggie, Angel. It felt good, sweet. I loved my doggie and saw her licking as a sign of love, although maybe she just liked my skin's saltiness.

2. My first human kiss was at day camp, maybe age 8. They were showing a movie and a pretty girl—I didn't even know her name—was sitting next to me. I kissed her on the cheek. She didn't slap me. She smiled.

3. In my junior year of high school. Laura was, like me, quiet. We liked museums and cafes. On our first date, we had the obligatory peck but I'm not counting that. After two hours at MOMA debating the extent to which minimalist art was aesthetic, political, or a shallow attempt

to give the finger to convention, we strolled out and, under a tree in Central Park, I felt a stirring, one born of kinship as well as sexuality, and I kissed her—for a long time. Not the slurpy, out-of-your-mind kind, the slow, gentle, savoring kind.

4. Of course, there was The Kiss at my wedding. I felt I was playing a role, the role of husband, with another character, the minister, ordering, "You may kiss the bride." As soon as I got the order, I kissed her—not too short or it would suggest a bad marriage but not too long or ardent or it would seem like showing off. It was the public display of affection appropriate to having just made a lifetime vow of fidelity in front of our well-wishers.

5. After a year, while we had agreed that no matter what, we'd kiss each other every morning and before we went to bed, we drifted from that. And the kisses became more sterile, until we stopped.

6. A few years later, as our ardor for each other dwindled, at a conference, I had a fling. The kiss was electric but even by the end of the conference, the wattage had declined. It became clear to me that affairs weren't the answer. They were sparklers that quickly fizzled and risked burning your hand.

7. It's now a half-century later and I'm writing to you from my deathbed. I mustered just enough energy to lift my head to reach the cheek of my wife who was leaning down. I'm glad I could kiss her, sad that soon, I never would again.

But looking back, I'm not sure that kissing is all that it's cracked up to be.

My Oxygen Valve

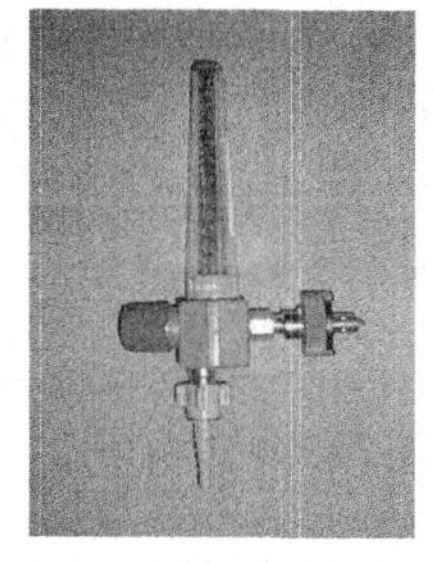

BrokenSphere, Wikimedia, GNU 1.2

The hiss from the oxygen valve calms me as I try to sleep.

When I get up in the middle of the night and neither deep breaths nor counting sheep put me back to sleep, I make up a happy story about myself. For example, I start out poor, lonely, and in bad health, but win the lottery, meet the woman of my dreams, get healthy, and live happily ever after.

But when I wake up for good, I realize I'm in hospice. Then I can't escape reality. I know they only put you in hospice if you have less than six months to live. In my case, I know it's a lot less but that's okay. Yeah, they give me plenty of pain medication, but still. Actually, I'll be relieved when it's over.

I work hard at distracting myself from The Big End. Unlike other people at my stage, seeing friends and family doesn't work—I don't want to make them sad. I prefer to end solo. I'm nice to the nurses but am glad when they leave.

I watch TV and that helps, I guess. And I try to delude myself that I'm going to heaven but I don't really believe it. Most of me thinks that man created heaven to deal with times like this.

Now, I think I'll distract myself by counting up my life's credits and debits.

On the good side:

As a kid, I remember my teacher saying I was the most considerate child in the class. She reminded me that when a girl fell off her bike, I not only helped her up, I held her hand until she stopped crying.

In the playground, when I played basketball, I didn't hog the ball.

When I was in college, when a date didn't want to have sex, I was respectful, not pushy.

As a car salesman, I discouraged people from buying a bad car, an unneeded accessory, and unlike most other salespeople, I fought with the sales manager to get my customer the best price possible, even though it meant I got less commission.

I gave talks at libraries and churches about how to avoid getting ripped off by a car salesman.

I took up magic and did little magic shows at children's birthday parties. For example, I'd learn how to put what's called a mouth coil inside my mouth while still being able to talk normally. Then, I'd pretend to be choking, reach into my mouth, and slowly pull out a multi-colored paper chain. It was 25 feet long. The kids loved it.

I lent a friend money to invest in what I thought was a risky real-estate scheme. When it did turn out to be fraudulent and he lost all his money, I told him he didn't have to pay me back.

When I retired, I planted lots of tomatoes and gave them to my neighbors.

I drove my neighbors and friends to their doctor's appointments and even to less important errands.

When my wife died, I let a stranger live in the spare bedroom for free.

On the bad side:

As a kid, I enjoyed squashing bugs.

As a teenager, I stole money from my mother's purse…a number of times.

I worked under-the-table so I could get food stamps.

I cheated on my wife…a number of times.

When money was low, I did push mean car customers to buy crap they shouldn't: extended warranty, side-body molding, crap like that.

Oh yeah, I try to suppress this but…I shot the guy who attempted to rob me at gunpoint. I faked bending over in fear, grabbed his gun, and shot him. I don't know if he lived because I ran away and never got caught.

I stared at the oxygen valve and then turned it off. Everything is beeping.

The Meaning of Life from Right Field

Many people think I have the dream job: even though I get just the league's minimum salary, play for a middling team, and play right field. I'm a major league baseball player.

Peter Bond, Wikimedia, CC 2.0

For 99% of the game, I'm just standing out there or in the dugout. Here were my thoughts one inning out there in right field.

$720,000 for less than one minute of action per game. Over a season, that totals just a few hours—hell of an hourly wage. And for what? To catch a ball or not, to hit a ball, usually not—Even top Hall of Famers get a hit only 1/3 of the time.

And for what? What could be sillier than catch the ball, throw the ball, hit the ball? That, when people are starving in Africa. Yeah but what could I do to help that zillions of other people couldn't do as well, and I wouldn't make much difference anyway.

And how about me? I'm a marginal player. Any day, I could get sent down to the minor leagues. And there, the minimum salary is $35,800, a 95% pay cut.

And how about after I retire, which could be after an injury, or at most 10 years from now when I'll be 40? Am I going to be like so many forgettable major leaguers: own a used-car dealership and become a tub of lard?

I guess I could always get a job coaching at least in a high school. Maybe that's the best idea—mentor kids using my best skill, baseball. I'd probably tell them to keep baseball as a hobby, not try to defy the lottery odds and aim for the pros. Even if they made it to the majors, they'd almost certainly end up more like me than Mike Trout.

I was still paying attention, fortunately, because I just saw the batter's stride and it looked like he was aiming my way. His late swing confirmed it, and yes, the ball came out to right field, but there was no way I could catch it. It was your basic line-drive single. I picked it up on one hop, threw it to second base, and waited some more.

Service Dog

EBTimes CC

I'm a lawyer, so I care that laws be followed. So when I saw someone bring a little mutt into the supermarket, I scoffed, "Dog in supermarket?!"

She said, "Service dog."

I scoffed, "Right."

She: "Want to see his tag?"

Me: You can buy those on the internet.

She: I'll bet most people think you're a jerk.

Me: Don't change the subject.

She: That's the real subject.

Me: I'm happy with my life.

She: Even though most people think you're a jerk?

Me: (I wasn't sure it's true but said), "Most people think I'm a good guy. Besides, that's not the question. The question is, why are you bringing a non-service dog into the supermarket?"

She: You *are* avoiding the real question. And you can't be happy if you're obese, eating yourself into an early grave.

Me: What gives you the right?!

She: You started it. You aren't worth engaging with. I'm done.

Me: Good.

I feigned indifference but as I walked away, my face twitched and I couldn't stop it.

I peeked to see if she noticed. She was looking right at me and smirked.

I tried to forget it. I can't. Am I a jerk? Am I eating myself into an early grave?

An Aspiring Campaign Manager

US Govt, Public Domain

Colin was running for student-body vice-president. Behind the curtain of the college's auditorium, Colin begged his mom: "I can't do this. You're the politician— You know how to BS 'em without their knowing. You're an actress, I'm a dick."

She literally had to push him onto the stage, and he delivered his memorized speech. He tried to build emotionality like Martin Luther King did in the I Have a Dream speech but Colin is no MLK. The audience's applause was perfunctory.

Colin had been encouraged to go into politics, not just by his mom who is a state senator, but because he majored in poli sci. He remembered a professor who said, "Yes, politics is ugly and, in the cosmic scheme, it should be ignored. But in the real world, government is where the power is."

But Colin's inept speech confirmed that he should be behind the scenes. So he applied for dozens of jobs on political campaigns but the best he could get was a minimum-wage temp gig as a "community organizer," which was puffery for telemarketer (wordsmithed as "phone-banking") and door-to-door canvasser in swing precincts. Mainly, he got door-slams and hang-ups.

Not only was the job frustrating, at minimum wage, Colin couldn't afford rent and so had to live with his mother. He asked the campaign manager for a raise: "Our candidate always preaches for a living wage yet you're paying me minimum wage?" The manager replied, "You're lucky you're paid at all. Millions of people are eager to volunteer." He thought, "I thought our party was against Darwinian survival of the fittest."

So Colin continued to live at home, couldn't motivate himself to look for another job, and was smoking more weed. But when his mother laughed on seeing him bring home a less-than-prepossessing date, he knew he had to find a better-paying job so he could afford to move out. "But how can I prevail over the zillion other wannabes?"

He decided to try to get someone to run for town council and offer to be the campaign manager for free. He asked all his friends and parents' friends but got nowhere. But then, recognizing, from his mom, the importance of politicians being good actors and today's valorizing of disability, he Googled to find deaf actresses who had played the deaf woman in the play, Children of a Lesser God.

He found three: One never responded, one emailed that she was too busy and lived too far away, but he convinced the third, Felicia Jones, an actor in amateur theatre. She said, "I don't want to be in politics but I'll run because it sounds fun. But if I'm elected, I'll say I can't take office because I realize I need to spend more time with my family." Colin agreed to the deal.

His next move was to contact his political marketing professor, who agreed to craft the campaign slogan: Forward with Felicia. Also, she created the stump speech, explaining to Colin, "It has to slam dunk in polling yet unobjectionable to moderates."

The speech:

> *Stand with me as we fight for a woman's right to choose. Stand with me as we fight for clean air and water. Stand with me as we fight for better education for our children, our future! I am here for all people, white as well as people of color, straight as well as gay, disabled and fully abled, all of us, all-in, together. As the Constitution says, "We the people."*

She explained to Colin: "I included that punch line to neutralize people from the other party. They like long-standing institutions. We'll never get them to vote for our candidate but it's a legal way to suppress their vote."

The professor told Felicia, "We can increase turnout, disproportionately for our candidate if we climb onto the media coattails: Felicia, keep slamming some politician from the other party that the media has turned into a boogie man."

No surprise, the media loved Felicia and when she won, it gushed. For example, the page 1 reporting in the local newspaper sounded more like an editorial: "Not only is Felicia Jones the first deaf member of the town council, she is a progressive voice. Voter Mary Johnson said, "Felicia will serve us well."

Only days later, Colin got a call from a state senator facing a re-election challenge. She said, "To run our six-month campaign, I can offer you $50,000." Even though he was thrilled with that, he sensed he could squeeze more, so he played poker: "I need $70,000." She agreed, whereupon he texted his mom, "I got 70K. I'm moving out."

Silenced

I was the last remaining conservative talk show host on my station. The others had been excised in favor of liberals, music, or sports.

pxfuel, free to reuse

People always told me I was a natural: voluble, argumentative without being offensive, leavened by just enough humor. But the reason I survived the cuts is that I had a large audience, which makes the station money.

But one day, I thought my voice was a little throaty. So I drank some tea with honey. It helped but not enough. Within three months, my voice had become not only hoarse but so soft that even if I raised my volume to max, it was too soft. I went to specialist after specialist, test after test. No one could figure out the cause. So the station let me go.

And it got worse. Within a month, I was mute.

My so-called friends slowly stopped calling me, inviting me. While I understand that it's not fun to have a friend who can't speak, it still was disappointing that my friends were fair-weather only.

I was lonely. So I created a dating profile. I disclosed my muteness, both because dates would find out soon enough and because I like being honest.

Not surprisingly, I got no responses—a mute, conservative, unemployed talk-show host? But finally, a Cathy responded. Her response included, "It probably won't work: You're a conservative mute and I'm liberal Chatty Cathy. But I love to talk and, with you, I won't have to worry about talking too much."

But Cathy should have worried. Even though I couldn't talk, I could communicate by writing and with facial expressions and body language. We met at a coffee shop and she did talk a lot. She didn't get the message from my body language but when I wrote, "I'd like to respond," she finally got it. Before long, we got into a political exchange, and here's how it ended.

She said, "With income inequality so great, how can you not advocate more taxes to redistribute to the poor?"

I replied, "The top 25% of earners already pay 89% of the taxes. And society is better if, except for a basic safety net, more money is left in society's bigger contributors' hands."

She had the last word: "I don't think we're going to work out." And she left.

I'm scared that I'll remain lonely and unemployed.

Oy

Bam Bam Gucci, Wikimedia, CC 4.0

I hate travel, not dislike travel, hate travel. The hassles, not to mention the cost, dwarf travel's pleasures. I'd pay *not* to travel. My friend told me that Prague was beautiful so I watched a YouTube video and I was done.

But my relatives guilt-tripped me
to go all the way to Israel for my cousin's wedding. Oy.

It sucked even before I left. Get someone to take care of the dog and water the plants. Deal with all the work that will need to get done while I'm away. Make sure I have everything: the right clothes, the hotel and rent-a-car confirmations, enough cash.

Then with traffic and that traffic being unpredictable, I had to leave too early. And even though I had some cushion, I was nervous driving to mass transit, finding parking nearby that wouldn't break me, hoping mass transit would be on time, getting on and then getting pushed around on mass transit. Oy.

I arrived at the airport and there's the TSA line—The world's longest snake and a COVID superspreader event. I struggled to keep lugging my carry-on while digging for and then holding my driver's license, my boarding pass, and my passport. Oy.

I was finally onboard and sighed relief. Soon though, the noise began. The loudspeaker was loud enough to ensure everyone can learn new, difficult information: "Insert the metal buckle into the fitting." And the spiel is getting ever longer—By the time she finished, we were practically in Israel. That noise was soon replaced by roaring engines—and I'm not exaggerating—at least an hour of baby crying. Oy.

Of course, on landing in Tel-Aviv, there was more security. Then I stared at the luggage carousel and stared some more. Finally my stuff came. Phew and yes, oy.

The next problem was my fault I guess but, God, there's so much to remember. I told the cab driver to take me to the Crowne Plaza Tel Aviv and he did. But it was the wrong Crowne Plaza Tel Aviv. I didn't know there were two Crowne Plaza Tel-Avivs. The cabbie should have asked me which one, right? Oy.

I had a few days before the wedding and If I came this far, I was going to see the sights.

First, I went to Old-City Jerusalem. Yes, it was pleasant wandering the alleyways, but the main tourist areas—the Wailing Wall, The Church of the Holy Sepulcher, and the Dome of the Rock—were crawling with tourists and almost as many vendors hawking Jewish, Christian, and Muslim keychains and refrigerator magnets.

I took a tour of Nazareth and the Sea of Galilee. It was cool to see Jesus's steps including where he supposedly walked on water. But the spirituality was broken by our tour guide having us take our break at, yup, a stand selling Jewish, Christian, and Muslim keychains and refrigerator magnets.

Next, I decided to go controversial—The West Bank. First, I had to go through a checkpoint and while waiting for my turn, I asked a soldier why the checkpoints. He proudly said, "One reason is that I stopped a suicide bomber whose shirt was laced with explosive."

Even though I'm Jewish, true to the Jewish tradition of "on the other hand," I chose the tour run by Palestinians, who insisted that the Palestinians have more historical claim to that land, that Israeli settlements are illegitimate, and Palestinian anger is increased because of Netanyahu's conservative government. He was so inaccurate, but I felt intimidated so I just thought, "Oy."

Overwhelmed by all that, I headed for the Dead Sea, touted for being so salty, you can float. So I floated—I can do that at home with water wings.

Having had my fill of tourist spots, I headed back to Tel Aviv for one of my favorite activities anywhere—hanging out in a cafe. The falafel was good, the women cute, and then I saw one in an Arab headscarf leaving…with her backpack still beneath her seat. Other people saw that too and watched nervously. But she turned around and got it. False alarm but oy.

Finally, it was time for the wedding. Despite half of marriages ending in divorce, I still get a little choked up at two people promising to be monogamous for richer or poorer, forever. The rabbi had just said, "Do you take this..." when BOOM!, a bomb exploded that must have been just a few blocks away. Everyone gasped, then shrugged, and the rabbi continued as if nothing had happened. "Do you take this woman to be your lawfully wedded wife?" "I do."

At the reception, we laughed, we ate, we danced, and I forgot about all the preceding "oys"—until I realized that I'd soon have all the oys of the return trip and then spend the next week trying to catch up with work while having jet lag.

I wonder where my parents will push me to next: Ukraine? Oy.

Being a King is Overrated

They killed my wife, the queen, but I got away.

Clker-Free-Vector-Images, Pixabay CC0

So I continued in my 22nd year as the King of Stryfia. I'm still in my prime but felt weighed down by the job. The old bridge could collapse but how would we pay for a new one? The people are already heavily taxed because of my government's inefficiency and corruption. When we needed to build a school, one of the bidders bribed our Minister of the Interior to get the contract. Then he ordered more lumber and roofing than needed. The only way we found out is that we saw that, deep in the woods, he had used the extra material to build himself a grand house. I made him make restitution and in appreciation for not going to prison, he built me a small cabin.

Stryfia is always facing the threat of war. Most leaders are too aggressive, not caring enough about the loss of life and property that wars cause. When I ordered the laying down of arms and using the money for things like schools and bridges, those leaders view that as weakness, an opportunity, and they invade and take our land. We're half the size of what we were.

Then there are mundane things a king must deal with. Like when a farmer complained that he was sold a sick horse. The seller insists it got sick after he sold it. I couldn't figure out what to do, so I told them to compromise and the seller to return half the money. Both of them left dissatisfied.

And alas, there are my children and my ministers. They all want power and lucre, and will flatter me, lie to me, do anything to get them. And in my heart, none of them deserve much.

So one day, during one of their many squabbles, ostensibly about what's good for the kingdom but really about what's good for them, I asked my son for his lyre, my daughter for her knitting needles and wool, my wisest advisor for some great books, and with my sweet doggie, went to my cabin in the woods. It's a year later and I'm still there.

Occasionally, I visit the castle and find that things haven't changed much. I'm sometimes tempted to return to the throne but doubt I can make much difference. So I plan to stay in the woods with my lyre, my dog, and my books.

The Dinosaur

I'm a dinosaur. I love classical music. I decided not to pursue a career as a professional pianist because it requires hours a day of numbing practice to have even lottery odds of making it.

Charles Parker, Pexels, CC0, free to reuse

But I can't capitulate to lucre so I took a job at Splendid Sounds, a cafe that plays classical music including live concerts, and sells classical CDs and vinyl, plus books and videos about classical music.

That means I have to live with roommates and can't afford a car. That is super-restrictive of my freedom but I've traded that freedom for the freedom to have a classical-music life.

I enjoy talking with customers, for example, explaining why Furtwangler's Beethoven's 7th is much superior to Dudamel's. Or discussing the differences among great pianists, for example, Kissin, Zimerman, Argerich, and Oscar Peterson, the unequaled jazz pianist. I could go on and on, and sometimes, I do.

One conversation stands out above the rest. It was with the rare young person to come into the cafe, an argumentative type. Even his posture leaned forward.

It started innocently enough. He asked whether we had a vinyl copy of Glenn Gould's recording of Bach's Goldberg Variations. I said that we had both the 1955 and 1981 recordings. Reasonably, he asked, "What's the difference?" My answer didn't sit well. I said, "The 1955 version reflects Gould's youth—bravura over wisdom." He said, "I'll take the 1955." I shrugged.

He said, "You have a problem with that?" I tried to deflect with, "I'm pleased that a young person appreciates classical music."

That mollified him a bit. He said, "It's not hip-hop but I believe in diversity, even in music."

Hip-hop is the one music I can't abide, so I said, "Perhaps it's my limitation, but to my ears, hip-hop isn't musical and is too in-your face."

He seethed, "It's music for the revolution—angry, inciting! And unlike you tight-asses, it's about the fun of drugs and sex. All Bach inspires is religious fervor, the foolish belief in a God."

I said, "Whether you're religious or an atheist like me, classical music, from motets through Bach, Mozart, Beethoven, Debussy, Ravel, and my favorite, Chopin, encourages reflection, peace, and to my ears, unbridled pleasure, all of which we could use in these times when so many people seem anxious, depressed or—and I hesitated just a moment for effect—on a hair-trigger."

"If you want an anesthetic, smoke weed."

I asked, "Then why are you buying the Goldberg Variations?"

"Just to try something diverse, in the same way I tried gay sex. But I think I'll pass." And he strutted out.

I stared into space.

Mousy

hippopx, CC0

My boss called me into her office. "We like your work but you're a bit, well, mousy, so people underestimate you. As you know, we're slowly reducing headcount by giving employees AI-assisted tools and I worry that unless you can be more assertive, you could be considered, well, expendable."

I was, of course, scared. So after work, I started to kill my inner mouse by watching a well-known loud-and-prouder. I then tried to imitate her. When I thought I was being plenty assertive, I recorded myself on my phone's video app. Still too mousy. I needed to summon some deeply buried inner rat.

Then I tried imitating the most assertive people I see on TV—certain senators and newscasters, that woman on Fleabag. I videoed myself again. Better but still…

Next, I tried the analytical approach. I thought, okay, what does charisma come down to?

Well, first, it's posture. I googled "deportment" and it said to pull my shoulders back and my chest out. But that would make me look like I was showing off my tits. I didn't want to do that.

Then it's the walk—I practiced striding instead of trudging. That I could do.

Tone of voice. They say that to sound authoritative, speak at the bottom of your natural range. So I practiced that until I sounded like a smoker but not quite like Greta Garbo 's gravelly—"I vant to be alone."

I kept practicing and being big and bad at meetings, including interrupting like Loud-and-Proud did.

Three months later, I was laid off. As usual, to avoid lawsuits, they do a group layoff carefully balanced by race, gender, age, and sexual orientation. They never give you a reason but you know that they don't lay off people at random. So I have no idea if I was still too mousy, too bad-ass, my work was bad, or something else.

I applied for lots of jobs and, in some interviews, I acted super-confident, in others, my natural self, and in most, somewhere in the middle. I got nothing until I applied for a job as payroll coordinator for the local diocese. I was my natural self. That was five years ago and I'm still there. My friends call me Church Mouse
and I kind of like it.

Behind Doors 1, 2, and 3

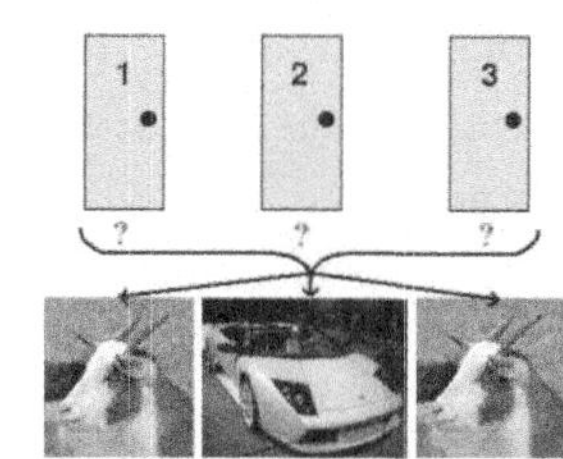

Kuxu, Wikimedia, GNU 1.2

I sat in my usual spot at The Graduate, the appropriately named Berkeley dive bar that caters to 20-somethings that prefer to drink and maybe think in a quiet rather than deafening bar.

At some point, a guy sat next to me, but I didn't notice. I was thinking, "What the hell should I do for a career?"

I had graduated six months ago, did the cliched trip—Europe plus Nepal—and came back no clearer on a career direction let alone a path to enlightenment.

I sat with my Long Island Iced Tea, a drink that gives big buzz per buck. Oozing into my softened brain was an image of three doors, like in the TV game show, Let's Make a Deal. And the host said to me, "For you, a special deal. I'll show you what's behind all three doors. The catch is, you have to figure out which is actually best for you.

"Behind Door Number One is WRITER!"

I picture my debut book, *Handled*, about how good people become bad politicians because of their handlers. It won the National Book Award and Nobel Peace Prize, and I was interviewed on both CNN and Fox, the *New York Times* and *Wall Street Journal.* It sold 10 million copies and I donated 95 percent of the profits to the Foundation for Ethical Government.

Or I spend five years procrastinating and finally finish writing the book but all the agents and publishers ghost me. So I work at a cafe, including cleaning its toilets and even with two roommates, I can't make the rent, so I'm homeless.

"Behind Door Number 2 is INVESTMENT BANKER!"

By age 30, I'm legendary for bringing amazing new products to the public—the zPhone, which makes the iPhone obsolete, InstaHouse, which builds lovely homes in one day for $20,000, and Vivace, a drug that increases healthspan by ten years. I'm worth $50 million and donate 95% to the National Association for Gifted Children.

Or, although I applied to all 12 first-tier and all 26 lesser investment banking firms, I got a total of one screening interview and was screened out. I'm now a bank teller.

"Behind Door Number 3 is FUNDRAISER!"

After taking a few sales courses, I get hired as an assistant fundraiser at my university but because I exceeded my annual quota in the first month, I was promoted to fundraiser and when I did it again, was promoted to trainer of fundraisers, and when all my trainees quickly exceeded quota, I became Director of Development. Then there was a bidding war for me among some of the nation's most prestigious nonprofits. I now make $2,000,000 a year and was named International Fundraiser of the Year.

Or, the only job I could get after taking those expensive sales courses was as a door-to-door solicitor for Save the Snail Darter. Door after door was slammed in my face and after a month, I had raised only $172, and they fired me.

I woke from my reverie to finally notice the guy sitting next to me. He said, "You looked deep in thought."

I said, "Yeah, I've been thinking about what career to pursue."

He replied, "I'm the manager of a soybean processing plant and could use an assistant. Interested?"

I said, "What the hell."

The Cynics Club

Elevate, Pexels, CC

The only requirement for membership in the Cynics Club was amazement at people's stupidity, especially around religion, pro sports, and the media. Typical comments:

"What kind of God would allow earthquakes that kill thousands, permit babies to be born with horrific diseases and scream for weeks and then die leaving bereft parents. There is no God, certainly no God finding solace in."

"How can they expect us to be loyal sports fans let alone those who will spend a fortune to sit umpteen rows away, when players are so disloyal—They'll jump ship for a few extra bucks when they're already richer than 100 fans put together."

"Newscasters are read-alouders. And their opinions are usually based on life in their out-of-touch bubble. Yet they're so confident that they're willing to manipulate our views on everything from education to crime. How much real-world experience do they have? Usually little. I'd like to see them spend just a week shadowing a cop, in an inner-city classroom, or at the Mexican border. After that, they'd cry at all their ill-founded manipulations."

But it turned out that maybe we were as hubristic and simplistic as we accused them of being. Our club's most beloved member was diagnosed with end-stage cancer. He found comfort only in the long-shot religious faith and sports-fandom of his youth. And he found himself more forgiving of the media. After all, we all have biases.

After he died, the club disbanded.

The Bellhop Who Refuses Tips

The manager of the fancy hotel had been frustrated. It had been a month since she placed the ad for a bellhop. The first person she interviewed failed the drug test. She hired the second one but on Day One, she had already received two complaints from guests. She tried to work with the young man but he said, "This shit ain't for me."

Rennett Stowe, Flickr, CC 2.0

So the manager continued to search.
When she saw a portly 75-year-old walk in for an interview, she sighed, but she was desperate. Laws precluded her from asking what she really wanted to ask, "Why would a fat old guy want to be a bellhop?" So she

just asked the standard, sanitized question, "Would you tell me a little about yourself?"

I said, "I was a lawyer for a university and just retired. I'm already bored."

"But why would you want to be a bellhop?"

"I grew tired of the university's greed: suing faculty researchers for the profit from the products they had worked so long and hard to create, suing the government for not giving them enough money, and defending against professors who sued because they believe they were denied tenure for non-merit reasons. I just want to be nice, to give. I don't need the money. I just want to make people happy."

After checking that I indeed had been a university attorney, she hired me.

I did my best to discern what each guest wanted. There were the hot couples who just wanted me to dump their stuff in their room so they could get it on. Then there were the nervous people who welcomed my describing the hotel's services and locals' favorite restaurants. Then there were people who tried to make me feel small. "Just put it over there." Then they'd hustle me to the door as though I was a fly to be shooed out. It all was okay.

What was most fun is that when guests tried to hand me a tip, I waved it away. Some just shrugged, "Whatever." Others said "Are you sure?" And occasionally, someone would ask why. I'd say something like, "You came to a fine hotel expecting to be taken care of. No one likes having to tip. Part of my taking care of you is to not get a tip. I just want you to feel cared about." And with that, I'd nod and make my exit.

The guests seemed to appreciate that but one person went far beyond. He said, "Tell me about yourself." I did and he offered me a job as general counsel for the nonprofit where he was CEO.

I thanked him but said, "I'm happy here, happier than I ever was as a lawyer."

It's a year later and I'm still glad I turned him down and that I still do my bellhop thing. Every morning I wake up with aches and pains from lugging people's stuff but it's worth it. What a privilege to be able to give pleasure to every person I serve.

Faking It

I hated my parents. They always treated my sister better than me—She got everything; I get yelled at.

Public Domain Graphics, CC0

And I hated school. Half the boys in my class had a hard time sitting still through it all. I don't know how girls do it.

Let me tell you what I did.

In the halls, as soon as I saw a teacher, I would stare at her, right through her eyes. Of course, they would freak out. In art class, I drew stuff that would make the teacher send me to the school psychologist. You know, like a picture of a boy shooting up the school.

With the shrink, I'd refuse to answer anything. I'd just stare at her. So they referred me to some other shrink and, again, I just stared. It was all easy-peasy—Just sit there.

My parents didn't seem to mind that the school district's "psychological services team" put me in an institution. I mean, yeah, my parents said, "Do you really have to?" But I think they said that to not seem like bad parents. I think they were glad to get rid of me.

At Hope Juvenile Growth Center (hah!), I got to see other interesting kids. And I didn't have to sit in school all day trying to stay awake let alone understand Shakespeare, geometric theorems, and being told for the tenth time that we white males are oppressors. We could learn pretty much whatever we wanted. I used articles I found using Google to learn more about the art of faking.

That was 20 years ago. What I am doing now? I teach psychologists, doctors, and lawyers how to detect fraud: embezzlement, welfare fraud, and yeah, kids who fake it.

Hilda the Hypocrite

In 3rd grade, Hilda volunteered to lead her class's recycling drive. She didn't do it because she cared about the environment. She did it because she liked being in charge of something.

With permission 18/1 Graphics Studio

She gave a speech about how "recycling can save the earth" and kicked off the campaign by ceremoniously emptying her desk's excess papers into the recycling bin—a vivid and public but easy way to show her "commitment." That made some kids feel guilty if they threw even a tissue into the trash rather than the recycling bin. Little did they know that at home, because

Hilda's apartment house's recycling bin was a few steps further than the garbage bin, she'd usually toss her family's recycling into the garbage.

In Hilda's high school history class, she gave an oral report on the importance of diversity. She dug up stories of people of color accomplishing great things. But when she became student body vice-president, which allowed her to pick three student senators, she chose three people of her race and gender.

After college, Hilda took a job at an environmental nonprofit. Again, her motive wasn't to help the environment but so she could tell her friends she's working for an environmental nonprofit.

When she became her workgroup's project lead, she stressed the importance of teamwork. But in practice, she rarely pulled her weight, yet when her boss wanted pay raises to be equal for all group members, she argued that she should get more because she was the lead.

In a Bible study class, Hilda spoke against abortion, even though as an environmentalist, she knew that overpopulation is a leading cause of environmental degradation. Besides, she had had an abortion and, if you count the morning-after pill, three.

When teaching Sunday School, Hilda urged her students to turn the other cheek even when the other person is wrong. Yet when driving, even when returning home from teaching Sunday School, Hilda often gave bad drivers the finger.

On Hilda's deathbed, she urged her family to work to support the environment, help the poor, and fight for the right to life. Tearfully, her family swore they would.

"Sub! Sub!! Sub!!!"

With permission, 18/1 Graphics Studio

After having been let go from my job as a fundraiser for an education nonprofit for "not making my number," I needed a win and fast. So while looking for another real job, I figured I'd substitute teach— There were ads all over looking for subs.

Yes, I was nervous. I remember us kids not treating subs so well but figured I could handle it, especially if I was prepared with fun activities to supplement what the regular teacher left for me. I figured wrong.

As I approached the classroom, two kids were in the hallway. When they saw me, they turned into the classroom and yelled, "Sub! Sub!! Sub!!!" More kids picked up the chant.

I had been raised to believe that if you treat people with kindness and respect, it will be met in kind. So although their behavior scared me, I mustered a smile as I entered the classroom, gently, without a word, motioned the class to settle down, and said, "I'm looking forward to making this a good day for you," whereupon a student made a mouth fart.

I gave him a schoolmarmy look and continued, "Yes, I'll do the lessons your teacher left for me." Kids groaned. "But I've also brought some special things for us to do that we should find fun." A kid said, "We're going to dance?"

I said, "Not quite, but..." At that point the kid climbed onto a desk and started dancing or, more accurately, twerking.

I figured I'd better get firmer, so I said, "Down." The student said, "I'm no dog. You can't talk with me that way."

He continued to dance, the class cheered, and I had to do something. So I took his arm and was about to say, "Get down!" But before I could, he stuck out his chin and scoffed, "I know my rights. You can't touch me. I'll tell the principal and sue your ass."

I didn't know what to do. My face was red, my heart was pounding, and embarrassed, scared, and, okay, a little angry, I padded to the principal's office and said, "I can't do this. I'm leaving."

The principal calmly said, "You are the paid professional. You need to be able to control a classroom."

I continued out the door and redoubled my effort to find another job as a fundraiser, but this time, for a cause other than education.

A Career Coach

Ironically, it was a success that made me do it.

My client used every tactic I taught him plus unethical ones like, on his references, listing his

With permission, 18/1 Graphics Studio

girlfriend as his boss. And he got the job.

I'm embarrassed that I hadn't previously reflected on what a sleaze I had been, packaging inferior clients so they get the job over more worthy candidates. Not only does that deprive worthier people of a job, but thereby saddles the boss, coworkers, and customers with a worse employee than they should have gotten.

I'm embarrassed to tell you what I did. After hours, using a phony voice, I left a voice mail at the HR department at the nonprofit that hired him and told the truth about him.

I felt good about doing that, like a Robin Hood stealing from the unworthy to give to the worthy. So I did that every time I had such a client.

And all was fine until one day, someone knocked on my door. It was a process server. I opened the envelope and a client who got fired because of my voice mail was suing me. I'm guessing the HR person told him that someone spilled the beans and he knew it had to be me.

Maybe this career coach needs a new career?

Following Church Teachings

I was putting out my jello mold for the church supper. To avoid it being the stereotype and to make it a little healthier, I made it in a heart-shaped mold and mixed in fresh cherries, well, frozen cherries, defrosted. But that's beside the point.

With permission, 18/1 Graphics Studio

Next to me, putting out her

tuna casserole was a woman I didn't know well, around my age, 35. I couldn't even remember her name, so I was glad when she was kind enough to not assume I knew it. She said, "Hi Mary, I'm Christine."

I prefer to be quiet but she was a talker, and before I knew it, she was telling me that she needed to move out of her apartment and was having trouble finding one she could afford, even a share.

Maybe it was because two weeks ago, the minister did the sermon on generosity. She quoted something from Corinthians, something like, "Each of you should give, and not reluctantly, for God loves a cheerful giver."

So without really thinking, I put on my churchy smile and said, "How'd you like to share my apartment? I'll only charge you $500 a month." No surprise, she jumped at it.

As soon as she did, doubts crept in: What if she plays loud music? What if she leaves the kitchen messy? And sharing a bathroom— I'll have to smell her, well, you know.

But I didn't anticipate this: Every night, there were, well, intimacy noises. Loud ones. They were especially loud when she had company but even when she was alone.

It wasn't just the noise, it was the reminder that, for some reason, I've never enjoyed sex that much. I certainly don't crave it. It's not because of guilt, even though when I was growing up, I still remember the Sunday School teacher pointing to the cross and only half-kidding saying, "This is what happens if you have premarital sex." When you're in the sixth grade, you kind of take such warnings literally. At least I did.

I tried to be Christian about it. I endured Christine's enthusiasms as long as I could without saying anything. After all, it would be unchristian of me to deny her pleasure, especially in her own home, even if it was my home too.

Then I tried raising the issue in a loving way: "I'm pleased that you feel comfortable living as you'd like, but I'm wondering if you just might be just a bit quieter when you're, well, enjoying yourself. Or at least put some music on so I'm not hearing quite as much." She was Christian about it and said she felt terrible that I've caused pain and promised to be quieter. And she was for a while but then started up again.

I hoped it would be just temporary, but no. So I tried again, this time, just a bit less kindly: "Christine, I'm having difficulty with the noise. It's even making it hard to sleep. So I'm hoping..."

A few weeks more of ever less kind begging and then I did what I'd think Jesus would think is the most Christian thing. I said, "Christine, I am pleased that you are happy here. I don't need this apartment that badly. It's yours. I'll find another place."

Waiting to Get Operated On

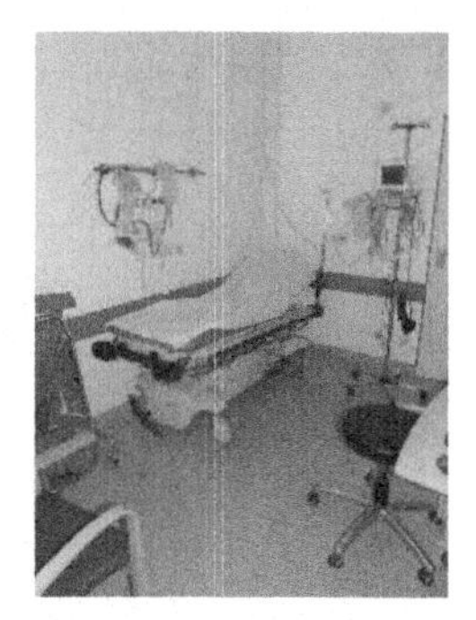

pxfuel, free to reuse

My dad was just walking along when he tripped on a raised sidewalk, broke his hip, and because it healed slowly—he was 86—it eventually got infected. They tried all the antibiotics but they didn't work well enough. He got sepsis—an extreme reaction to infection—and he died.

I was a runner—It was as much a part of my daily ritual as brushing my teeth. I averaged five miles a day. I took only Sundays off. But eventually, my knees gave out—bone on bone. I needed a knee replacement but was scared. Yes, I was a little younger than when my dad had his hip replaced, but still. And the recovery from knee is tougher than from hip. But I had no choice—Much of the time, the pain was a 7 or higher.

The procedure went well but four months later, I was still sometimes using a cane. I worried whether I'd always be using that sign of old age for everyone to see. I finally did get off the cane but just months later, I lost my balance going down the stairs—in my own house, for God's sake—and broke my hip.

I'm writing to you from the hospital. waiting for them to wheel me into surgery. I'm picturing my dad: his robustness, his decline, his death. I am terrified.

Kissy-Poo

I can remember it like it was yesterday. In the bed, Melissa turned to me: "Kissy-Poo?"

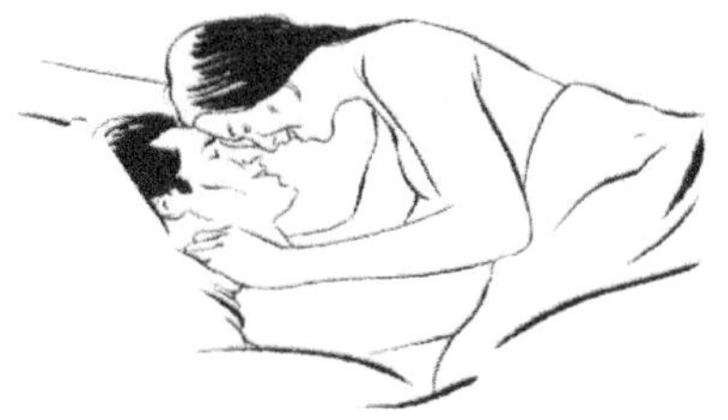

With permission, 18/1 Graphics Studio

"Again? I smiled.

And she hopped on me for the third time that night.

I moaned, "I'll love you forever." She whispered, "I want your baby." I laughed, "Three babies!"

Melissa was my first love. I had hoped it could be that way with other women, but the fireworks never exploded. But Melissa was so pretty, so funny, so good in bed!

Two years later

My lawyer argued, "Your honor, when my client was at work, in violation of the divorce decree, she absconded with the armoire."

Her lawyer countered, "Your honor, she was so distraught by her husband having hidden $25,000 that he didn't list in the Disclosure of Assets."

My lawyer tried again: "My client had reason to be distraught. He's being required to pay a ridiculous amount of alimony, excuse me your honor, spousal support. He felt the armoire was tiny compensation."

One year later

Here I am again, giggling in bed, this time with Cindy: Again I'm thinking, "Should I ask her to marry me?"

A Pregnant Nod

Jen finished her last fight of the day. She told the author, "You really should use 'unimportant,' not nugatory." Such wasn't in Jen's fantasy when she dreamt of being in book publishing. But proofreader is as far as she has gotten.

With permission, 18/1 Graphics Studio

And now at 38, because of some combination of personal choice, peer pressure, and the tick-tock of her bio clock, Jen's priority was becoming a mom.

Jen would love a partner but her track record said, "Long shot." So she visited a sperm bank. She thought, "I'm going just to look." Those are dangerous words, like when someone says they're going to the animal shelter "just to look."

After reviewing dozens of profiles and mulling how much to compromise on the sperm donor's intelligence, looks, and personality, she settled on #462.

Kyle was born normal, but a normal baby is an abnormal challenge, for example, hours of inexplicable crying and the resulting sleep— deprived mom who, in this case, stopped giving a shit about whether the comma should go inside or outside the parenthesis.

After just three days, Jen told her mom that she's thinking of giving the baby up for adoption. Whether or not that was a ploy, it worked and Grandma offered to sacrifice her new empty-nester freedom for parenthood round two.

But in just days, when Jen came home and reached out her arms hoping that Kyle would be eager to see her, he nuzzled into Grandma— every night. So Jen cut back working to half-time.

One day, Jen sat bored on a park bench with Kyle in the stroller, her brain going to mush. A guy pushing a stroller asked if the empty spot on the bench was available. She thought, "Is he unshaven because he's cool or because he's slovenly?" and muttered, "Okay, I guess."

Talky, he said he was divorced and wished he could meet a working woman so he could quit his job and be a house husband.

Internally, Jen screamed. I don't want this guy. I don't want to be a parent. I don't want to go back to work. I don't know what the hell I want."

But all she did was nod.

Singing Success's Key

The dozen people in the audience clapped unmemorably, Marianne smiled, and headed off-stage to her table in the corner, where the waiter brought her usual: a salad and a Bud.

With permission, 18/1 Graphics Studio

She was grateful for that. Most places expected her to sing just "for exposure." At least Folk You fed her.

And they didn't mind Marianne taking long breaks. And this night, she did and mused, "27. That's almost over the hill. And my dad tells me to give it up and go to college. But I have no idea what I'd major in, what career I'd be good at. And when I read the small print at the only borderline-affordable college near me, it says that average time to a degree is not four years. That's the *expected* time. The actual *average* time is 6.2 years. And while it says that 83% of students receive financial aid, an average of $30,000, the small print says that 70% of that is loan, which has to be paid back plus interest." And she plodded back on stage.

A week later, while reading a trade magazine for the music industry, she found an article that she hoped would provide an answer. Its title: To Max Audience Appeal, Create AI-Formula Music." It said, "Your best chance of a hit is for the topic to be love, and the lyrics must not be happy or sad but go from sad to happy or happy to sad. The melody and chords must mainly be in a major (happy) key with just a few phrases in a minor key for contrast. And both melody and chords must be super-simple and repetitious to maximize the chances of the song becoming an earworm, which boosts prospects for word-of-mouth marketing."

And Marianne created an album of songs that fully conformed to the artificial-intelligence formula. And she became a major success, including a national tour, performing in stadiums across the country.

After a performance, in front of a bank of microphones, the CNN reporter asked, "How'd you come up with these amazing songs?" Marianne said, "I dunno. It's just a feeling thing, organic, you know. I just followed my gut, followed my passion. You know, do what you love and the money will follow." The reporters nodded and took notes.

An Ambivalent For-Profit Executive

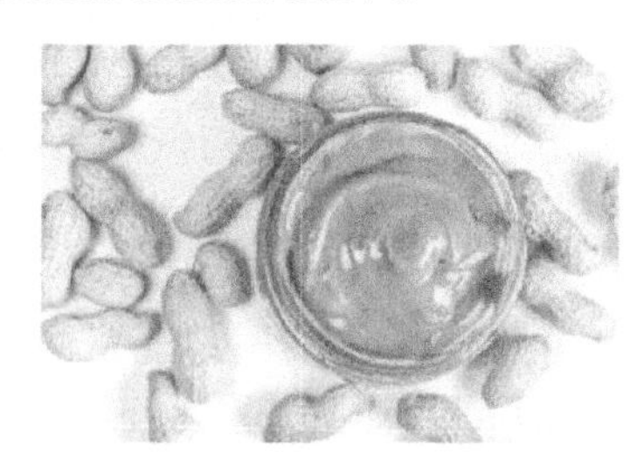

Marco Verch, Flickr, CC2.0

In his Wassily chair that sat on a Karastan rug, Matt sipped a cab from a Zalto glass. All that isn't surprising in the home of a senior vice-president at Better Brands, even though he's in charge only of the peanut butter division.

Matt rarely got home before 8, by which time he was usually exhausted. But today it was just 6 and he felt he had some bandwidth left. So he decided to step back and think about his job.

"I like the status— It feels good to tell people that I'm a VP at a Fortune-1000 company. And yeah, I like the comp, especially the stock. It keeps going up and that reflects my team's effort to create and promote good products at a fair price. Besides, I simply like my job— lots of problems to solve and most of my supervisees think of me as a good mentor and advocate.

"On the other hand, I have mixed feelings about having to keep costs down. Yeah, that means that my quality peanut butter— no additives, no aflatoxins— is affordable. And yeah, it's important to protect shareholder value— I mean, most people who invest in our company do it through mutual funds and ETFs— They're saving for a home, for college, for retirement, or a cushion for unexpected expenses.

"On the other hand, controlling costs means I have to do things that make me sad, like replacing employees with technology— for example, our new AI customer service: better answers, faster, cheaper, and happier customers. They love getting their problem solved quickly and without having to wait on hold— and we save a lot of money. But employees are human beings. Most of them were doing the best they could.

"On the other hand, would society have been wise to not use the plow so it could save jobs for people who tilled with a shovel?

"I need to stay put and be grateful for my job. I will, though, donate some more money to Junior Achievement. It supports budding entrepreneurs, which leads to better products for us all.

"Okay, back to the work. Let me think a bit about renaming our peanut butter ... We should ride the populist wave. Hmm...Maybe, "People's Peanut Butter?"

And with an easier mind, Matt took another sip of cab.

A Widower

U.S. National Archives, Public Domain

Both Arthur and Sharon had rewarding careers. After being a fighter pilot having flown a sortie over Haiphong Harbor, he opted for a civilian career, which he spent in the Two Rivers Unified School District, first as a clerk and slowly moving up to be its assistant director of human resources.

He was pushed to take early retirement and resented it because that's what employers do to get rid of deadwood without getting sued for age discrimination. He wondered, "Am I deadwood?"

Privately, Sharon was glad that Arthur retired. Although she liked her job, she had long preferred to quit and play with Arthur: travel, take dance lessons, visit the grandkids.

But that plan didn't work out and not because, like some in their age group, one of them got a heart attack or a cancer diagnosis. Sharon literally got run over by a bus. On her bike, the bus changed lane and didn't see her. The bike frame was crushed so it wrapped around her neck, and she died of asphyxiation.

Arthur developed a routine-walk his dog Lola while the coffee was brewing, then linger over the newspaper, shower, read while listening to his favorite music, and so on. At bedtime, Arthur called Lola into the bed and he tried to fall asleep always listening to the same CD: A Child's Gift of Lullabies. https://bit.ly/3IxhyjS

Arthur spent a lot of time thinking about Sharon— gentle, genuinely interested in him, and that all the way to the end, they enjoyed their tender version of making love.

Arthur thought he'd spend his last years with that routine but then his best friend had a stroke and became wheelchair-bound, living in fear of the next one.

So Arthur decided to come into schools to describe what it's really like to be a fighter pilot, for example, "While being barely old enough to rent a car, you get to control a huge, snorting beast in hopes that your work will save more lives than you end." But all three local schools politely turned him down. He figured that the schools don't want anything that seems pro-military. The local Rotary club did let him speak.

Next, Arthur thought of tutoring. But despite querying the principals at those schools, he only got one referral. He figured that was because he was male. The one kid was Adam, a 12-year-old who disliked reading. They read Top Gun together, Adam asked questions and treasured the book, especially because Arthur autographed it. Arthur also felt good about it, not just because it motivated Adam to read but because the wide-eyed Adam made Arthur feel almost heroic. But after finishing the book, Adam's mom thanked him and thus ended Arthur's tutoring efforts.

Arthur then returned to his simple life, adding gardening, volunteering at the animal shelter, and writing his memoir. Its last line: "I tried."

My Wasted Potential

With permission, 18/1 Graphics Studio

It wasn't until I was 70 that it happened. It was a random moment: I was planting a tomato when I couldn't get the truth out of my mind.

It's not acceptable even to think it: I am a genius who wasn't allowed to make the big difference I feel I could have made.

Despite growing up in a slum, a child of new immigrants, Holocaust survivors who spoke no English, I was reading on the 5th grade level in the first grade. My IQ was 150, was admitted to a prestigious high school, college, and graduate school.

Way back in 1974, my undergraduate senior project showed that toll booths should be replaced by drive-through toll-paying, which would have saved millions of drivers time and immense pollution—All those cars idling. But although I wrote a detailed proposal to the transportation commission in New York, Philadelphia, Chicago, Los Angeles, and San Francisco, I never even got a response.

My Ph.D. dissertation demonstrated that the laws of genetics don't get suspended when it comes to human intelligence. My study was among the first to show that, like most characteristics not just in humankind but across the animal and plant kingdoms, genes and environment both matter a lot.

Funny, the part that my professors seemed to like the best were the three lines that weren't academically rigorous: "No poodle and pit bull breeder could claim the average difference between the two breeds is all environment .... Every mother knows, even in utero, that their babies start with different personalities ... Fighting the achievement gap just by changing environment is like fighting a boxer with one arm tied behind your back."

Although my thesis won the campus' Dissertation of the Year, no mainstream media would publish the results. I submitted it to 11: ten no responses and one that said, "We're concerned it could be perceived as racist."

When the COVID pandemic began, I wrote an article contending that we should, with clear eyes, evaluate the wisdom of allowing natural immunity to occur rather than lock down society. The article raised the possibility that more deaths might be prevented and economic and psychological costs reduced. The article also provided data that indicated that lockdowns restrict people's getting the micro— exposures we all get to pathogens, which trigger immune responses and thus prevent serious illness. Unfortunately, someone used social media and letters to my wife's employer claiming I was a "COVID denier" and a "death monger." My wife, understandably afraid of losing her good job, asked me to pull down the article and I did.

I still have much I could contribute but have become pretty inert. Maybe a little of it is my age, but more is that I'm scared that yet again, I'll get the 3 Cs: censured, censored, and canceled. I feel like a boxer who's gotten knocked down in the first nine rounds. It's hard to motivate myself to come out for my tenth and final one.

So here I am in my garden.

In Search of the Secular Grail

Like most people, I was looking for the grail: happiness. We spend more time at work than on anything else, so I gave a fair amount of thought to choosing a career.

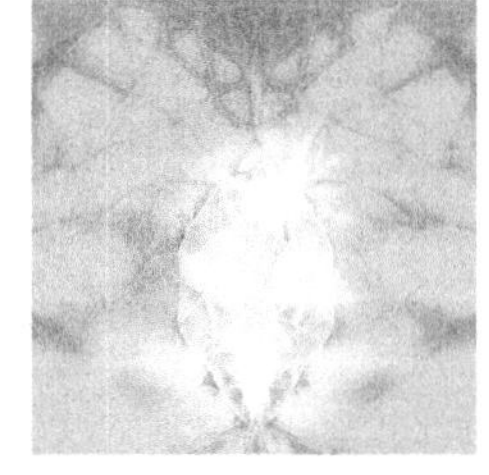

PublicDomainPictures.com, CC0

I rejected MD because I tend to the hypochondriacal—I'd "get" my patients' diseases. Besides, I'd worry too much about whether I got the diagnosis right, would the treatment work, and I'd feel terrible if they got worse, let alone died. No doctor career for me.

I rejected law—Too much arguing, fussing over details, too many ethical temptations.

I rejected business: I believe in the net benefit of capitalism but personally don't care enough about profit to be in business, self-employed or working for a company.

I rejected nonprofit work. Too rarely does the money bestowed by donors yield enough benefit. And most nonprofits' collaboration-centric style of decision-making is too glacial for my speedy nature.

I rejected government work—too bureaucratic, too *much* job security—To get fired, you practically have to commit a felony. That causes a torpid workforce. I'm not torpid.

I finally settled on landscape architecture: aesthetic, practical, indoor and outdoor. But in the trenches, it's not all flowers, trees, and man-made waterfalls. It's dealing with customers: persnickety homeowners and government and companies that ever change their mind yet don't want to pay for the changes. And it doesn't matter enough which shrub or whether the "water element" goes in the southeast or northwest corner. Then there are the government regulations—maddening. Most are rarely worth the paperwork and cost, let alone the weeks or even months waiting for approvals. I've stayed in landscape architecture but it isn't my grail.

The best I've been able to come up with is, after work, settling into my easy chair with a cup of hot chocolate, listening, on loop, to a favorite song. These days, it's Peter, Paul, and Mary singing Puff the Magic Dragon. I find a wisp of the grail in the lyric, "Puff, the magic dragon lived by the sea, and frolicked in the autumn mist, in a land called Honalee."

Campaign Meeting (Una reunión de campaña)

52-star U.S. flag. Gaiole, Wikimedia CC 1.0

The area's campaign manager smiled, "Here you go: 52-star flags, t-shirts, caps, and bumper stickers. You are not to display these until the day after the election. Then, it's loud and proud. We don't want to hurt our party's candidates. The polls show that the voters don't favor DC as the 51st state nor Puerto Rico as the 52nd.

"Now get out there. We must ring every single doorbell in every swing precinct. If a white answers, you say, "It's time your government cared about people." If a Latinx answers, you say, "It's time your government cared about Latinx people." If a Black answers, you say, "It's time your government cared about Black people."

To further rally the troops, the campaign manager gushed, "I see a future in which all students are required to learn Spanish, we get a government that truly reflects Latinx interests, and that California, Texas, and maybe even New York become the official or at least unofficial New New Mexico! In the meantime, que empiece la guerra! Let the war begin!" The campaign staff and volunteers whooped.

The Muffin Man

U.S. Army, Public Domain

I'm 35, a computer programmer, and forgettable. I mean, last week a coworker told me about a party he went to. When I said that I had been there, he said, "Oh, I didn't notice you." Yup.

I'm not too tall or too short, too fat or too thin, too handsome or too ugly, too quiet or too outspoken. I'm just there, buried somewhere in the middle.

When I was younger, I tried to stand out—tell lots of jokes, wear bright clothes, praise people—That's what *How to Win Friends and Influence People* tells you to do. I even bought a red Toyota MR2, the little sports car.

But none of it really worked. Today, I mainly just work and play video games.

Recently, I tried a different tack—I started baking muffins. It's easy and enabled me to fantasize. Like in The Glass

Menagerie, maybe a caller will come and I'll make a new friend.

True to my thorough self, I made batch after batch: chocolate muffins, blueberry muffins, blueberry walnut muffins, lemon muffins, lemon walnut muffins, and my signature: blueberry, buttermilk, cornbread muffins. Soon, my freezer was filled with muffins.

What to do? Well, last Saturday, I defrosted them and took them and a card table to the train station. I set out the muffins and a sign that said, "Free. Enjoy!" I was hoping I might make a new friend or at least the muffins would find a home and my freezer would be free for God knows what.

Well, most people looked at me like it had to be a scam—Was I like a Jehovah's Witness giving a Watchtower but then you had to hear a pitch? Or was I crazy and the muffins were poisoned? A woman stared at me a while, saw a policeman nearby, and strode to him.

Next I knew, the cop was in my face. "Do you have a license to sell food?" I said I wasn't selling, I was giving. He said, "You're not allowed to do that either." So I packed up my muffins, put them back in my freezer, and played a video game.

A CEO Talks with a Clerk

Akshay Gupta, Pixabive, CC0

I was being a good boy—leading by walking around. I stopped at a half-dozen desks and at the next one, had the experience of a lifetime. Here's a paraphrase of our exchange.

Me: Hi, I'm Ron, the CEO. How are you"

She: *(seeming uncomfortable)* Fine, thank you.

Me: You want to tell me what you're working on?

I assumed she'd tell me about her work but…

She: I'm leading the effort to unionize the workers.

Me: I've been dispirited about that. We pay you well, good benefits, job security, have an open-door policy. And many businesses that unionize get worse. Many U.S. industries have been decimated, with huge loss of jobs when they unionize: steel, cars. And even if they stay in business, the workplace becomes more adversarial and the workers seem *less* happy. When I go into Safeway, unionized, the workers seem unhappy, yet when I go into Trader Joe's, which isn't yet unionized…

She: You make much more than what we workers make. That is unfair!

Me: I worked hard in school and colleges, took out huge loans not just for college but an MBA, worked my way up from entry-level trainee, was smart enough to become expert at the technology and finance, work 60 hours a week and don't get overtime. Did you put in as much effort? Were you and your would-be unionized rank-and-file as smart and hard-working? I get paid well because the board, who sets my salary, knows that very few people could do what we do and add so much value. Could you do my job?

She: You were privileged by birth, race, and gender. Don't you lecture me!

I walked away shaking, returned to my office, sat with my head in my hands, and decided to tell you about this.

The Broken Hearts Club

Andrew Demenyuk, Attributed Free License, Deposit Photos

It wasn't much of a club actually—only three members. But we like it despite or probably because we're all women.

Jeannie has pined for guy after guy but none of them wanted her as more than, as she put it, "a sperm receptacle." She continued, "I'm jealous of all those women with rings on their fingers, prancing around with their baby carriages." Tina asked, "Are you sure you're not better off without all that—Remember, better solo than so-so."

Heather's husband died in, as she put it, "a fucking motorcycle accident." She said that now six months later, "I'm still grieving. I can't make myself do anything." Jeannie asked, "Is that just an excuse? If so, for what?"

Tina's off-again/on-again boyfriend is, as she put it, "off permanently." She exclaimed, "I was so perfect?" Heather asked, "Would he agree?"

Mainly, the Broken Hearts Club grouses, occasionally about their insecurities but mainly as Jeannie said and the others agreed, that "men suck." Society's mind-molders—the colleges and especially the media —promulgate that. So "men suck" has become an ever harder-wired "truth."

But all three members knew that, as Heather said, "Bitching does no good. Let's move forward." So while they found it more fun to complain, they were, as Tina said, "Good, bad-ass women" and they discussed how to move forward.

Jeannie promised not to go to bed with a guy until at least the third date.

Heather swore, "No more bad boys."

Tina said, "I need to make myself stop thinking about Tony and start putting myself out there again."

They all agreed that guys just aren't that important, even if one doesn't suck.

The Broken Hearts Club meets in a cafe and, today, a guy, a cute guy, ambled over. He smiled, "I'm bad—I've been listening to you. Could I sit in?"

Jeannie pursed her lips. Heather flushed. Tina giggled.

I Won't "Make the Most of My Looks"

My parents, my high school friends, even some idiots in college told me that "If you made the most of your looks, you'd be pretty." Well, fuck them! My college courses, well, woke me. I refuse to conform to the patriarchy wanting me to wear clothes to accentuate my "figure," that I gotta deal with long hair because guys like it, and that I need to keep dieting to be a size 8. Fuck them! Watch Barbie!

TMagen, Wikimedia, CC 4.0

I'm 30 pounds overweight and I like food, wine, and weed enough that I'm not going to deny myself so I can appeal to men, or to women, or to non-binaries for that matter. They either like me for who I am or fuck 'em!

And I do speak out. At meetings, I won't get interrupted — I do love being loud and proud. And I do call 'em out as racist, sexist, homophobic, transphobic, whatever.

Yeah, when I ran for president of my local chapter of the National Organization for Women, I lost to some Barbie doll. So I quit and joined the Socialist Women's Action Network, and now I AM the chapter president.

My advice to you: Don't take shit from no one. Don't compromise. The time for revolution is NOW. Fight!

Teardown

Ever more often, they cast me as the evil or goofy guy who is foiled by superior women.

Ruca Souza, Pexels, free to reuse

In my previous role, I literally played a monkey complete with grunting and beating my chest. The metaphor: I'm a mindless conformist—monkey see, monkey do. In contrast, my female counterparts were bold and preternaturally spunky.

In my current role, I'm a sleazebag guy manipulating three women to think I'm engaged to all three. Of course, they, with a low-income woman's help, triumph over me, reducing me to a whimpering moron.

The play was a full two hours long and we all gave our hearts out. Far beyond just memorizing our lines, we milked our roles for maximum laughs and pathos. I thought I played my role well, being, as appropriate, sleazy, befuddled, or hysterical.

Yet after the curtain fell, they were all so matter-of-fact. We had just completed a successful, demanding run. Were they all really so blasé or were they still acting?

They certainly were no more than flatly polite to me. They maintained that affect throughout the two hours that it took for us to tear down the set—one of the myriad unglamorous parts of being an actor.

In any case, when I finally got back in my car, I swore, no more acting. Of course, I've said that the last few times.

David, Episode 1: Disinformation

pxfuel, CC0

"This monorail, the MonsterRail, is the world's largest. It is the culmination of a decade of effort and yes, money to move people out of their cars and into mass transit—Oh, I'm supposed to say just 'transit.' MonsterRail will be a beacon shining the world onto a greener, cleaner future!"

The audience erupted, at least in part because the mayor's advance team recruited her passionate supporters and because the CEOs and spouses of the MonsterRail's suppliers and contractors were invited, down to the CEO of Apogee Bolt, David Hayashi and his wife Amelia. The media was, well, onboard but rampant accusations of media bias precluded their cheering, especially when the cameras were rolling.

The mayor cut the ribbon and the dignitaries boarded MonsterRail. It climbed the 172 feet so it provides a view of the city and the ocean. Amelia said to her husband, "David, it's so quiet!" David smiled, "It's all because of our bolts," and they giggled.

As MonsterRail rounded the first curve, they heard a crack, then another, and another, and suddenly, MonsterRail rolled over and before anyone had time to scream, it plummeted the 172 feet amid screaming and wailing. David had given Amelia the window seat and that turned out to be her undoing. The impact smashed the window and thrust Amelia's head out and when MonsterRail then rolled over, it crushed her head.

The joint report from the National Transportation Safety Board, National Highway Traffic Safety Administration, Federal Highway Administration, Federal Railroad Administration, and Federal Transit Administration determined the cause: inferior Chinese bolts, used, rusted bolts that were supposed to be used only in non-load-bearing applications such as to hold up railroad ties in residential backyard staircases. The sole supplier: Apogee Bolt.

> *Apogee Bolt's proposal made clear it would use top-tier, German- or Japanese-made titanium bolts. The ones used on MonsterRail were grossly inferior, used, rusted pot iron Chinese bolts that were plated to look new and excellent. They even had a sticker with the premier Japanese bolt manufacturer's logo on each one.*

Pending trial, David Hayashi was released on $3,000,000 bail.

The media loved it. Anti-corporate? Perfect! For a week, the Apogee Bolt story remained front-page news.

David tried to visit the crash site but the guards refused to let him onto the site of an investigation. So he took pictures using a telephoto lens, which confirmed that the bolts indeed were sure to break.

David thought, "We would never sell such bolts, even for a backyard. How the hell did it happen?" He talked with the warehouse manager and all the warehouse workers. None could explain it. The only person David had hadn't talked with was the night watchman.

11 PM, when the watchman's shift began, David showed up. The watchman looked surprised and scared. So David pushed, "How did those bolts get into our warehouse. Tell me!" And the watchman did: "A guy wearing an Apogee Bolt badge said that he was there to replace the bolts for MonsterRail with higher-quality ones. I was skeptical so he showed me a sample. It was really shiny—It looked great. Still, I was going to say no and tell him to come back tomorrow, but he said that the bolts had to be ready to ship first thing in the morning and he'd give me $100 for my trouble. So I said okay."

David went to the media but none of them ran with the story. They assumed David was doing a PR campaign to defend himself and to bias potential jurors. A few media outlets did a quick investigation but dropped it…except for one small newspaper, the New York Sun, which was at the brink of going bankrupt. Its editor authorized a Hail Mary, giving most of the paper's remaining money to a young, aggressive, let-the-chips-fall journalist to find out the truth.

And she did— The Russian government had wanted defective Chinese bolts to be used in the high-visibility MonsterRail so that when it crashed, future projects would more likely go to the Russian steel industry, which was struggling despite the boost from the Ukraine war. So the Russians sent an operative wearing overalls and a phony Apogee Bolt employee badge in a truck with a phony Apogee Bolt sign that was full of those dangerous bolts.

The Department of Justice was reluctant to drop the charges against David and Apogee Bolt's other executives —That would embarrass the DOJ. But when the major media finally picked up the story that the Sun broke, the DOJ was forced to drop the charges.

David spent much of the next month at his wife's grave.

David, Episode 2: Reservations

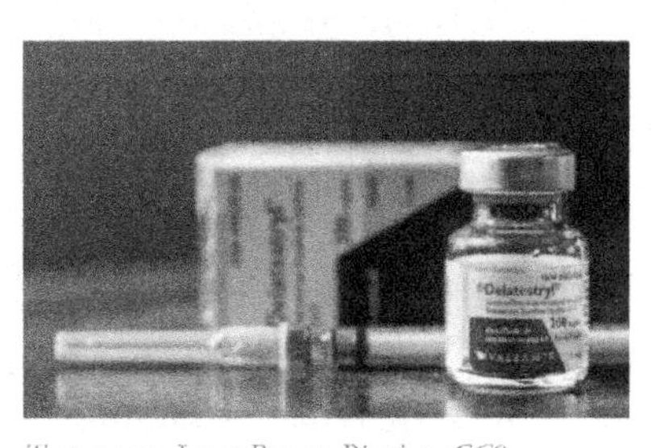

Testosterone, James Ronan, Pixabay, CC0

"Stop telling me what I can't do. I'm 21!"

"You're acting like a child and so I need to treat you like one," replied her father, David.

"You want me to be like you? Work 70 hours a week selling bolts, including the ones that made MonsterRail crash?"

"You know as well as I do that the Russians snuck into our warehouse and substituted defective Chinese bolts for our excellent ones."

"The main point is your crazy 70-hour workweeks. We aren't human doings; we're human beings."

"Human beings don't smoke dope every day, do no work but just complain about 'fucked capitalism' or brag about how non-binary you are!"

"How dare you! I'll have you know that I've started sexual reassignment hormones."

"Did college do this to you? Is it because your mother died in the MonsterRail crash? Is it the damn American culture? Japanese kids don't do these things! They're responsible human beings."

"You just don't get it, dinosaur. This isn't Han Dynasty Japan or yes, America's 1950s clueless, capitalist, racist, sexist, homophobic America. Yeah, you're a dinosaur. Excuse me, I have to take my testosterone."

And head high, Mari strutted out, slamming the door.

David couldn't sleep and the next morning, he crawled to work wondering if his daughter was right. He looked around. The managers were mostly Chinese, Japanese, Indian, and white, the warehouse people mainly Black and Latino. But he thought, "I swear, we hire and promote on the merits. But is Mari right that we need to do even more? That we need to sacrifice merit for equity? I cannot, I cannot believe that but can I be sure?

"And does the world really need Apogee Bolt? There are plenty other bolt manufacturers. Sure, our bolts are good and fairly priced, but so what? Is this what David Hayashi should be doing? Should I march with Mari? Should I quit and open a cafe?"

That night, David shared his reservations with Mari whereupon she whispered, "I was lying about the sexual reassignment."

He asked, "Mari, want to go out to dinner, maybe veggie burgers?" She replied, "How about Japanese?"

David, Episode 3: Resigned

PixforFree.org, CC0

David and Vicky giggled as they rose from his office sofa. He admired her as she put her clothes back on.

They worked hard to avoid giving away their affair. After all, he was the CEO and she was his admin.

David's infatuation with Vicky had dulled his dissatisfaction with her work. She tried, she really did, but her reasoning was too often a beat off. For example, she wouldn't realize that he'd need a break between a contentious meeting with the union and his next appointment. She would occasionally screen out a call that she should have let through. She'd too often send a routine email on to him rather than answer it herself.

After the fog of infatuation had lifted, so did David's rose-colored glasses. After all, he worked 60+ hours a week and her job was to help. Net, he thought she was barely a neutral.

He gave her feedback, first gently, then firmly, and finally, the affair notwithstanding, he felt he needed to put her on an improvement plan, which she correctly recognized as CYA preceding termination.

She was afraid of losing her well-paying, prestigious job—administrative assistant to the CEO. So she consulted a lawyer, who said that even though the affair was consensual, she had a claim because of the CEO/admin power imbalance.

Her lawyer asked if, to avoid it being he said/she said, she could get a couple of her female friends at work to say that that wasn't an isolated incident but that David had created a hostile environment.

Vicky let the process server into David's office. The server said, "David Hayashi?" As soon as he nodded, she dropped a manila envelope on his desk that was stamped in red, "You have been served."

David read the Order to Appear, stormed out of his office, and seethed at Vicky, "You stupid gold-digger!"

The case settled out of court —Vicky got $100,000, a transfer to a position as the admin for a female vice president, and that she'd be guaranteed that job for at least two years.

David was dispirited and much moreso when the board forced him to resign: "We can't risk media blowback or the company getting boycotted by the feminist community."

David searched hard for another job but every application was ghosted except for one—"You're eminently qualified but we can't take the risk of hiring someone who was forced to resign because of accusations of sexual impropriety and of having created a hostile work environment." So at age 51, David was forced into retirement.

He had to give up his lovely condo—Not only had he now been unemployed for a year, his company stock had collapsed even though the defective-bolt claim turned out to be Russian disinformation.

David's daughter tried to be supportive. "Dad, hire a PR firm. And get your supporters to storm the shareholders meeting." "Mari, I appreciate your support but that's just not me. I need to accept today's world and be grateful I won't be homeless."

Now what? David considered writing a memoir but decided it would be too egotistical, besides almost no one would read it. Hike the Pacific Coast Trail? Too much, even part of the trail.

He decided to take up photography. He started just by taking pictures on his phone of anything that seemed interesting: a dandelion sticking up from the concrete, a pink sunset, and then a tired old man. That was it—He'd take un-posed portraits of retired executives. He'd ask them to curate their portrait: "What do you see when you look at yourself?" One of them lamented, "I can't believe how old I've gotten." Another said, "I can see why I'm invisible to women."

David's reaction to his selfie: "I tried, so hard. Maybe things will get better." But not really believing it, he got himself a glass of wine.

Odd Man Out, Episode 1: The Prom

Collagist, Pixabay, CC0

The prom was coming up. Not going would be final confirmation that I'm a loser.

I can't stand how I look. Let me try combing my hair with the part on the right side. Terrible. On the left side? Worse. No part? Maybe. Tousled like the guys the girls like? I'll try that. Or maybe it's my smile. Try bigger? Too big. Smaller? I guess.

I thought that a girl named Margie was cute. In class, without thinking, I intercepted a note that she was passing to someone. I opened it. "I have my Santa Claus now—my period." I was so embarrassed. I gave it back to her, said I was sorry, but she turned away.

In the lunchroom, I looked at Rebecca—I guess for too long. She got right in my face and said, "Stop it. You're creepy."

I decided to go the prom by myself. I thought that at least a few other kids would come alone, but I was wrong. I was the only one. I stood there and watched—Guys got so close to the girls. There was a girl who was standing alone and I asked her to dance but she said she was with a girl who had gone to the bathroom.

I went to the bathroom to look again at my hair and to try out other smiles.

I stood some more and then a chaperone asked me to dance. That made me feel like even more of a loser. I thanked her but said I just couldn't.

I overheard some kids talking about an after-party. I looked one of them Keith—a popular guy—in the eye but he didn't see me or maybe he looked away. Anyway, I sure didn't get invited to any after-party.

I left the prom early and stared again at my mirror. I hate myself. I'm going to play some more Worlds of Warcraft.

Odd Man Out, Episode 2: The Dorm

I somehow knew things wouldn't get better.

Collagist, Pixabay, CC0

My roommate was going to be a guy named Dirk. Who would name their kid, Dirk? Probably a jerk. I laughed at my stupid rhyme but then realized I was only half joking.

When Dirk showed up, he *was* a jerk. He acted like he owned the room. He dumped his stuff onto the floor and hung a huge poster of a hunky guy and a half-naked girl on a motorcycle. Practically the first words out of Dirk's mouth were, "I scored this fucking amazing weed. Want some?"

I didn't mean to answer like a mouse but I peeped, "Thanks. Maybe some other time." His answer, "Dude, we're roomies. It's the sharing culture. Like all-in, we, together, there's no I in team. Right?" As he hung his stuff in the closet, he pulled out my gray jeans. "Dude, these would like totally go with my black shirt. Okay if I borrow it sometime?" I murmured, "Sure."

I knew it had to be an act but still. Some people put on an act for their whole lives.

Dirk said, "I met these two amazing girls at orientation. I'm going out with one tonight—I hope you don't mind if I bring her here afterward." I didn't know what to say, so I said nothing. I guess he sensed my reluctance so he said, "Hey, how about I set you up with the other one? Hey, you can take your pick. I'll take the other one. Who knows, maybe we'll both get lucky." I desperately wanted to say no but I didn't want to seem like the total dork I was, the total dork I am. So I muttered, "Okay." He said, "Cool."

With his black shirt, he wore, yup, my gray jeans. The thought of his dick, well his underwear, next to my pants' crotch? Ugh!

The four of us just walked around campus and when we got back to the dorm, he stopped in front of a red, chrome-tricked-out Harley. He asked his girl, "Wanna ride on my (and he waited to let the sexual double entendre sink in) bike?

She laughed, "Will we *all* get a ride?" Dirk laughed, "Could be! Hey, let's forget about the motorcycle ride for now. Just come up to my room, I mean *our* room." The two girls looked at each other, suppressed a giggle, and the four of us went upstairs.

We sat around awhile talking about nothing and then he started to kiss his girl. My girl giggled and looked at me. It felt wrong, way too fast, and I didn't even think I liked her but I somehow felt I had to kiss her. It got exciting, fast, but I was nervous. Could I get it up? I did and then I lost it. I felt like dying.

To make matters worse, Dirk and especially his girl, were making wild noises. When it subsided, he said, "Hey, want to do switchzees?!" I whispered no. The two of them giggled and went at it again. I decided I'd never date again.

Fast forward to the end of the semester. I had gotten my parents to swing for a single room so I didn't have to deal with Dirk. But I didn't make any friends and I didn't date. Also, I didn't like a lot of my classes—Most were hard or irrelevant. Dirk had given me a baggie of "primo stuff" as an apology that we didn't work out, and I started smoking it, and more often.

I finally opened up to my dad and said I'd love to drop out of college but knew I'd be unemployable except for a McJob. He asked if I wanted to just take a break and take a job in a plant nursery—He knew I always liked plants. I was afraid that if I dropped out, I'd never go back to college but end up with a life carrying sacks of compost, but I said I'd try it.

Odd Man Out, Episode 3: My Fair Lady

Even though I hated college so much that I dropped out, the first thing I saw when I first came to work at Growing Up plant nursery made me think I shouldn't have dropped out. What did I see? Staff carrying bags of compost into little old ladies' cars.

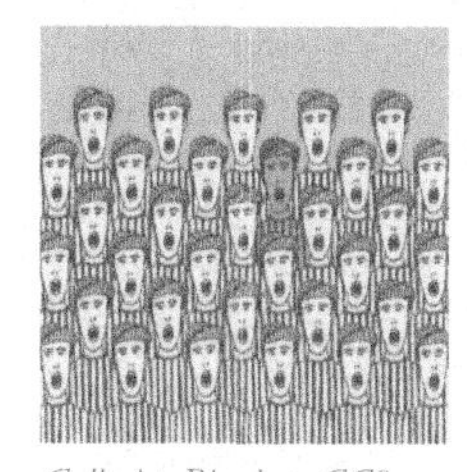

Collagist, Pixabay, CC0

Because the staff didn't know me, the owner asked me to spend my first day as a secret shopper. I'd learn what the nursery was like from the customer's perspective and be able to report back on how the staff was doing. The owner said he was worried that his nursery was struggling while a similar one nearby had just expanded.

I noticed that the staff didn't upsell. If someone bought a rose bush, they didn't ask if they might also need fertilizer or pruning shears. But worse, I noticed staff taking very long breaks, hiding in the shed. Worst of all, when I bought a plant, gave the cashier a $20 bill and acted like I wasn't paying attention, she gave me too little change.

When I reported back, the owner said, "I don't understand. I pay more than my competitor, I train my staff well, praise often and criticize sparingly. Why are they doing this to me?" He asked me to visit the competing nursery, The Greenery, and see if I could figure out what he was doing wrong.

The staff at The Greenery was very different. They all were working hard yet seemed content and eager to help customers. One staffer, Naomi, seemed particularly good and she was around my age, so I went up to her and said I wanted to buy a tomato plant. She asked me a few questions and then, on her phone, used ChatGPT to find a couple recommended varieties. She had one in stock, sold me that, and yes, asked if I needed fertilizer or a tomato cage.

I asked Naomi how she got hired and she said, "The boss doesn't rely on ads—There's too much lying on applications. He asks us and his friends to refer people who they think would be great. That works well. But to tell you the truth, I'm ready for a promotion. Unfortunately, my supervisor isn't going anywhere."

I called the owner of Growing Up from there, told about how they hire and about Naomi. He said, "Great, from now on, I'll hire that way, and would you put her on the phone?" He chatted with her and said, "Pete said you're ready for a promotion but can't get one at The Greenery.

Might you be interested in being the supervisor here at Growing Up? I can give you a 20 percent raise over what you're making now." She was delighted.

As I was watching Naomi, it struck me that although she was around 30 pounds overweight, a lot for someone in her early 20s, I still found her attractive.

The owner wanted me to learn the business from the bottom up, so when I started actually working at Growing Up, I was doing lots of schlepping of bags, and Naomi was my boss.

I'd try to time my breaks for when Naomi might be there, and we talked. First it was just plants, then family, hobbies, and so on, but finally, she said that her main interest is to lose weight: "I've tried and I've tried and I'll lose a few pounds but always gain it back and more."

Partly because I was attracted to her despite her weight and partly because I liked the idea of mentoring someone, I said, "How about my coaching you?" She said, "Kind of like Henry Higgins coaching Eliza in My Fair Lady. Let's try it."

I started by asking her what approach might work for her. She said that she had to throw out all the sweets in her apartment and then stay conscious, with every bite, whether she needs that next bite.

We agreed that once a week, she'd take a picture of herself on the scale and show it to me. She said that knowing she'd have to do that would help motivate her.

She lost eight pounds but slowly gained it back. I guess the novelty of the mentorship wore off, or maybe she needs a professional weight-loss coach, or something.

But like I said, I found her attractive even at 30 pounds overweight. And I liked her more somehow because she tried to lose weight but, like most people, couldn't keep it off. That made her more human. So I asked her on a date.

We're still dating and, last month, we took a step forward. We decided to ask the owner if we could open a little cafe inside the nursery's houseplant area. Staff and customers could sign up to give little talks about some aspect of gardening, and we'd sell coffee and warm muffins that we'd make in the staff kitchen. Perhaps because the cafe was easy to set up, even though it's rarely crowded, it's making a little money and we're having fun. We've even talked about getting married but agreed for now to move in together and try a one-month renewable "marriage" contract. I guess we're like our nursery's name: Growing Up.

Odd Man Out: Episode 4: Compost

Alamy, CC0

I tried to deny the significance of having developed a paunch by age 23. I would, for example, rationalize, "I still can easily lift sacks of compost to put in customers' cars." I suppressed that overweight's toll usually doesn't become apparent until later.

I liked my job for other reasons. First, my having struggled in college didn't matter on my job at the plant nursery. All that mattered was my reliability, work ethic, and that I was low-maintenance. School just wasn't my thing. In addition to the social-life problem, the school psychologists labeled me various things—dyslexic, ADHD, auditory processing deficit, even developmental delay, what used to be called mental retardation. But bottom line, I couldn't understand and didn't believe it was worth struggling to try to understand literature, let alone quadratic equations.

I also liked that I could play little games as I worked, like arranging the plants in order from nicest to worst and rating customers by their demeanor. I also loved seeing the new hybrids and reading their labels that while inflated, offered hope that this rose, this peach, this tomato will indeed be the best yet.

When Naomi got promoted to store manager, I was offered her job as supervisor, including a nice raise. I was afraid to take it— I liked my current job and never felt I was the manager type. But the gurus and motivational speakers in the media always urged aspiring, thinking big, "Dream it and you can do it!" Plus, I thought about how cool it would be to tell my friends and especially my parents that I got a promotion—They had relentlessly pushed me to go to college because "without college, you'll never have more than a McJob."

But my instinct was right. I hated the new job. First off, there was a lot to learn—like plant knowledge, inventory management, and employee rights. That was hard. Even harder was dealing with the people. Those ratings I gave to customers often turned out to be right. For example, the haughty ones often were that way and they got to me. One said, "You don't know- how to fertilize citrus?! That's why I'm willing to pay so much more for plants than at Wal-Mart— to get expertise. I need your supervisor."

I was no happier with the employees. For example, some would come in late or no-show, sometimes without even calling in. And when I called them on it, they'd make some excuse that likely was BS. Yet I couldn't call them a liar and I wasn't confident enough to fire them. So I just burned inside.

After my first day as supervisor, I came home exhausted and hating myself. My parents said, "Give it time. It's just your first day." I gave it a week but finally told Naomi that I needed my old job back.

I was happier, even when, maybe especially when, I was carrying sacks of compost.

Odd Man Out: Episode 5: Weed

On the bus, people move away from me. The smell from the compost bags I loaded into customers' cars stayed on my clothes.

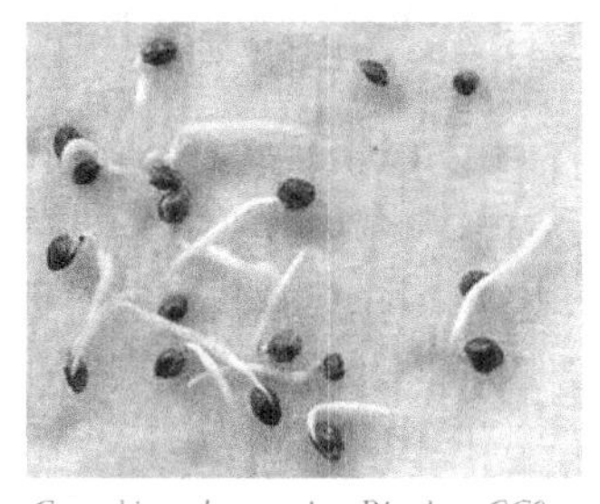

Cannabis seeds sprouting, Pixabay, CC0

One day, I got home, checked the mail, and stopped when I saw the envelope from the property manager. "Oh shit." I had decided to not pay last month's rent because I was dying for my splurge—a pizza and an 1/8th of weed. But now I'd have to pay the rent or they'd start with the eviction warnings.

The next day, I was in the nursery's propagation shed when the stereotype of an old hippie stoner appeared—Iron Maiden t-shirt with big belly sticking out, wild hair, a cross hanging from his pierced ear. I said, "I'm sorry. Thia shed is for employees only."

The hippie said, "I know, but I need a favor. My name is Kush. I make a few bucks selling weed but if I have to buy the stuff, I barely break even. But when I try to grow it from seed, I can't make it work....but." He pulled a baggie with a wet paper towel and just-sprouted marijuana seeds in it. "These are Ghost Train Haze—ultra primo. Just grow them for a month until they're bigger—You work in a nursery; you know what do to—I can grow them from there."

I said, "No way."

Kush said, "How's 200 bucks?"

No.

"350, final offer. 100 now and 250 in a month when I pick up."

I thought of my rent and even pizza, and breathed.

"Cool" and with that, Kush put the seed-laden paper towel and a hundred-dollar bill on the potting table and started out.

"Hey, come back here!" But Kush kept sauntering out.

I was tempted to pocket the 100 and throw away the seeds but thought about what Kush might do to him if in a month there were no pot plants. So I planted them in a flat and put it in the least noticeable spot.

Two weeks later, my luck ran out. No one except me ever came to the propagation shed. But that day, the owner was touring his sister who was visiting from out of town. The owner asked me to demonstrate propagation. My heart pounded as I was setting up and they were wandering the shed. The owner's sister stopped, giggled, pointed to the flat of marijuana, and exclaimed, "I didn't know you guys grew weed!" I was fired on the spot.

When I told my parents, they focused less on the weed and more on the chance to push me yet again to try college. I argued that I hated school, was bad at school, but finally agreed to take the Intro to Horticulture course at the community college.

But that was the same for me as high school and the other college. I thought, "Why do I need to learn the Krebs cycle and insecticides' chemical method of action to grow and sell plants?" That all seemed both irrelevant and too hard, and after a week, I dropped out.

I couldn't bear to tell my parents, at least without giving them some good news, so I applied for more nursery jobs. But the only one that was hiring was Wal-Mart. The job was okay and because at Wal-Mart, customers not staff loaded their cars with compost, I felt good that at least he didn't come home smelly.

Odd Man Out, Episode 6: A ChatGPT Hallucination

Jeff, who had been forced into early retirement because of a perceived racial slight, shuffled into Wal-Mart. "I'm wasting my time with this gardening shit, just waiting to die."

Antonio Mendes da Silva / MMSH CC 4.0

I, who had been fired from the Growing Up plant nursery for growing marijuana and now work in the Wal-Mart nursery, stared at a rose. I wasn't just admiring it, I was wondering if the rose and the $20-an-hour Wal-Mart job would be the best I'd get from life.

Half-heartedly, Jeff asked me, "Do you have a fragrant yellow rose bush?"

I admitted, "I don't know but let's see what the Internet says." I learned that tactic from Naomi, my former boss at Growing Up nursery. ChatGPT confidently recommended the Peace rose but having read plant labels and smelling the roses when he worked at Growing Up, knew that Peace had little fragrance and told that to Jeff. Jeff replied, "Ah, another ChatGPT hallucination." So I Google-searched "fragrant yellow roses" and the Sunsprite variety came up. I recalled that one being very fragrant and said, "We don't have Sunsprite here but Growing Up Nursery does. I used to work there."

Jeff was impressed. Unlike some employees who would have faked it, I admitted that I didn't know the answer and didn't just accept the ChatGPT answer when my experience indicated the ChatGPT was wrong. Plus, I was willing to do the ethical thing—send a customer to another nursery. So Jeff asked me, "How'd you like to do a little rose project for me? I have about 20 rose bushes. How about you buy Sunsprite, plant it at my home, fertilize my roses, and cut the dead blooms? I'll pay you $30 an hour." I smiled.

After finishing the project, Jeff invited me in for a beer. I was shy and didn't know what to say, so Jeff filled the silence by describing what he used to do: fundraise for a nonprofit. I asked, "How do you fundraise?"

Jeff was pleased at my curiosity and besides, Jeff was eager to share what he had learned over a lifetime. So he started candidly, "#1: Fundraising is sales but it's easier than sales because people are suspicious of salespeople but they don't think of fundraisers as salespeople." Jeff shared a number of nuggets. I was fascinated but said, "I could never do that. I'm not a people person." Jeff responded, "That's okay. People-people tend to talk too much and that hurts the chances of a sale."

I left Jeff's house mulling and decided to apply to wholesale rose nurseries as a salesman, and one hired me. Not surprisingly, that company put Growing Up Nursery on my prospect list. There, I told my former boss, Naomi, how her having modeled good salesmanship impressed me. She placed a large order, including extra Sunsprites. And I thought, "Maybe I'm not doomed to $20 an hour at Wal-Mart. Thank you, ChatGPT for hallucinating."

Odd Man Out Episode 7: Living On

A rose hybridized by Marty Nemko that is currently under test.

I learned a lot of uncomfortable truths about roses from selling to the nurseries. Their buyers would complain, for example, "Roses need constant spraying—Perfect for Saddam Hussein." and, "Planting a rose bush requires a weightlifter, not a grandma."

But I had grown to love the rose bush, that romantic flower factory. So I tried hybridizing—crossing varieties to create roses healthy enough that they don't need to be sprayed and small enough that even grandma could plant them in a window box.

I had read that the odds of creating a commercial rose were one in 10,000 and that finding that one requires a few years of diligent work and then a few more to build stock—It takes that long create enough plants to be worth a marketing campaign. 20,000 plants is the magic number.

It took me 13 years but finally I came up with a miracle: a gorgeous red produced in quantity on a glossy-foliaged compact plant that shrugs at disease. I named it, *I Love You.* And for the past four years, the grower, Flores Flower Farms of San Joaquin, California sent me annual reports.

When I got the report that the stock had grown to 20,000 plants, I flew cross-country to San Francisco and then made the long drive to see his field of *I Love You* rose bushes. When I arrived, the owner, Victor, shocked me: "I am so sorry. There was a fire and all your roses were destroyed. I'll show you." And Victor showed me a huge field of destroyed rose plants.

For me, that was the last straw. I had had a life of setbacks: career, romantic, and after my second round of chemotherapy, the doctors didn't think that more torture would be worth it. So I joined suicide's fastest-growing demographic: middle-aged white men.

It turns out that Flores Flower Farms, quickly seeing that the *I Love You* rose was a breakthrough that would earn millions of dollars, he moved the field of plants far from the road so that when, sooner or later, I came to review the field, I'd be shown a different field of rose bushes: one of useless rose varieties that Flores deliberately burned for just that purpose.

Flores Flower Farms did make millions on *I Love You* but my legacy lives on in countless blooms and happy grandmothers.

Odd Man Out, Episode 8: "I Did It for The Family!"

Malcolm Manners, Wikimedia, CC 2.0

Victor felt guilty, and with good reason. He had contributed to my suicide. At the end of a hard life, I had finally hybridized a breakthrough rose, *I Love You,* and had Victor's Flores Farms build stock so it could be commercially introduced. Victor realized *I Love You's* multi-million-dollar potential. So, by showing me a field of burned roses (not *I Love You* but an inferior variety) he got me to believe that all the *I Love You* bushes had burned.

Victor suppressed thoughts of his theft and causing my suicide, and just went on with his farming. Yes, he had considered using the ill-begotten money for profit-sharing and charity but ended up spending most of it on his family: the diamond cocktail ring his wife had been craving, the Lincoln Navigator SUV he wanted, and yes, putting aside money for his son Anthony's college education.

But the day came when Victor could no longer suppress his guilt. Anthony, soon to start his senior year of high school, was starting summer vacation and wanted to make some money. Rather than work fast-food, Anthony asked if he could work on his father's farm. Victor was flattered and on Anthony's first day of work, toured him around, including the hidden field where the *I Love You* rose bushes were growing —-Even though Victor had no right to those roses, he wanted to show off "my greatest plant."

Anthony asked, "But you don't hybridize roses. Who did?" Victor lied and deflected with humor, "Oh I do lots of things you don't know about." That deterred Anthony for the moment.

But a few days later, Anthony was helping to clear the field of inferior rose bushes that his father had burned. Anthony thought, "Why did dad never mention anything about a burned field? And why did the burning stop exactly at the field's perimeter? Anthony concluded that the fire must have been deliberately set. And why had the *I Love You* rose bushes been in a hidden field? If the I *Love You rose* was his dad's proudest achievement, wouldn't he have planted it prominently?

Anthony asked his dad about it and Victor worked hard to maintain his salesman's plastered pleasantness. But when Anthony pushed, and pushed, Victor's face reddened. And now, Anthony was sure that he understood: "So that's why that rose breeder Pete committed suicide. You caused it!" And Victor screamed, "I did it for the family, for you!" whereupon Anthony slugged his dad and seethed, "I will not use your blood money to go to college. What I'm tempted to do is go to the cops." And Anthony stormed out.

Odd Man Out: Episode 9: Mite

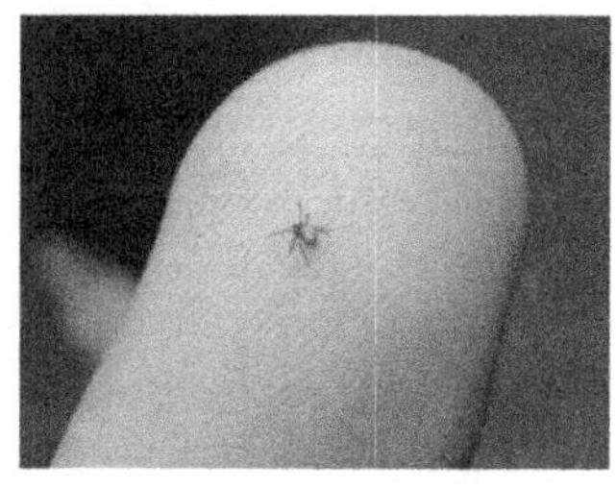
Brennan Palzoid, Flickr, CC 2.0

Anthony had just discovered his father's having stolen millions of dollars from the inventor of the breakthrough *I Love You* rose bush. Anthony threatened his father, "I'm going to the cops!"

Terrified of a long prison sentence and having to give up his Flores Farms, his father muttered, "Anthony, I'll give you the whole field of *I Love You* rose bushes and you can grow them and keep all the profits—Start a nonprofit if you like. That way, good can come from my bad and I won't spend my life in jail."

Anthony knew that whitewashing wasn't exactly saintly, but he nodded.

It was July and the one-year-old bushes needed another year until they were saleable. It was an inspiring time for Anthony to start growing that field of roses—It was covered with velvety, classically formed red roses on compact glossy plants. They almost looked like miniature Christmas trees with perfectly spaced ruby ornaments.

To avoid Anthony changing his mind and turning him in, his father taught him everything he knew about rose growing, for example, the rule of fertilizing: St. Patrick's Day, Memorial Day, Independence Day, and Labor Day, and that there was no need to buy expensive rose fertilizer—General-purpose fertilizer at half the price is fine. His father explained that the miracle of the *I Love You* rose bush is that beyond being gorgeous, unlike most rose bushes, its leaves stayed healthy without spraying and that saves money and effort. Of course, Anthony, a Gen Z'er, was more impressed that *I Love You* would be an eco-rose.

Anthony entered *I Love You* in the International Rose Society's competition for Rose of the Year, sending plants to the testing sites all over the world.

Fall came and Anthony harvested the rose blossoms to sell on the roadside stand in front of the nursery. Then the bushes went into dormancy so in spring, they could be reborn.

May came and *I Love You* won Rose of the Year. Immediately, orders poured in from wholesale nurseries—$430,000 just in the first month.

Growers ship roses when they're dormant—December and January. Unfortunately, the July before they were to be shipped, most of the leaves on the *I Love You* bushes started curling and turning gray. Anthony called his father out to the field—He took one look and the diagnosis was clear—spider mites. That field, inland from Flores Farm's other fields, was hotter, drier, and not windy— perfect for spider mites. He said, "Spray the field with the stuff in the shed labeled 'miticide.' It became illegal—It's a little worse for the environment I guess, but it works so much better than the stuff the government still allows, so I've kept some." Anthony, having become an environmentalist from his high school courses and watching TV said, "Can't we use the legal stuff?" His father replied, "Maybe. It's riskier, but maybe."

Anthony and the farm workers applied the legal miticide as directed: every ten days. But August came and the leaves were grayer and more curled, and the telltale webs on the leaves' underside were thicker. Anthony called University Agricultural Extension and they said, "No guarantee but as the weather cools and the air gets moister, you should be okay, probably." The "probably" scared Anthony. He was tempted to try the now-illegal miticide but because of Extension's cautious optimism, his wanting to walk his environmentalist talk, and not wanting to break the law, he decided to stay with the weaker stuff.

In September, the leaves started defoliating. He called Extension again but it offered no solutions. And by November, when it was time to start harvesting the bushes to fill the orders, three-quarters of the plants had been weakened enough that they were unsaleable.

Dispirited, Anthony said, "Dad, I just can't deal with this. How about you take back the land and the roses and just give me enough money for college?"

His father agreed, Anthony enrolled for the spring semester at the University of California at Merced, and picked Computer Science as his major—Everyone was saying that the future is in computers, especially AI.

Anthony was scared that college, especially at the University of California, would be hard, and he was right. Before he'd be allowed even to take the prerequisites for the computer science major, he had to take calculus. Its syllabus said the course would "emphasize analyzing data by means of linear, quadratic, polynomial, logarithmic, exponential and trigonometric functions." (That is taken from an actual UC Merced calculus syllabus.) That was enough to scare Anthony but the first class session terrified him. Practically the first words out of the professor's mouth, "You know, the product rule for differentiation" made Anthony's heart pound. "You know? I don't know!" (That quote is from an actual first lecture of a UC Merced calculus course)

Anthony also took Introduction to Sociology, which he could comprehend, and it radicalized him to do more for farm workers. Looking at all the courses ahead of him and that only 72% graduated even if they took six years, Anthony decided to drop out and try to start a nonprofit on behalf of farm workers.

But what should his nonprofit's focus be: tutoring farmworkers' kids? Teaching juvenile hall teens to grow roses? Anthony decided, in light of his father's lapse, to teach ethics to farm workers.

Anthony had to get a grant affiliated with a nonprofit and that took 13 long applications until he got one. Then, Anthony had problems getting farmworkers to show up for the workshops. Most of the farm workers had after-work activities they understandably prioritized, like spending time with their kids. Or they just were tired from work. Anthony is wondering if he should go back to college.

All because of a mite.

"I Wanted My Husband to Die"

I always flirted a lot but was married, so I didn't cheat. Well, I did once, but it was no big deal.

The problem was our marriage. You see, I'm a normal, fun-loving person. I love

The Advocacy Project, Flickr, CC 2.0

travel, dancing, doing things with family. My husband liked none of that. Mainly he just liked to work.

And when we conversed and I would talk about normal topics—friends, family, pop culture, spirituality, clothes, decorating, cooking, gardening, even current events—it was clear that he just wanted to escape to his bedroom… to work.

He was just like his father. He didn't work for the money. He'd do it for free. He'd *pay* to work. Work was just what he cared about. He actually said, "The meaning of life lies in productivity." And I knew he'd never change.

Of course, I thought about divorcing him but that would have been too painful, especially given who he was: He would have been very hurt and he was very smart. Even if we had started out agreeing to have an amicable do-it-yourself divorce, it would have devolved into a war, with him hiring a killer lawyer and giving him all the ammunition he needs. In defense, I'd hire my killer lawyer and years later, we'd both have been pounded and poorer.

When I was 72, my bad back started to be a real problem. It became hard to bend over and to get in and out of the car. I walked like an old lady. It was a reminder that life's clock was ticking.

A year ago, my husband asked me, "Do you wish I were dead?" Of course, I said no but it got me thinking.

Not long afterward, he had a stroke and said, "I hope I die. I don't want you to have to care for a vegetable." He did become kind of a vegetable. The main reason I didn't put him in a home was that I was afraid my friends would think I was cruel. Maybe I am.

Last week, he died, and today the people who came to the house after the funeral just left. I was good: I put on a sad face, I reminisced, I told them I was grieving. But if I'm honest with you, my main thought is, "How soon can I start to live, even to flirt?"

Hopeless

When I was a kid, on weekends, I'd sleep until 11, sometimes noon. Now, alas, at age 63, I'm getting up at 6 and without an alarm clock.

Wilfredor, Wikimedia, CC

I was forced into early retirement by a Woke manager and now I start my day with a 6:30 walk. I find comfort in taking the same route every day and when I see people's newspapers having been dropped far from their door, I toss them as close as possible to the door without hitting it and so possibly waking the person. If I play shrink with myself, I do it to reassure myself that I'm not a bad person, even if my Woke boss thinks I am.

Well, one morning, a woman about my age, in a ponytail and kimono walked, or I should say limped, out her door. I found her attractive despite or maybe because of her limp—It made me feel less insecure.

She said, "Hi. I'm Mollie. I also get up early. I sit at my window, so I see you every morning. Thank you for tossing my newspaper to the door."

I nodded and she said, "Forgive me but I'm a psychotherapist so I can't resist asking: Am I right that you always seem sad, or maybe it's worried, or even angry?"

"All of the above."

I was sure that would scare her off but she said, "Would you like to come in for a cup of coffee or tea, or even hot chocolate?"

I thought, "She must be lonely but so am I, and she is kind of attractive." She sensed my interest but hesitation, so to push me over the edge, she turned back toward her door and waved for me to follow, and I did.

As I was walking in, I reminded myself to be nice. So often, I'm argumentative and worse, my arguments are often not PC—That's why my woke boss "encouraged" me to take early retirement.

But I couldn't restrain myself for more than a minute. I saw that her dining room table was covered with papers, and TurboTax was on her laptop's screen. I said, "What a pain. We get so little for all our tax dollars and worse, they make us take a week or more of our lives to figure out how much to pay."

She said, "Death and taxes. Inevitable so why not just lie back and enjoy it?" I couldn't believe that a woman would invoke that sexist quip. Even I wouldn't say that.

I tried again to be conspicuously nice, what the French call, politesse. Alas, before long, I was back to my reflexive curmudgeonliness. The city had just ripped up the sidewalk on my street to make it compliant with the Americans with Disabilities Act. I said, "They have money for that but not for the police to come for any of the countless smash-and-grabs and catalytic converter thefts?!"

She said, "Even as a psychotherapist, I know that changing people is very hard, let alone in your personal life, but how'd you like me to try to get you to see our glasses as half full?

Alas, after our fourth date, in which she made dinner for me and had taken an hour to clean up, I snarked, "I see you're planning to use your kitchen floor to perform surgery." She sighed and not out of offense. "I've failed. I knew I shouldn't try to change you."

I replied, "I'm the one who failed. I always fail with people. I think of myself as a good person but although I try, I really try to be nice, I can't sustain it." And I got teary.

She came to me, took my hand, and walked me to her bedroom.

Coloring Inside the Lines

So many self-help gurus, celebrities, movies, books, and TV shows urge us to color outside the lines.

Raka C., Pixabay, Free to reuse

Yet I've resisted. Whether by temperament or choice, probably a combination, I've generally colored inside the lines. I do that not just because it's safer but because I believe that lines usually have been created for good reason and perhaps revised to make them even better, having stood the test of time and of consensus, even of protest. So I have always believed that I'm more likely to be happy if I at least default to coloring inside the lines.

As a child, I colored inside the lines literally. My mother kept the butterfly I colored-in on the fridge for weeks. My friend's butterfly had jags that extended randomly outside the lines. I thought he spoiled the butterfly.

In high school, I did what was assigned. For example, when we were told to write three reasons John Kennedy was a good president, I did it. But my friend convinced the teacher to let him, instead, write three reasons Johnny Carson is a good comedian. I believe that my friend would have gotten more out of the regular assignment.

I followed the advice that we got at college-student orientation. I didn't drink or do drugs, well a little. I didn't fall behind in my classes and did get involved in a few of the time-honored extracurriculars they suggested: I wrote for the student newspaper, joined the future businesspersons club, and went on the college's study-abroad summer trip.

I married a well-adjusted woman who had a good job, and we put a few hundred dollars a month in an S&P 500 fund for a few years until we could comfortably afford a modest home in a fairly-priced, safe suburb.

I stayed with the same company for much of my career, having gotten a few small promotions. I kept learning, focusing on things that would make me a better employee.

When I retired, I redid the backyard by copying my favorite award-winning garden that I found with a Google search.

I've just finished writing my will, leaving my modest estate to my wife and kids, and some to charity.

I'm glad I've colored within the lines. Well, most of me is glad.

Turning Down Harvard

At age 6, my parents bought me a Harvard tee shirt. At 10, they took me on a tour there— What I mainly remember was the triple-scoop ice cream cone that they wouldn't let me have.

With permission 18/1 Graphics Studio

In high school, my parents advised me, "Every Ivy has a crew team and few kids are willing to get up early in the morning to row."

I managed to dissuade them: 'Would you get up every morning at 5 to freeze your ass off?" But I took as many Advanced-Placement courses as were offered, even though that sacrificed extracurriculars and teenagers' less formal pleasures. I took the SAT three times.

One of my friends even took up the tuba, explaining: "My college counselor told me that even Harvard's marching band struggles to find tuba players."

In April of my senior year, I got the email from Harvard: "Your notification is at your portal." For two days, I couldn't make myself look at it. Finally, "We are delighted to..."

The message's last sentence: "We invite you to campus on April 24 for Discovery Day, where you'll meet your fellow admits, tour campus, visit classes, and enjoy a celebratory dinner on us."

At Discovery Day, all proceeded as I expected except for the classes. I thought, "Useless shit taught badly. And those teachers are no doubt among Harvard's best. After all, they're trying to get us to come here rather than to Yale or wherever. This is what I worked so hard for? This is what my parents are going to spend $300,000 on?"

The dinner was a buffet, with bar-height tables to encourage meeting and greeting. I told a number of students what I was feeling, for example, "Even though the Harvard diploma is a big deal, it's crazy for smart people to spend yet more time at a student desk, taught esoterica but boringly."

Schooled in the art of politeness, the students listened respectfully and one even paraphrased me: "So, you're wondering whether Harvard is the right choice for you?" My typical response: "If Harvard, education's pinnacle, is like this, I'm wondering whether any college is the best use of our time." Each student took the first opportunity to escape to talk with people who'd cause less cognitive dissonance.

When I returned home, my parents spurted, "So, how did you like The Mighty Crimson?!" I muttered, "Fine" and walked out. And I walked and walked until I had an idea:

I was going to start a charter high school. Instead of a curriculum larded with what students didn't care about, my school's curriculum would emphasize relationships, money, choosing a career, plus what individual students wanted to learn. There would be virtual mornings at which the students, at home, would complete self-paced simulation— and video-rich modules taught online by transformational teachers from all over the world. In the afternoon, the students would come to a community center for extracurriculars.

I submitted my charter-school application to the school district, which didn't respond for a month, and when it did, imposed two pages of requirements that were impossible to meet.

When I told my parents, they resumed the pressure: "Just try Harvard. Otherwise, what are you going to do, work at McDonald's?"

I'm not sure what I'm going to do.

A Modern Odyssey

Jeramey Jannene, Flickr, CC2.0

Hi, my name is Odysseus. Yeah, my parents named me after the Homer character. I guess they were hoping that would inspire me to become brave and clever, but while I was a marksman in the Army, now I just sell beer at USC football games at the Coliseum.

My girlfriend Penelope is the clever one. She's a fundraiser for USC. She set up a friendraising event, where alumni who bought season's tickets to the football games would get to meet some players. The stars blew it off but a few no-names showed.

One of them, Swifty Smith, a second-string kick returner, flirted with her disgustingly. He stared at her breasts and smirked, "I'd like to eat those for dessert!" Because she didn't want to upset him and risk a scene, she politely said, "That's flattering" and she turned to pitch a potential donor.

Unfortunate for her, Swifty, not the sharpest crayon in the box, took that as a sign of encouragement.

I had left to visit the nearby Calypso College when I got a text from Penelope: "I'm walking back to our apartment and I think this football player who was at my fundraiser is . . . Help!!"

Swifty had pulled her into an alley and smirked, "I've seen you do anything for a guy. Jesus, I saw you following your boyfriend around as he was selling beer!"

She pretended to flirt with him and purred, "I'll tell you what? I'll let you have me... under one condition: We meet at the Coliseum when it's empty. You see, I have a thing for guns. The two of you will shoot a rifle from the goal line. The one whose shot lands closest to the 50-yard line can have me.

There, Penelope said, "To be fair to each of you, Swifty, you go first and Odysseus will sit in the stands behind you so you don't get distracted. Then you'll reverse." Swifty nodded, not quite understanding. So Penelope made it easy for him: She handed him a rifle and said, "Just stand here at shoot at the 50-yard line." And I went with the other rifle into the stands behind him.

Swifty focused on getting the rifle's sight on the 50-yard line, whereupon, grateful for my marksmanship, I got a bullseye and he died right on the goal line.

We were grateful the Swifty was a lightweight kick returner and not a 300-pound lineman, so we were able to drag him and drop him down into the Coliseum's giant recycling bin.

The cops could never figure out what happened to Swifty. Not long after, Penelope got a great job offer from Cornell and so we moved to Ithaca, where we lived happily ever after.

At My Child's Little League Game

I wish I didn't have to come to my kid's games. Baseball is so boring and besides, Timmy is one of the worst players on the team.

pxfuel, DMCA, free to reuse

And he's on the bench. Finally, the coach let him pinch-hit and he struck out. The coach said, "Good try." The coach is of the everyone-gets-a-trophy school. Maybe that's okay—They're just kids, but seeds get planted early and later, the plants are hard to root out.

So now, I have to wait there for three more innings and then, being a "good" dad, I gotta find something positive to say to him. But what can I say? He sat on the bench the whole game except when he struck out. What can I say, "Nice try?" "Good going?" "You suck?"

My mind wandered: What if Timmy were good? Well, I'd have to go to more games but, if he were good, I'd be more invested, maybe even enough to coach him. But father coaching son? Risky. I do know I wouldn't be one of the obnoxious parents who browbeat the kid and then tell the coach that the kid should get more playing time.

What if Timmy were in the Special Olympics? I'd feel more supportive. I mean, if he were a paraplegic, it would be bad luck, not his fault.

What if Timmy were a girls' softball player? I dunno. Who has it better today, men or women? I'd get in trouble for even asking the question. I'd get in trouble even for asking, "If a guy checks the woman box, should he have the right to play women's sports because he says "I now identify as a woman?" And what about the people who claim to be non-binary? What if that were Timmy?

The game was over and all I could think of saying to Timmy was, "How nice that you all shake hands with all the winning team's players." But that feels like such a dishonest gesture. That's not real sportsmanship.

As we drove home, I wondered if the lessons Timmy was learning at Little League are a net good? Should I encourage him to try other extracurriculars? Or should I let him do what he wants after school: go to his room and read and listen to music. Yeah, that's what I'll do.

"Hey, Timmy, how'd you like to forget about Little League so you have time to hang out in your room after school and read and listen to music?"

He cried, "I love Little League."

I sighed, "Let's get your ice cream."

Should I Pay the Ransom?

Some parents are lucky. Their teen's rebellion is minor—maybe trying a cigarette, coming home a bit after curfew. I'm not so lucky.

Sheila Sund, Wikimedia, CC 2.0

When my son was maybe six, I used the old trick of giving him two choices, both acceptable to me: "Do you want broccoli or string beans?" He threw both bowls onto the floor.

My son is now 16 and is throwing away much more than vegetables. He refuses to study. Even though he's smart, despite grade inflation, his GPA hovers over a C. And forget about getting him to study for the SAT or do extracurriculars other than weed. And if I'm honest, he's that bully that parents tell kids to avoid. He gets off on scaring kids and because he's strong, he backs it up with his fists.

So last night when midnight passed and he still hadn't come back home, I wasn't very worried. That had happened occasionally and besides—and I hate to admit it to you—a wisp in me was thinking, "If he got killed in a car accident, I could manage to survive."

He didn't get killed. He got kidnapped. You see, I'm the CEO of a nonprofit and, nonprofit or not, executives' kids are prime targets for kidnappers.

They want $1,000,000. The cops just told me that's a bargain compared with the typical ask. I said, "Maybe I'm getting the nonprofit rate." The cops didn't smile. They just explained that not paying upps the chance I'd never ever see my son again, but from a public policy perspective, they'd like if I didn't pay.

Despite my son being a miscreant, most of me wants him back even if it costs me $1,000,000, my life's savings. But the cops giving me a pro-social rationale for not paying is making me think. What would you do?

Lingering

I've always lingered. It's my nature not to hurry even though I'm a cab driver. If a customer says, "Go! There's a big tip in it for you," I nod but drive only a little faster than normal.

pxfuel, DMCA, free to reuse

I linger over everything:

I linger over my coffee. The first sip is the best and I let it linger in my mouth but I'm still enjoying my coffee a half-hour later. And if I'm reading the newspaper, add an hour.

No surprise, my girlfriends always have loved that I linger doing you know what.

Then there's nature. I love staring at a leaf, a brook, or a flower.

I linger over my memories. For example, today, I thought about the first girl I kissed. It was at a party in Cindy Matthews' basement in the 5th grade. You could get the cassette player to play the same song again and again. It was Unchained Melody. I danced with Rita Brand for what must have been 20 repetitions.

Today, I spent an hour thinking of all the fads that had come and gone: pet rock, hula hoop, koosh ball, Rubik's cube—I could never come close to solving that. Are those toys really better than the many others that didn't make it? How important is luck?

I don't think artificial intelligence is a fad. I don't really understand it but am guessing that it'll be good overall but lots of people will lose their jobs. When I retire from being a cabbie, will my replacement be a driverless vehicle? Will I get replaced even before I reach retirement age?

I've loved lingering but I've now been a cabbie for 40 years. Should I have lingered less?

A Confrontive Career Coach

Jeffery Rauschert, Wikimedia, CC4.0

My parents stressed that you give a greater gift by telling people an uncomfortable truth about themselves than a pleasing lie. My parents walked their talk and I'm grateful for it. They pulled no punches when I was too long-winded, not thorough enough, or too argumentative.

My training to become a career coach stressed the opposite: be accepting, supportive, and provide a safe space. While I didn't argue with my instructors because I wanted to graduate, their rationale didn't shake my belief in the power of constructive criticism over "support."

So as a career coach, I made what I believed was the ethical choice to be direct and sometimes— to shake a client from too— confident complacency— confrontive.

For example, a client was a bored Social Security administrator. The more I learned about him, the more I realized that, in his soul, he was entrepreneurial. For example, he said he used to be a ticket scalper and later admitted that he still does it "a little." I suggested, perhaps too bluntly, that he needed to sacrifice the security of his ill-suited career as an administrator and become an ethical entrepreneur but not a scummy one. I'm sure he inferred that the "scummy" referred to him. He got angry with me, but fast forward a year and he was running a moderately successful online business selling used books that he sources from libraries that are dumping excess inventory.

Another client, a clinical social worker, blabbed on and on about how spirituality-centered she was, including chakras and Wiccan retreats with naked sage-burning dancing in the woods to banish evil spirits in favor of world peace. She said that for the last two years, she's been trying to make a related activity her career: doing "healings." She's 33 years old and I asked how much she has made, net, per year? Answer: $3,000. I said, "You have a hobby. Do you want to continue living off your boyfriend's income? Is that spiritual? You need a career, not a religion." She hated me... for a session. Then we explored more remunerative and, yes more conventional ways to do healing, and she decided to enroll in a course using progressive exposure to help people overcome phobias.

Then there was the aspiring singer. She sucked and while I didn't use those words, I did say, "You're paying me for candor. Well, sure, Bob Dylan succeeded with a bad singing voice but you ain't no Bob Dylan." She walked out right then.

Indeed, my confrontive approach was poorly received by too many clients and my practice slowly withered ... and withered.

So one evening, after my last client of the day, I reflected and decided I'd be conventional: I'd be a "supportive" coach.

So when an old guy blamed ageism for his career problems, I put duct tape over my mouth. It would have done more good to remind him of his tech-lightness and admitted declining learning speed and memory. He said, "I have CRS: can't remember shit." But I played Mr. Support: "I can imagine how frustrating it must be to be the victim of ageism" blah, blah, blah.

When clients wanted to use "creative writing" to hide their employment failures and gaps, I remained silent and merely helped them write the resume they wanted.

My practice rebounded but I reflected on my new approach and felt it wasn't ethical and was less helpful. But the Catch-22 is that too many clients wouldn't tolerate a confrontive career coach.

So I decided to close up shop right after I saw the client who I most believed warranted confrontation. Speaking unvarnished to you dear reader, he's unintelligent and lazy but thinks he's smart and that any lack of drive comes from racism, capitalism, his parents, his boss, everything but him. He claims that the one internal cause of his torpor is immutable: "I'm depressed." But it's clear that his depression isn't physiological— He has drive for things he finds fun. An appropriate job and work ethic would go a long way to curing his "depression." I told him as much and, yes, at the end of the session, he said, "This is our last session."

As soon as we got off the Zoom, I deleted my practice's website, tossed out my business cards from my desk and wallet, and unlisted my phone number.

I'm now an eligibility worker for the unemployment office. Here I can and indeed am paid to be confrontive. Having been a career coach, I know the lengths that some unemployed people will go to to get money. For example, a few clients who had bad track records at work, lied and listed their friends or relatives as their boss— "Oh, John was a wonderful employee."

Now, for example, when a claimant for unemployment money says that they contacted the required three employers to try to find work and I sense it's BS, I say, "Okay, I'll call them now" and pick up the phone. Often, the applicant says something like, "Uh, well maybe I didn't." I feel good about being a good steward of taxpayer dollars. I'm a career coach who has made a good career change.

An Arguer

I endlessly tell myself, "Stop arguing. You rarely change people's mind. More likely, you make them hate you. I mean, think of just your recent failures: How stupid of me to disagree with the CEO. So what if he insisted that we could get the software out by Christmas and I said, "*Next* Christmas if we're lucky." After that, I was out of his inner circle.

Mohamed Hassan, Stockvault, CC0

My wife keeps begging me to travel with her. But I find travel much more hassle than it's worth. I don't have to stand at the Roman Colosseum to "feel one with antiquity"— I can watch a Stanley Tucci video. But it caused a fight that she still brings up as an example of my "weirdness."

A friend runs five miles a day. He's 45 and admits that his knees are starting to bother him. I told him that I've seen many people in their 50s and 60s, especially runners, who need a knee replacement, which is no fun. He said, "I'm aware" but he hasn't reduced his running by a step.

When I complained to my kid's teacher that he's bored and needs higher level work, she said, "All the incentives and pressure are for us to bring up the bottom." I said, "That's a formula for societal dissolution." She didn't change a thing.

In a meeting on climate change, I said that it's magical thinking to believe that to keep the planet's temperature from rising a degree or three, the world's 195 countries will dramatically hurt their people lives, even their ability to heat their homes affordably in perpetuity. The response: Students called me a climate denier, implying I'm like those monstrous Holocaust deniers.

A cousin frothed that she finally decided to have kids. I probably could have gotten away with saying evenly, "That's nice." But idiot me had to say, "You do know it's one of the biggest sacrifices— your freedom for 18 years. And that assumes that after college, Junior doesn't crash back on your sofa.

So I guess I shouldn't be surprised that I wasn't invited to the family's Christmas dinner. I am that uncle that everyone tries to avoid.

So it's Christmas night and, candidly, I'm happier sitting at home. To be honest, the older I get, the more I prefer my dog. Besides, I don't see the big deal about turkey or ham. I'd rather have a burger.

Redistribution

Jensen Art Co. Pixabay, free to reuse

I'm a welfare worker and feel like a thimble facing a tidal wave of people who feel unable to cope. And most of my colleagues feel that way.

So I've half given up. Yes, I still try hard, with my teaspoon, to bail water from our drenched, leaky ship, but a few months ago, I started to do something I'm doing, I guess, mainly in frustration with our task's difficulty.

I created a fictitious client and had the money that I'd get for clients sent to a post-office box I set up for myself under the fictitious client's name. So I'd get food stamps (now obfuscatorily called SNAP or EBT), transportation vouchers, housing subsidies, and cash payments. It adds up to almost as much as my salary. And I got away with it.

How could someone who had gone into welfare work rationalize such dishonesty? First of all, I gave away a lot of the money that I stole to friends who I felt would make better use of it—like pay for a job-training course and not drop out. Second, what I "reallocated" was a drop in the ocean—The government spends literally trillions of our tax dollars. Finally, what I kept of the money feels like payback for the stressful job we're asked to do while being paid less than a garbage collector.

So I did it again and again until I had created 20 fictitious clients. Not only did I get away with it, my boss praised me for serving more clients. He didn't care much about the clients, but the more clients-served he can report to the state, the better he looks. Plus, that enabled him to fully spend his ever-larger budget. Absurdly, the department gets penalized for not spending it all.

Not only did I get praised, I got promoted to manager, whereupon I hired two of my friends with acceptable degrees who were beneficiaries of my largesse. They plan to do what I'm doing.

Looking

DavyNin, Flick, CC2.0

Rupert was sure that finally, he'd be in demand. After all, there are four widows for every widower. At age 80, most men were dead or pending. But no, Rupert was far from in-demand.

It wasn't that he wasn't nice. And sure, his torso looked like a D but that belly bulge was smaller than most guys' his age. The problem was—if we are to be honest—that he was ugly. His face was asymmetrical, his lips too thin. He didn't even have eyebrows anymore.

Rupert was lonely and decided to take one last shot at looking better.

He went to Weightwatchers. It was hard but the size-2 teacher kept praising him. In five weeks, he lost eight pounds.

He usually wore too-formal bow-tie clothes, but as part of his personal renovation, he visited Macy's, where the 35-year-old saleswoman picked out an outfit that she insisted looked "awesome" on him. The $1,200 was almost more than a retired accountant could swallow, but he did.

He even wondered if Botox would help. The cosmetic surgeon tried to upsell him to a face lift—"It could make all the difference." But he declined, yes because of the money but even more because, especially at his age, he was scared of surgery.

Rupert had stayed away from the senior center during his personal renovation but finally, the day of truth had arrived.

He showed up a bit early and resumed the position—in the corner. And voila, a woman did come up to him and said, "You look great and well-rested. I love the new outfit, and did you lose a few pounds?"

He beamed and they went on two dates but then, the next moment of truth had arrived. They had had dinner at his place and after, he looked her in the eye and reached for her hand. She said, "You're very nice but…"

Rupert never returned to the senior center.

Down

Pickpik CC

Both of my helicopter's engines died and I crashed on a snow-covered forested mountaintop over Bhutan. The chopper burned but miraculously, I escaped unharmed but with no food and water, and it was freezing, and I was in the middle of a blizzard.

I looked down in all directions and saw a dot of light a few miles down. Could it be a house? What was the best route down? There were no paths.

I started down and the snow got deeper—like two feet deep. I goose-stepped back up—Finally, what I had thought were silly exercises in bootcamp came in handy.

I tried a different route. For maybe 20 steps, it seemed good, then I felt the front of my boot not touch anything—One more step and I would have been off a cliff.

Finally, I got lucky. Step after step seemed solid. The dot of light had become larger. But the blizzard got worse and I couldn't be sure what would happen with each next step. Step, good. Step, good. Step, good. Then step, crunch—My boot had broken through ice into frozen water. I stepped back and saw that it seemed like a small lake. Another disaster averted.

But now, my boot was sopping and freezing. Would I get frostbite and need my toes, even my foot, amputated? That pushed me to go faster.

The blizzard had become so thick that I could no longer see the light. But what I did see was, on the snow, a small brown pile. I leaned down—dung! I couldn't imagine what animals live up there.

I continued on and soon could see what that light was. It was a house, with white smoke coming from the chimney!

I knocked on the door, a woman answered, and I saw what that brown was—dog poop! There was a cute, little, what seemed to be a Lhasa Apso. I explained what happened and she handed me her cell phone. I was surprised that she didn't invite me in—I obviously was frozen and Bhutan is supposed to have the world's highest gross domestic happiness.

But I guess the woman was scared or at least put-off by seeing a man in a singed U.S. Marine Corps uniform, so I gratefully took the phone and called the nearest Marine Base, Khanabad, Uzbekistan. The person there said that someone would pick me up "soon" in, yes, a helicopter.

I knocked on the door to return her cell phone and, yes, hoping she'd invite me in, but she just took the phone, bowed, and closed the door.

Behind the Smile

Pete Simon, Flickr, CC 2.0

I want to succeed, so I say the right thing but inside…Well, here are examples:

I smile and say, "Good idea!" But I'm thinking, "So-so idea. I won't act on that."

I smile and say, "Nice outfit." But I'm thinking, "Stupid fashionista, you look ridiculous. You're trying too hard. You're so shallow."

I smile and say: "What a lovely baby." But I'm thinking, "What vacant eyes with no curiosity, and ugly to boot."

And I started doing misanthropic things… and they got worse:

First, I withheld information that would help a coworker.

Then, for a promotion, I bad-mouthed my competitor. That person would have been a worse manager but still…

I sabotaged our website so it went down. It's not like it provides a crucial service. It's just a sports-betting site and shutting it down saves the stupid bettors from losing money, but still.

Then, driving home one day, I was switching from one podcast to another and inadvertently—I didn't mean to, I swear—I ran over and killed a child.

I went to his memorial and, OMG, if any kid deserved to live, it was him. He was gifted and beloved, a rare combination. I swore I'd be good from then on.

So I donated a painful amount to Hoagie's Gifted, a wonderful resource for parents and teachers of gifted kids. I was kind to everyone at work. I didn't just share information but gave ample earned praise and shared credit for accomplishments even if I had done most of the work. And yes, I smiled a lot—I knew that made people feel good.

But I kept seeing stupidity and laziness in and outside of work and slowly, I again got angry and, yes, evil. What put me over the edge was this coworker who is so confident, so loud-and-proud, so interruptive in meetings, yet is stupid, really. Also, and this surprised me, I found myself bored—It's more stimulating to be nefarious than nice.

So I returned to my old ways and—this is so embarrassing and I really don't know why I did this —Driving home one day, I saw a kid in the middle of the street pummeling and pummeling a smaller child, even though that child was curled in a ball and screaming. I ran over the pummeler and drove away.

No one caught me and, continuing to be honest with you, I don't feel bad.

Senator Cruz

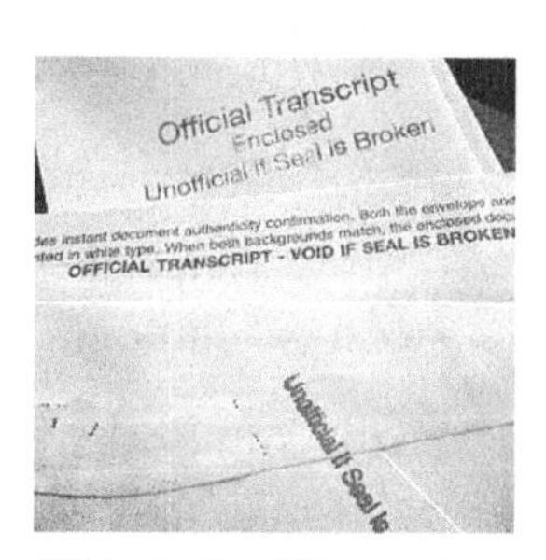

Wikimedia, Tony Webster, CC 4.0

Hi, my name is Alexander Crews. I saw my father struggle. He's an irrigation installer and is seeing his income drop as more installers—legal and illegal—are willing to work for less…and for cash.

That made me decide I would try to get into Harvard. That would guarantee me a good career. Unfortunately, I was far from guaranteed to get in. So first, I did the usual things—sign up for a ridiculously hard course schedule, took the SAT three times and with a prep course, and served soup to the homeless. But my GPA and SAT were still much below the average compared with Harvard entrants of my demographic background.

So I changed my name, legally, from Alexander Crews to Alejandro Cruz, joined my school's Latino group —La Lucha—and wrote my college application essay on the oppression that my family and I suffered.

I got into Harvard.

The problem is that I struggled at Harvard. After three years and many threats to expel me, my GPA was still 1.9. and the dean warned, "One more chance." I was desperate so I paid a work-study student in the records office $1,000 to make my transcript say I have a BA with a 3.9, magna cum laude. Then I dropped out.

Because I did badly at Harvard, I was afraid that if I applied for a job appropriate for a Harvard graduate, I'd fail, so I decided I'd run for town council.

I only subtly mentioned my Harvard "degree" in my stump speeches and media interviews but ahem liberally laced them with my political party's Focus-Group-Tested Phrases: forward, together, all-in-, brighter future, stand for justice, and so on.

The election was tonight and I won—the youngest person by far on the Springfield town council. I know I should be thinking about how to become a good councilman but can't help thinking about how quickly I can run for state senate.

It All Came Down to the Sex

I always had a big sex drive. I was embarrassed when, even after two powerful rounds, I'd often paw at the guy for a third.

Sasin Tipchai, Pixabay, free to reuse

So it was ironic that Jack was the first guy I thought of marrying. Even in the first weeks, he wasn't that eager even for Round 1. My luck, otherwise he was perfect: intelligent, kind, and okay, rich.

Things got, ahem, limp pretty quickly. After just two months, we were down to a perfunctory once a week. We tried everything: communication, fantasies, porn, costumes for God's sake, even a sex therapist. But as we walked out of the session with the shrink, we laughed and agreed that retail therapy would be more therapeutic.

But because Jack was otherwise great and, by that time, my biological clock was ticking pretty damn loud, we got married. Within months, we were down to near-zero and Jack said, "Please, go have affairs. True love means letting you do what you need to."

To save his feelings, I said I wouldn't do that, but I did do that. First it was just a fling at a conference, then one with a coworker. But then there was Antonio—He was as eager for Round 3 as I was.

When Jack walked in on us, he cried and somehow that made me, right there, tell him that I needed to leave him for Antonio.

A few months later, the infatuation fog with Antonio had lifted for both of us and, as I'm writing to you, I'm thinking of asking Jack if he'd have me back. But no matter how good Jack is, can I accept a life of celibacy or affairs?

Payback

Tony Webster, Wikimedia, CC4.0

Mark finished doing his income taxes, finally, including having to pay more atop what had already been withheld.

And he thought about all the other taxes we have to pay: sales tax, property tax, park user fees, and then there are the car "taxes" that we don't think of as taxes: tolls, car registration and license fees, excise tax on tires, and usurious fines for a speeding ticket or even for forgetting to stuff the parking meter. Those give the government a one-two punch: more tax money and pressuring people out of their cars and into mass transit. That's also why they charge heavy taxes on airplane tickets and car rentals.

What pushed Mark over the edge was a $95 parking-meter ticket. After he quietly paid, he decided he would take on a project that he believed would do more good than any he had ever done. He bought a can of spray foam that's used to seal basements so rodents don't get in. Then, in the middle of the night, he inserted the can's tiny straw into the credit-card reader of dozens of parking meters to jam them up.

But a surveillance camera caught him and his license plate, and he's now serving a nine-month prison sentence. There, sympathetic fellow prisoners told him that he would have gotten away with it if only he had worn a ski mask and parked his car further away.

When Mark gets out, he plans to jam the machines that automate red-light and speeding tickets.

Like Mother, Like Daughter?

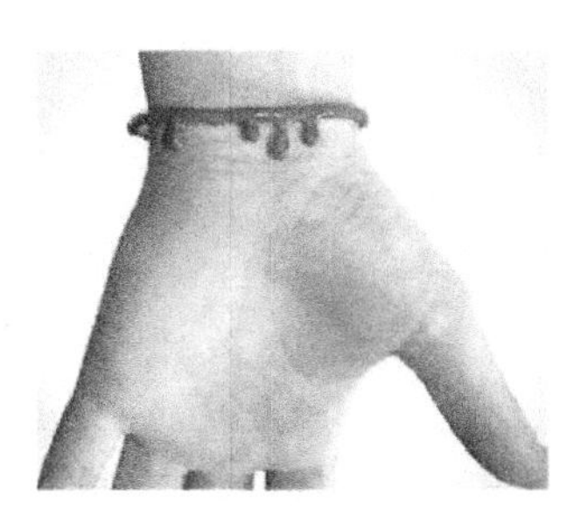

Oddity, CC0

I wanted to be sure that my daughter, Crystal, would live up to her potential. She gets mainly C's on her report cards, so I emailed her teacher asking for her to get tested for the gifted program.

But the teacher emailed me that she thinks Crystal is an overachiever, working hard, creating neat and thorough work, but that her reasoning ability— key to giftedness— is pretty average.

I didn't want to accept that. Looking back, that was because I was scared that was true of me and that I only got an Ivy League degree because I killed myself. So I demanded that Crystal be tested for the gifted program.

When the school psychologist emailed me— I guess she couldn't face me— Crystal scored just slightly above average.

Still, I wanted to be sure I was giving Crystal every opportunity. So I asked if she could try being in the after-school program for gifted kids. They said no ... until I threatened to sue. I guess that scared them, so they agreed.

But that turned out to be my bad. Crystal struggled there and at the end of class on just the second day, when the kids were let out to the schoolyard to go home, one kid pointed to Crystal and said, "Too dumb." Other kids thought that was funny and so they chimed in and circled her: "Too dumb! Too dumb!! Too dumb!!!"

I figured, okay, maybe that wasn't the right program for Crystal, so I signed her up for the after-school Math for Girls course offered by a local female-empowerment nonprofit. I thought that maybe I was pushing Crystal too hard, but when I saw her working hard on her Math for Girls homework in addition to her regular homework, I felt okay.

But not for long. One night, just before bedtime, I heard her crying in her bedroom. The door was locked, I knocked, and she yelled, "Go away!" I kept knocking, and finally she screamed, "See if I care!" She opened the door and I saw that her wrist was slit. But it turns out it was fake— It was a decal she had bought on the Internet.

I sent her to counseling, and then I went too. I've since eased up and think that will make her more successful and definitely happier. To tell the truth, I'm also easing up on myself.

A Smiler

I was always serious until my mother said to me, "Smile and the world smiles with you. Weep and you weep alone."

Clker-Free-Vector-Images, Pixabay, Free to reuse

I wanted friends and had few, so I started smiling. And gradually, kids started to like me. I could relax only when I was back in my room—Smiling is tiring if you're not a natural.

I carried it through college, where I was not only popular but got to be the head of the college's Equity Club, even though behind the smile, I sometimes wondered whether, in practice, equity would mean anti-merit hiring, promotion, and admission to college and even medical school, which would hurt our health care, all our products and services. But at meetings of the Equity Club, I put that out of my mind. If you're thinking such things, it's hard to smile.

At work, I worried at how lazy some people were, but I smiled and I got ahead.

Then I met Adam. He was the one person at work who rarely smiled. I asked him why and his answer hurt me: "Because I'm honest and if you're busy smiling and making nice, you're not solving problems. You're just another phony glad-hander who goes along to get along."

I was embarrassed and so I started being more sober. No surprise, little by little, people seemed to like me less and I didn't get the promotion I thought I deserved. I felt that I was a more worthy, substantive, and honest person but that wasn't fun and increasingly, it was lonely.

For now, I've made the obvious choice: balance, but I worry that if half the time I'm focusing on being nice, is that really the right way to live? On the other hand, I'm human. Shouldn't I be allowed to make compromises so I can be a happier person? I dunno. What do you think?

Wannabes

I'm a delivery driver for The Carbonic Collaborative. That's a fancy name for a company that refills CO_2 tanks for soda fountains, margarita makers, and helium balloons.

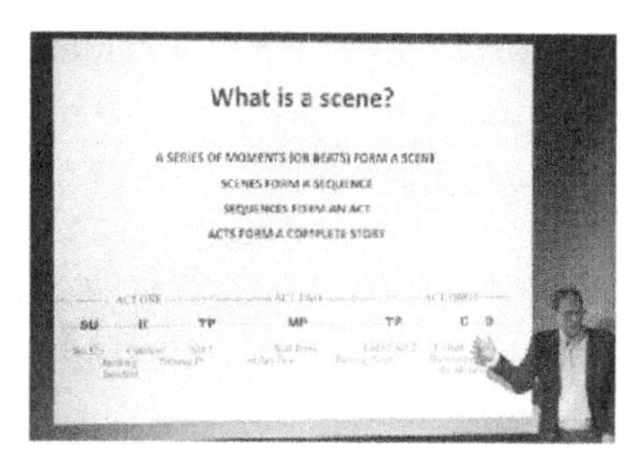

Vancouver Film School, Flickr, CC2.0

But like most people, I have a creative itch that needs to be scratched. So, after work, for the last three years, I've taken screenwriting courses, one of them twice even though it cost $1,495 a pop. To avoid being accused of giving false hopes and perhaps to avoid getting sued, the trainer always says something like, "Of course, it's not easy to make a living as a screenwriter." That gives just enough hope for us wannabes, too much hope.

In between screenwriting courses, I reread screenwriting books like *Story, Crafty Screenwriting*, and *Screenwriting 434*, written by Lew Hunter, the legendary head of UCLA's screenwriting program. In a recent year, nine of the ten top-grossing films were written by graduates of his program.

Along the way, I wrote a screenplay, which took me a year. I entered eight contests and won one.

I leveraged that by applying to screenwriting programs, including my long shot, the aforementioned UCLA. And I got in! The tuition would break me as well as make me take out a huge loan but I wanted to live my dream. How could I not?

So I packed my bags and relocated from Milwaukee to UCLA. I did well in the program and the pressure of deadlines resulted in my writing five screenplays in the two years. (I since learned that the average working screenwriter gets one done in *two months*!) At the bottom of each screenplay, the professor used Hunter's famous and just encouraging-enough send-off: "Write on!" Hunter himself gave me an amazing letter of endorsement to send to literary agents along with my "inventory" (the industry term) of scripts.

I queried 28 screenplay agents. The results: 13 no-responses, three perfunctory nos, and a yes from a third-tier agent.

She sent my screenplays all over Hollywood. For months, crickets and then finally, a film production company, a major one!, bought an option to do The Ugly Club: a story of three ugly high school kids who became cheerleaders and struck a blow against lookism. But the option expired and they never made it into a movie. The explanation: "We couldn't get a bankable star."

On the tail-between-my-legs drive back home to Milwaukee, I had plenty of time to think. Was this all a waste? The idea popped to mind that I could teach screenwriting. After all, I did win a screenwriting contest — even though it was a minor one and the prize, $750, wasn't much more than the entry fee for all the contests I had entered, let alone the cost of all the workshops and books. I could also pitch wannabes by saying that I did get into and graduate from America's premier screenwriting program, left with an amazing letter of recommendation, got an agent and a script optioned. But that's all deceptive. Could I make myself tell students the understatement, "Of course, it's not easy to make a living as a screenwriter."

Author's note: Some of this story is autobiographical. I read those screenwriting books, Lew Hunter did read four of my scripts and wrote me a wonderful letter of support. I did send it to 28 agents. But I never got an agent, let alone had a script optioned. Looking back, I think of my few-year screenwriting addiction as a hobby fueled by the hope I'd get a film made.

A Tagger Defends Graffiti

Late at night, I sneak out of my apartment with my spray cans—red, white, and black. I climb billboards, highway overpasses, even fire escapes, and I tag 'em, mainly just my nom de guerre—That's one word I remember from history class. It means warrior name. I don't know why, but I call myself, *KAO*. (See my tag to the right?)

Eric Verspoor, Flickr, CC 2.0

I was getting bored with those places so I asked myself, "What's the coolest place I could tag?" The Statue of Liberty! But there were too many guards, so

I did it on the ground just before the entrance to the main parking lot. There, at midnight, there are no guards. My KAO looks cool. My friends think so too. I can still say I tagged the Statue of Liberty.

Then I got an even better idea. Late at night, there always are cop cars parked next to the police station, but no one's around. Like Beyonce did at the Superbowl, I climbed on one. From there, it's easy to tag the car's roof. Cops deserve it. But I got caught.

The judge asked me why I do it? I made up something like, "We have no power. We have no money. We have no chance. Tagging shows that I have some power. Plus, I get to show my friends around—'See, I did that, and that, and that.' They all think it's cool. Also, tagging gets me high without drugs. You get it, right?"

The judge got it. He gave me 10 hours of community service.

A Sighing Marriage

Albert and Sophia waved good-bye to their daughter as she drove off to college. Now, with the nest empty, they had to face their marriage's mediocrity.

With permission, 18/1 Graphics Studio

They managed to stay together because they accepted their schlep-through-life marriage. It helped that both have a rewarding career. Albert researches the genetic basis of altruism and one of its roots: impulse control. Sophia is developing a bracelet for autistic people that vibrates each time their cortisol level— a proxy for anxiety— rises.

Albert and Sophia sat at the breakfast table and she said, "We should try to improve our relationship."

Okay...

How about we start with money? You sigh when I buy a mere $20 candle."

We should be saving more.

You "invested" in Bitcoin and look what happened. At least I get pleasure from the candle.

We have about $200 a month in discretionary money. How about I invest $100 and you spend $100.

But no more Bitcoin.

Is Procter and Gamble stock safe enough for you?

Our government is ever more anti-corporate. I'm not comfortable betting on a U.S. company.

Okay, how about $90 in an India ETF and $10 in Bitcoin?

Sophia sighed. "Okay. Let's turn to a harder issue: communication. When I talk, you only half pay attention and I sense that you want to end the conversation as fast as possible."

That's only when you complain. We usually don't get anywhere because we've already tried to solve these issues ad nauseam.

Haven't you ever heard that sometimes, people just want to be heard?

How about, each night at dinner, either of us can talk for a few minutes uninterrupted and the other person has to listen carefully."

Fine. That's something else worth a try. But now, the killer topic: sex. We're down to once a month and I know you're doing it only out of obligation. As far as you're concerned, we'd be celibate.

He sighed, "We've tried everything. Should we try a sex therapist?"

Okay, and let's see how well the money and communication experiments work.

They gave each other a perfunctory hug, he went to his laptop, and she phoned a friend.

The sex therapist ended the first session with, "So, shall ve meet ze same time next week?" Albert and Sophia looked at each other knowingly and Sophia bravely said, "We'll get back to you." The therapist sighed.

When they left the office, both broke out in laughter. She imitated the therapist's officious, European accent: "You neet to communikete better unt maybe try a lubrikent or even peacock fezers."

Albert smiled, "Sounds like Dr. Ruth. We would have gotten more benefit from retail therapy. See how I encourage you to spend?"

And they laughed. She said, "See? The therapist brought us together on something!"

The communication and money tactics worked well enough but the lack of sex remained a thorn. They decided not to separate but Albert said, "Should each of us try to have an affair?" This time it was Sophia's turn to sigh and she said, "I guess."

He found Samantha, a marketing manager, to be not smart enough and too sexual.

She found Ethan, a philosophy professor, to be not sexual enough plus, "He smells wrong."

Albert and Sophia agreed to stop that experiment and continue schlepping through life but augmented by the aforementioned money and communication tweaks and by spending more time doing the things they enjoy doing together like watching movies and also, accepting that they'll find the greatest reward in their career.

Albert said, "I think this all is making our marriage better than most." Sophia sighed.

A Shrink of Faith

P.poschadel, Wikimedia, GNU 1.2

Nearly every day, after I've said good-bye to my last client, I drop the mask and sigh. I'm no good and maybe my field is no good. True, my clients like having someone to vent to, who won't interrupt them, who rarely challenges them. But how often do my clients get better? Yes, they may get clearer on what their mother, their father, whomever did to them umpteen years ago, but is their life better? Not often enough, and their wallet is always thinner.

I finally screwed up the courage to, in confession, tell the priest that I feel I'm a waste. In addition to the absolution requiring just a few Our Fathers and Hail Marys, he asked if I had ever thought about incorporating religious faith into my psychotherapy practice. I hadn't but as I contemplated asking my clients to seek God's help as part of their plan, I doubted it would be more helpful.

Should I do something that's more likely to make people happy, like become a baker or a jewelry maker? My parents and friends would quietly think less of me—I'm not bold enough to do something like that.

Or maybe I should just take some continuing education courses. They're offering all sorts of techniques, like eye-movement desensitization and reprocessing therapy, dialectic behavior therapy, equine-assisted therapy, hypnotherapy, mindfulness therapy, and neurolinguistic programming. Or are those just yet another round of entrepreneurs with insufficient data trying to make a name for themselves? I think I need to pray.

Intermission

Luke finished playing the Appassionata sonata, bowed, and strode offstage for intermission.

With permission 18/1 Graphics Studio

In the dressing room, he thought, "The note mistakes were no big deal, but was I fully present? Did I take enough risks? Did I look stupid waiting so long at the piano before starting? And my bow was too long— The applause wasn't that loud. I hate theatricality."

"Three minutes, Mr. Francis."

Luke continued to think, "Ugh, Putin. He's like Hitler. We've tried to destroy the Jews from the beginning: The Romans, the Crusades, the Inquisition, the Pogroms, the Holocaust, the double standard for Israel even compared with Iran. Enough— You have to do Gaspard de la Nuit— It's hard. Think of Argerich playing it, Pogorelich. You'll never come close. How much does it matter?

Luke strode on stage as if all he did during intermission was sip water. Of course, the audience expected him to follow the ritual: bow with a modest smile and begin. But after Luke bowed, he stared at the audience and asked them, Does music matter? And even if it does, does it matter much whether I play a little differently or a little worse than other pianists that you can watch and hear for free on YouTube? Even if I luck out and play my best, it's worse than Argerich, Horowitz, Arrau, Rubenstein, Zimerman, and pianists I've never heard of. And think of the millions of suffering piano students, violin students, saxophone students for God's sake, sacrificing some of life's meaning, its pleasures, trying just to learn the notes of hard stuff, even easy pieces like Fur Elise, let alone create magic with the music. Or even rock music, blues, punk, hip-hop, show tunes. They'd be better off studying science, maybe even watching cat videos. What does matter? Does excellence matter? Does making people more equal matter more? Less? Is peace the answer? If we're peaceful, will Putin try to take over the world like Hitler wanted to except that we bombed the shit out of him? I'm not sure what matters or even what's right. So I'll just play.

The Last Conservative

Dani Blanco, Wikimedia, CC 4.0

Most people think I should retire. After all, I am 75 and my views are—as one Woke teacher put it—troglodytic. Another called me, The Last Conservative.

Indeed, in today's Woke era, teachers are urged and often required to valorize the redistribution of yet more from society's contributors to those who have contributed less.

Yes, I hold some conservative views: Merit should trump demographics, companies are net better for humankind than government is, and attempting to cool the planet demands unrealistic, permanent worldwide compliance and costs a fortune that could be more wisely spent.

Even though the union forces me to pay its dues, I refuse to be a member—I believe in merit pay, not that everyone gets the same and lifetime job security even if you burn out. And I don't believe in union dues used for political purposes let alone to support mainly liberal politicians.

I do hold plenty of liberal views: pro-choice, pro-gay marriage, anti-materialist, and I'm an atheist. Hey, I even play the guitar and use it in class: Every period, I welcome the kids with something like Puff the Magic Dragon, Over the Rainbow, or Edelweiss from the Sound of Music.

And once the bell rings, I really get started.

For example, I rewrote the Wizard of Oz, Oliver, and Sound of Music so my class could perform it in one-period school assemblies. I convinced one of those "evil" corporations, Bally, to donate an arcade-sized Ms PacMan machine to use as classroom rewards. The teachers laughed and said the corporation would never do it. I can just imagine the teachers' faces as the delivery guy wheeled the Ms PacMan past their classrooms.

Sorry for sounding defensive but maybe you'll forgive me if I tell you all I've gone through.

I used to share my views with the teachers in the break room. Now they won't even talk to me.

I had my classes evaluate the opportunity costs of attempting to cool the planet. Well, a Woke parent complained to the principal, who then asked me, "Bob, isn't it time to retire?"

But it was a student's question just a few days later, that blew things up. The student raised his hand and asked, "How come Rachel is so smart?" I explained that like most characteristics, intelligence is significantly affected both by environment and genes. https://tinyurl.com/3p99p8tk

Well that accurate and moderate statement triggered the parent, who got a half-dozen parents to join her in storming the principal's office. She called me in and I heard the Mob's unbelievable stupidity: "He's an elitist." "He's a eugenicist!" "He's a racist!!" The ringleader said, "You fire him immediately or we go to the media!"

The principal caved.

I'm not litigious—unlike Lefties. Every time they don't like a court decision, they sue or burn down a city. So yes, I retired, and started to write a blog under a pseudonym—John Galt, the hero in Ayn Rand's Atlas Shrugged. https://tinyurl.com/589a5xsr But a Silicon Valley techie found out it was me, organized a mob to scream in front of my house at midnight, and orchestrated a social media campaign to destroy any chance of my finding a job in today's Woke world.

So now, it's my dog Reagan and me. I just mope around, play my guitar, read the *Wall Street Journal* and keep revising my book, *The Silenced Majority*, even though I'm pretty much the only person who buys copies, which I give out at UC Berkeley's Sproul Plaza, where kids hang out during the noon hour.

I toy with the idea of putting a gun in my mouth in front of that parent's house but know I'm too responsible a person to actually do it. If I do it, it will be in my bathtub.

Off

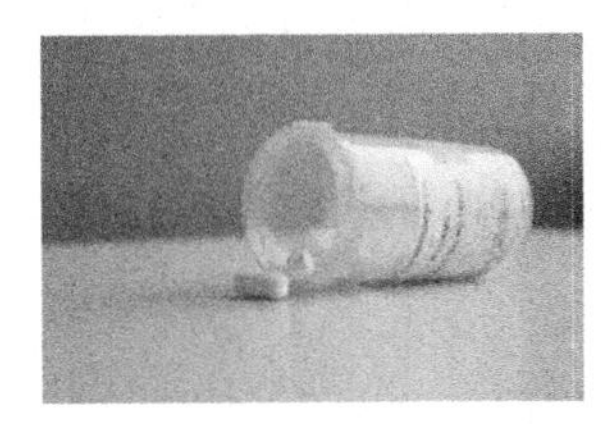

Charles Williams, Flickr, CC 2.0

I'm 87 and have had an okay life but now the aches and pains are getting worse, nothing immediately fatal, they're just wearing. And things can only get worse from here. I'm done.

So I asked my doctor if he'd give me the suicide pills. He refused, citing the too-restrictive rules. I pleaded, "Deciding when to die is our most intimate decision, even more than whether to have an abortion. The state shouldn't tell me when I've had enough. Please."

He said, "If you tell anyone I did this…" I swore I wouldn't.

But it's easier to ask for the pills than to take them. My hand was shaking so much that I was afraid I couldn't get them into my mouth. So I gulped some whisky to calm down, and it worked.

Of course, I was expecting to get sleepy and then go off into the forever sleep. But it felt the opposite. First, my pains decreased and then they were gone. Then I felt more energy. I looked in the mirror and saw myself rapidly getting younger. I kept staring until it stopped — I looked about 25!

I thought, this must be a dream. Is this what you feel like when you go to heaven? But I pinched myself and it felt like a real, earthly pinch.

Once I accepted that it was real, I had to decide what to do. Was I getting a second chance at life, starting again at age 25? I decided no graduate school, no marriage, no albatross mortgage. So I lived a modest bachelor life, signed up for a course on ethical entrepreneurship, and lived in a modest apartment — for a month.

Then, I started to feel those aches and pains. I looked in the mirror and I was aging. And soon, I was back to where I was at 87.

I didn't want to go back to the doctor for another set of pills. Instead, I took the pistol that I had long kept under my bed for security, had a couple of swigs of whisky, decided to write this to you, and now I think I am going to pull the trigger.

Made in the USA
Las Vegas, NV
27 October 2024

10221860R00174